Book of Dreams

Kevin Craig

duet

interlude **press**

CHICAGO

Published by Duet of Interlude Press
An imprint of Chicago Review Press Incorporated
814 North Franklin Street
Chicago, Illinois 60610
ISBN 978-1-951954-19-2

Library of Congress Control Number: 2022942098

Cover and interior design: CB Messer

Printed in the United States of America
5 4 3 2 1

For Dave, Manny, and Geordy, my brothers, because this story seems like something that could have happened to us all those years ago. And for Michael, who kept pushing me.

*"Books… they're kind of a compulsion for me.
To find a great bookstore is a great thing."*

—Philip Seymour Hoffman

Chapter One

I'M TRAPPED IN MY BEDROOM again, waiting impatiently for the screaming to end. Honestly, it feels like they could go on forever. I sit cross-legged in the middle of the bed and rock back and forth—my therapy position.

Mom and Dad are down the hall in the living room, arguing about "dividing assets." Again. She claims the contents of the den, and he gets the credenza in the dining room. This is sheer madness. Not once, in the hour since the blowup began, have either of them volunteered to take me. Through the whole argument, the tallying of their lives, my name—my existence—hasn't even come up.

As I sway to the sound of their chaos, I visualize all the shouted inventory items vanishing from the rooms in which they now reside. In my post-divorce imaginings, this leaves the condo pretty much empty except for the bedroom at the end of the hall on the right—my bedroom. Left untouched and abandoned by both my parents, it is still occupied by yours truly. Nobody fights over its contents. I don't make either list.

I usually just chill at home on Sundays and catch up on homework, but I need to get out of this hellish place. I need to stop feeling sorry for myself. I jump off the bed, grab my backpack, and leave my bedroom.

As I walk down the hall, the raised voices become much louder. In the epicenter of the storm, they swirl into a din of slings and arrows I run through to avoid being stung.

"I'm going out," I say as I walk past my mom, who wields Grandma Sophie's Tiffany lamp over her head. Her usually perfect long bob of dyed blonde hair looks like a rat's nest. She's a mess.

I'm a ghost.

"I don't care if she was your mother," Mom says in what couldn't possibly be a response to my announcement. The impeccable makeup she prides herself on is showing signs of impending disaster, especially around the eyes. *It's called waterproof mascara, Mom.* She does have perfect cover girl cheekbones, though. They help to detract from the makeup disaster. "She gave it to me and I'm keeping it. The Tiffany is mine."

"Dad," I say as I reach the door. My dad towers over *everyone*. If he wanted to, he could just reach out, grab me, and stop me in my tracks. He's the giant older version of me. I got his looks—dark brown hair, puppy dog eyes, and collagen thick lips without the injections—and my mom's height. I don't complain about scoring his looks, and I *can't* complain about being stuck with her height. "Going downtown. I'll be home by ten."

"It stays in the goddamned family. If you get the Tiffany, I get the Fabergé."

They both dart toward the Fabergé egg on the mantel. I shake my head and turn away to slide into my red Converse high-tops before slipping out the door unseen. Unheard. Unnoticed. Story of my life.

I'd give anything for this to be over, to be sitting on the other side of the divorce proceedings—or, at the very least, for my parents to be done with domestic cohabitation. But they keep making up and prolonging the inevitable. Dividing the assets has become a weekly entertainment in our family. It's a kind of sport in which neither parent ever argues for possession of the same thing they claimed the last time, a battle in which I am never included among the spoils of war. I desperately need normalcy in my life.

A walk downtown has always saved me. Getting lost in its chaos soothes me. It's good just to escape—on the subway, or by the power of my own two feet if I feel the need to walk off some of the stewing hostility my parents provoke in me.

I head for the subway that will deliver me to my sanctuary. I consider texting my best friend Noah and asking him to meet me, but I decide against it. I even consider texting Logan, my boyfriend. We could use the *us* time. I certainly miss his lips since the last time I kissed them, which was this morning at Carbonic Coffee. But if I text him, I'll have to explain why I'm escaping *this* time. I'm not up for talking right now, explaining, defending. I prefer a silent trip into my own thoughts while I wait out the storm at home.

The farther I get from its epicenter, the better I feel.

In three short stops, the subway releases me to the downtown city streets. I can be anonymous here. I breathe a sigh of relief, stuff my hands into the pockets of my hoodie, and walk into the afternoon. It soothes me to be surrounded by strangers as they go about their business. Is that weird? As full as the sidewalks sometimes get down here, a crowd always makes me feel the calm that comes with being alone in my thoughts. The chaos itself is soothing.

I take a turn down Elm Street. It's a particularly dead part of the downtown core, sketchy enough that I probably wouldn't walk here after dark. There's nothing to see besides a couple of restaurants at the far end of the block and a framing place on this end. Otherwise, it's just a bunch of abandoned storefronts awaiting demolition and the inevitable encroachment of gentrification, another city block that will soon become another pile of condos.

Halfway down the street, I see a glow coming from one of the storefronts. I know the building has been empty for ages, and yet the light in the window suggests life inside. I cross to the opposite side of the street so I can see the whole storefront as I approach.

As I come upon it, I stop dead and look at the facade in disbelief. It's a bookstore—only one of my most favorite things in the known universe—and it's just sitting here glowing, beckoning, waiting for me to make my way back across the street and step inside.

It's too good to be real, a balm for my battered soul when I feel particularly abandoned by the two hostiles back at the condo who are probably still flinging family heirlooms into the air about them. I cross the street, stand in front of the window, and take a deep breath. A bookstore. Heaven. A haven.

Through the glass of the front door, I see a big string of bells hanging from the other side of the doorknob. The bells seem like a warning, an omen. Only geezers use these things, in case they drop dead of old age or boredom. Someone enters their store, the bells crash all over the place, and they're brought back to life.

A wave passes over me—a premonition: *Curiosity doesn't only kill cats, dude*—but I ignore it. As shoddy and dank as the place looks, it's *still* a bookstore.

When I open the door, a rush of hot air escapes. It smells of mold and old wood, old pages and ancient leather, and like something close to a bakery. I wonder if this is an antiquarian bookstore, like the one Dad took me to in Paris last year. Shakespeare and Company. Man, it's just too good. The literal smell of heaven. Give it to me now.

But is there also an underlying, foul odor? Is there a stink here, beneath the smell of books, or is it just me?

I'm a book addict. There. I said it. It will one day be my downfall. The older the better, too; give me an old book, and I'm in nirvana. Mr. Clancy says I'm a dying breed. I may be seventeen and naive, but even I know that books will be around long after the apocalypse hits. Yep, books and cockroaches. And that old relic guy from the ancient band with the big-lips logo, Keith Richards.

I walk inside. The first thing I see is an all-white cat sprawled on the hardwood floor. It stretches inside a thin shaft of late afternoon sunlight. Spreading away from—or drifting toward—the dirty old thing is a cloud of dust motes. It looks as if the cat and the motes are fighting to possess the dying light.

The cat lifts an eye in my direction long enough to say telepathically, *Don't screw with me, I'm busy here.*

Eight rows of thick wooden shelves are filled with books that look older than Great-gram Imogene—if that's even possible. She's like ninety or something.

I go right to the closest shelf and start to browse through the books, caress their spines.

I get this spooked-out feeling as I peruse the shelf, though. What bookstore isn't jam-packed with color? Everywhere I look, I see various tones of only two colors: brown and black. And with all the dust motes floating around in the dying sunlight, it appears as though a low-lying fog is creeping through the store.

On one of those rare occasions when I was forced into a fishing outing with Dad, I learned that low-lying fog is a good thing—brings the fish out for a feeding frenzy, or something like that. What do I know? I'm *so* not a sporto. Low-lying fog in a bookstore, though? Not so much.

I have my hand on an old, bedraggled copy of a Russian classic—*The Brothers Karamazov*—when I hear the rumble of a throat clearing. It sounds like stones in a washing machine, or a cat stuck in a car engine when the ignition turns over. I've never heard a death rattle, but I'm pretty sure something behind me just made one.

"That'd be a good pick right there, son."

The hairs on my arms reach away from my body, and I retract my neck like a turtle, only I can't make my head disappear inside my shell. The voice is way worse than the throat-clearing. The cat agrees. It snarls and hisses at the old man like he isn't its friggin' owner.

Just as I'm about to tell him I've already read everything by

Dostoevsky, something shiny on a shelf nearer the back of the shop catches my eye. In this dull, dark ocean of books, dust, and dereliction, it's almost a eureka moment to discover something that stands out so much. I walk toward it.

The old man, who is not yet in my sight line, scurries behind me; I see him move up the aisle in my peripheral vision. As I reach out to grab the book, he steps between me and it.

"You don't want that one, son," he says, objecting to my choice before I even have a chance to touch it. His voice comes out in a hiss this time.

Who tells a kid that? Of course it automatically becomes the only thing within a twelve-block radius that I *do* want, and I haven't even seen the title yet. I deke him and make a grab for the shiny-shiny.

"Ooh! *The Book of Dreams*! Sounds awesome. Is this like the Tibetan one?"

"Young man," he says, "I'm going to have to ask you not to touch that particular book."

My hand lingers by its gold spine, and as I move to haul it from its slot on the shelf, the old man's hand engulfs my own. The hand, as white as bone and, well, also extremely bony, appears disembodied next to the black cuff of his suit. It is cold and covered with those age spots that all old people have. The hair already standing up on my arms now stands up electrically. Ice courses through my veins, as though his touch actually lowers my body temperature.

Who the hell is this old coot to tell me what books I can or cannot touch? *It's for sale, dude. If it's on the shelf in plain view—in a bookstore—it's for sale. End of story.*

I wrench out of his skeletal grip and step back from the shelf with the book in my hand. *Finally.*

"Don't say I didn't warn you, Gaige," the old man says as he turns and heads back to the front of the store. I think I hear him tsk. "Just know, son, some books once opened can't be unopened."

"What the hell does that even mean?" I ask. Now I feel brave. I won the standoff. I have the book. Dude is too weird, though. I watch his back as he moves toward the counter. He's impossibly tall and skinny, like a basketball player who has just returned from a ten-year stay on a desert island where he lived on insects and water. Like, he-should-be-dead skinny. His all-black suit is three sizes too big for him and covered in dust. His aura itself is dust. It mingles with the motes that fill the empty, sunlit spaces in the store. And what is with the long, greasy gray hair? Dude totally creeps me out.

I turn my back on him and make to crack open the gold book cover. My heart races. I'm desperate to see what's inside.

"You read the title wrong, too. Take another look, son. It's *MY Book of Dreams.*"

I stop what I'm doing and return my gaze to the cover. *My Book of Dreams.* Huh? I'm certain it read *THE Book of Dreams.* Positive, even.

What was it that Shakespeare wrote? *Something is rotten in the state of Denmark.* I think he also wrote, *By the pricking of my thumbs, something wicked this way comes.* Thankfully, my thumbs have not yet been pricked. Between scary giant, his pissed-off cat, the dust-fog, and the book, my Spidey-sense is telling me to get the hell out.

But I'm also intrigued. Too intrigued. Like I said, I'm a bibliophile. And this book is *so* calling my name. There's something about it. It's a four-car pileup, and I'm a rubberneck.

I spot a chair at the end of an aisle, take my prize over to it, and sit down with the book.

He just called me Gaige.

"Hey, wait," I say. "How did you know my name? You just called me Gaige."

"If you haven't looked inside that book yet, you can still leave it be and pick another. The Russians are fine reads, if you ask me. You still have prerogative on your side, Gaige. You can even leave empty-handed if you wish. It's not too late. Choose wisely."

Talk about creeping the hell out of a kid. What the hell is even wrong with this dude?

"How the hell do you know my name?"

But I don't wait for an answer. None of the alarm bells that should ring in my head are doing their job, at least not properly. Or they're ringing, and I'm just not listening. The shopkeeper has suggested that this book is forbidden, and I have never been one to accept that kind of shit. I dive in.

After I flip through the first several pages, though, I want to close the book again. The pages are all blank and emit a rotten smell. It's as if the book hasn't been opened for decades, and all the badness that has ever lived in this ancient bookstore has come to rest within its yellowed pages.

"It stinks," I say, more to myself than to the man, who now seems too far away to carry on an actual conversation with. Like I would want to. He totally gives the creeps a bad name. "Why does it smell so bad?"

Apparently, he's listening. "That's a question you really have to ask yourself, young man. You have things to hide in that little head of yours? You have things to be ashamed of? You sure that smell ain't coming from inside yourself? Skunk smells his own stink first, Gaige."

I stand and walk toward him, book in hand.

"Stop saying my name. How do you know who I am, anyway?"

"I'm just saying, that book knows you better than I do. I'm a silly old man who tried to warn you not to dance with the devil. Now you're dancing, young fella. Now you're dancing."

Talk about weirdness.

"What the hell are you even talking about?" I put the book on the counter and thumb through its empty, yellowed pages. "You trying to scare me? Who put you up to this, anyway?"

The bells on the door ring. Not just a little bit, but like somebody has taken them off the door, slammed them against it, and then stomped on them for good measure. I pivot to see who's come in, but the doorway's empty. Nobody there.

Then I jump as something brushes against my ankle. I feel a flush of embarrassment when I look down and see that it's only the pissed-off cat wrapping itself around me. Someone needs to be petted, and petting is probably not something the old man would ever stoop to do.

When I reach down to pet the cat, though, it hisses and snaps at my finger. Bitch draws blood with its dirty, stinking fangs.

"Ouch! Jesus." Not my thumb, but I've definitely been pricked now. I'm still waiting on my stubborn brain to kick in and heed that Spidey-sense. Any time, now.

"You wanna watch out for Lilith. She'd sooner eatcha than

look atcha. Clean that out before it gets infected. Cats are filthy creatures, fella boy. Rabies."

I suck on the bite and roll my eyes at Lurch.

"Gee, thanks, dude. First you try to stop me from buying a book, then your cat bites me. *Then* you try to freak me out about rabies. Customer service in this store is tripping."

"You have bigger problems than an old cat bite, Gaige. You let some stuff in and you let some stuff out when you done opened that book. I'll say it again—I warned you."

"What do you mean? It's just an empty book filled with empty pages that stink like shitty bad breath or something."

"No. It's out now. Your book is never empty. It's the book of your dreams, you see. They're there, son, filling up them pages something fierce and fast. You just have to look to see—"

"Fuck off," I say as I push the book away, but cutting him off mid-sentence doesn't stop anything from happening: the pages in front of me are now filling with words. He was right. There they are, line after line after line coming into view. The words swirl about before falling into place, and the swirling is so intoxicating, I just want to slip inside…

"Can't leave it now." His voice startles me, and I jump back. I can feel the grating vibrations of his laughter deep within my bones.

"What the hell? I'm out of here. You're a freaky old man. I don't know how you did that. I actually don't give a shit how you did it. It's a cheap carnival trick. I'm out."

I make for the door, but the old man comes out from behind the counter with a bag in his hand. He slides the gold book into the bag as he steps between me and the door.

I look into his face for the first time. Ever see those skeletal people in old horror movies, you know the ones—they're not dead, but they're so skinny and frail and gray, you just know they're gonna keel over in the next ten minutes and start eating brains or something? Dude's like that. Hollow cheeks. Empty eyes that look just as dusty as his black suit. His lips are slits of white, gashes in his ghoulish face, and he's got a disgusting old-man turkey neck, too. His long hair, falling in greasy strings around his face, completes the macabre look.

I think about screaming, but I know the sound of it in this dank place would terrify the hell out of me. So I muffle it. I eat the scream like I've never eaten a scream before.

Here I am. Right in front of the door. Lurch looms over me. I'm not getting through him. Just as I know he's scrawny and near death, I also know he's like frigging Gibraltar, a man of stone. Something in my head and my heart tells me not to mess with him, not even touch him.

He reaches toward me. I think for a second that he might kill me, but he extends the hand with the bagged book in it.

"Here you go, young man," he says. "You can't leave without your new purchase."

"I'm not buying that piece of shit. Get it away from me."

"Son, it's already purchased. It's yours. Bought and paid for. Told you not to open it. They usually don't listen, Gaige. Not usually. Why, in recent memory, I only recall one child ever taking heed of my words, putting that book back on the shelf, and scurrying out of here empty-handed with their tail between their legs. Just one. Naughty child, they were. Since you ain't them, you bought this book just like all the others before you. Now take it. Take it and be gone."

He nudges the book into my belly, pushing it against me like he's attempting to lodge it deep inside my abdomen.

I back off and push back. "I don't. Want. It."

"Take it and go, Gaige. You stopped playing with choice when you opened it, young man. It's imprinted now. A broiled chicken can't escape back to the coop. Done is done is done. Take it. And go."

"Broiled what, now?"

His eyes burn into me so intensely that I do the only thing I can think to do. I reach a hand toward his and grab hold of the bag.

"There you go. Now get and be gone."

"You're a crazy old man," I say. I know. Weak-assed, right? I sure showed him.

"Maybe so," he says, interlacing his long fingers and steepling his hands. "But I don't dance with devils, Gaige. I leave that to my customers. Now take the book you wanted so badly and be gone from here. It's time I close up shop for the day. Your parent folk should be just about done with the Battle of the Bulge by now. Be gone with you, boyo."

He steps aside and allows me to leave. My head buzzes like I'm trapped in a dream state, about to fall; like I haven't quite slipped off the edge of an abyss, but my arms are flailing madly as I attempt not to go over. The buzz fills the air around me and swallows anything sane left of the moment.

Suddenly, I'm outside the store without remembering how I got here. I can hear the muffled ringing of the bells on the other side of the door, but I can't see the old man or his cat through the glass. I step away from the door and look at the bag in my hands. My shoulders slump in defeat.

Then his last words wash over me once more. He not only knows my name, he also knows what the hell's going on in my life. He mentioned my parents' fight. It just isn't possible.

"Shit. I don't want this damn book."

Chapter Two

WALKING AWAY FROM THE STORE is one of the hardest things I've done in a long time. I don't know why. I only know I don't want this book. I want to toss the bag on the ground, walk away, and never look back. I want to take back the last ten minutes and walk past the store that shouldn't even have been there in the first place.

But I also want to see what the words say, what the hell the book is about.

So I decide to take it home. I put the bag under my arm and walk down the street to the subway station, where I descend the stairs and board a train. I get off at my stop and climb up to street level, walk the half-block back to my building, take the elevator up to our seventeenth-floor condo, and step inside.

The shouting has ended, just as the creepy old man suggested. The silence feels stilted, though. It's as though the electricity of the earlier fight still floats in the air about the place, still radiates a heat from my parents' spent anger.

My heart races. I'm not shitting: it feels like I'm smuggling something illicit into the house. Like it's not a book in my backpack, but a pound of cocaine. I breeze past Mom and Dad as they sit silently on the couch in the living room, just staring at a cake-baking show on the TV like it's the most interesting thing in the universe. Neither of them says a word, nor do they acknowledge my presence. I don't say anything either, for fear that one of them will suddenly give a shit and ask where I've been, or worse, what's in the bag.

I only feel safe once I'm inside my bedroom with the door closed. I sit cross-legged on my bed, take the book from the bag, and place it on the duvet in front of me.

Oh, how I want to open it. But I can't bring myself to do it. I didn't realize I could actually be afraid of an inanimate object. Surely the old man can't make it do the same trick when he's not even here.

I *don't* hear anything coming from inside the book. Of course I don't hear scrabbling—*that* would be impossible. And it would mean that I'm more unstable than I thought. Books don't make noise. *Books don't make noise.*

I guess words don't usually just materialize on pages where there weren't any words to be found a minute ago, either, but we've already crossed *that* bridge. Maybe, if I just look it over, I'll figure out how the old man performed his magic trick back at the store.

I stare at the gold-toned cover and its ornate design. Looks like a typical, old-fashioned book. I run my hand across the embossed title. *My Book of Dreams.* There's no author name under the title, or anywhere else on the cover. There's no description or publisher marking on the back. The only words on the whole cover are the title, repeated once on the book's spine.

In the end, the compulsion is too strong. I flip the cover over. Nothing: a once-white page, now yellowed with age. The musty stink I smelled earlier quickly makes its way to my nose. It's so pungent, like a swamp. Like death. I imagine the stank filling my bedroom.

I turn the page, and it's the same thing again. A blank. But this page is darker, stained, older, like I'm getting closer to the stink, going back in time.

I flip over another page.

The swirling words come to life once more and begin to not quite settle on the page. It's intoxicating to watch. Mesmerizing.

I see Logan's name, Noah's name. *I lost so much time that first day… I'm not sure Logan believes me… Don't cross the line… I don't know where it is I go, but I know I'm not alone when I get there…*

The scrabbling I heard before I opened the book gets louder, closer. More urgent. I'm inside the words now, on the other side of them, but I don't know how I got here. It's dark, like impossibly dark, but not quite pitch. And warm, everything gives off heat. But I can see things within this inky substance, amorphous walls, the ground beneath me. The ceiling reaches down toward me, almost aglow. Despite the darkness, my surroundings begin to take form.

A voice comes out of the darkness, just a little more than a whisper. "You can only go so far in, Gaige. Be careful. Stop there. Stop!"

"Who said that?" My voice sounds like it's far away, but also everywhere. It's like I'm talking from inside a conch shell. Instead of the sound of the sea and wind, it's my voice, lost somewhere deep inside an impossible labyrinth.

But that doesn't make sense. It's a book, not a shell. *You can't go inside a book, Gaige. Stop making no sense. Stop making nonsense.*

When no one answers, I try another question. A barrage of them, even.

"Where am I? Hello?" I'm walking on a soupy black surface that gives just a little with every step I take. It's like wet tar, like the ink from the swirling words I read has dissolved into puddles. Every surface is covered in the same viscous black goop. "Who's there? Hello?"

"Don't go any farther. Please. You must stop."

I look around desperately, attempting to see a shadow I'm not even sure is here. It sounds like a kid about my age.

"How do you know my name?" I ask. I do as they say, though. I freeze, forbidding myself to move farther into the darkness. Like I would want to.

"The book's imprinting you. You're imprinting it."

"What does that mean? Why can't I see you? Where are you?"

In an effort to see them through the darkness, I begin to take another step forward despite their warnings.

"No. Wait."

From somewhere beside me, a face begins to emerge from the gooey substance. As it comes into focus, it almost seems to form from the substance itself: not here, and then here.

It's a kid about my age, maybe. Smaller, almost petite. I can't tell if it's a boy or a girl. Their thick, shoulder-length hair is jet-black and blends with the viscous shininess of the surroundings.

If not for the waves running through it, it would disappear in the darkness. The waves pick up a luminescence that seems to be coming from the substance itself, like everything in this place is faintly glowing. It's hypnotic.

"Why are you here? Who are you? Did that man do this to—"

"I was the one. The kid who put his book back. You don't get away once he picks you, Gaige. I didn't buy my book. I put it back."

I feel something deep inside of me sink in despair. If they're in here and they didn't even take the book, what the hell is going to happen to me? I literally *chose* this.

"Holy shit," I whisper. I hang my head in defeat.

"No. Wait. It's not over yet. You didn't go too far—yet. I can keep stopping you. But you have to listen."

"I don't understand."

"They stop listening, Gaige. I keep them away. I do. But eventually they go deeper. They get drawn in by all the things. Sooner or later, they go through to the Other Side… and they never come back. He keeps feeding it. One kid after another."

I reach out to touch them, but they pull back like my hand itself is a fire that'll burn them to the ground.

"No. Don't touch me. Don't *ever* touch me. I don't think it would be safe. I'm of the Other Side now."

"You're what?"

"I'm of the Other Side. I'm made up of this substance now, this Dark Ichor. I don't know how I stay here, at the threshold. He keeps me here to amuse himself, to torture me. I don't know where I go when I'm not here talking to you or the others. It keeps happening and happening. And I almost stop you from entering… until I don't. I keep trying. But none of you listen for long."

There are inky tears in their eyes now. They look broken. I just want to grab them and hug them.

"We can get out together," I say. "It's obvious—I can just go back the way I came and take you with me. Can't I? I *can* get out, right?"

"I can no longer go to the Outside World."

"The outside wor—"

"This is where I am. The only place I can be now." They come closer and gesture to me. "You're sleeping, Gaige. You're dreaming this. These are your dreams. I am no longer of the Outside World. I'm only in the dreams of the other kids he chooses now. I'm of the Other Side."

"I'm not dreaming. I would know if I were dreaming. I came in through the…"

I don't have to finish the sentence to know I'm seriously surfing on the edge of reason. It's not like I walked here. There's no logical explanation for the way I entered this dark place: through the ink of the words I struggled to read as they took shape.

"He will attempt to entice you, Gaige," they say. They back away from me a few steps. "But try to remember that you can't go in any farther. Whatever you do, don't go any farther than this. It's what he wants. He's trying to make sense of this place. You're just another guinea pig to him. He'll make you want to go inside so badly. But you have to fight it."

They step forward again and drag their foot across the soft, murky black ground, leaving a line there, a little trench in the pliable substance that makes up this place.

"This line in the Ichor will stay here." They snap their fingers in my face to make sure I'm listening. "Do you see this line, Gaige?"

"Yes," I say. I make a point of looking down at it, taking it in. "I see it. In the substance, the Dark Ichor. Don't cross the line. Got it."

As I say these words, though, it's like I've already said them, like they're a warning from somewhere far away. Then I remember. They were one of the strings of words I read as they swirled about and landed on the page.

Were they the words from this dream? Did I see this dream before it even happened?

"You mustn't cross the line if you want to get back out to the Outside World. Do you understand me, Gaige? He wants you to cross the line to help him understand how this place works. But if you do, you'll never leave. Like the others. He'll entice you inside. You'll see things that aren't real. Don't be sucked in."

As they say these words, they almost begin to dissipate. They fade back into the darkness until they are barely visible. The last thing I see is the waves of their black hair. I feel like I just might fall into them, if they don't disappear completely.

"Wait! Wait. Don't leave yet," I beg. "What's your name? Will I see you again? How? How will I see you?"

Their androgynous face fades back in from the wall of goop, and for the first time, I realize just how beautiful they are. They pull me in just as much as the words that brought me here, just as much as the book did. I want to follow them. It's as though they understand what I'm feeling, because they put up a hand to stop me.

"No. Don't touch me."

"What's your name? I need to see you again. I need to know your name."

"Mael is my name. I've been here far too long. I have so many questions, but not now. Maybe later. You need to listen to me. Follow my words if you want to escape."

"I will," I say. Then, because I'm me, I add, "I'll try."

"Are Batcavers still around? Voodoo? Klub Domino? Club Z? Twilight Zone?" they ask in an excited barrage, as though they can't help themself. Like they're desperate for info from beyond this place.

"I'm sorry. I don't know what any of those things are. I'd have to Google them."

"I was a Batcaver before I was taken. Everything black. A club kid, street kid. Punk. Please tell me Kensington Market is still around."

"Kensington Market will always be here," I say. "My boyfriend lives just on its outskirts, near Bellevue Square Park. The one with the Al Waxman statue."

"He got a statue? I loved that neighborhood. Sorry. I miss the Outside World." This statement seems to bring them back to the moment. "Don't get lost in here, Gaige. Just… remember to stay back from the line. You have to remember."

In an instant, they're completely gone. Every fiber of my being begs me to follow them into the darkness, but I force myself back.

I glance at the line Mael drew on the ground. When I look up again, a burst of sparks illuminates the space beyond, and I see a swaying field of tall grass, an impossibly huge, sprawling, lone northern red oak tree in the far distance, and wildflowers springing up everywhere. It's like the scene is being drawn by the substance, created from it. And it's all so very familiar, but I can't quite place it. It's a memory, I think, but it's just outside my reach. Something about it reminds me of Logan, fills me with longing for him.

As I take a step toward it, there's a boom, and something that almost looks like lightning in negative crashes down and throws it all back into darkness. I force myself to step back again. I have to listen to Mael's words. I won't cross the line. I'm done.

As soon as the decision is made, I find myself back on my bed with my head down, staring at the book sitting on the duvet in front of me. I slam it closed and push it away.

Chapter Three

I STARE AT THE BOOK and consider my next move. My first instinct is to burn it—to destroy it, start running, and never look back. But I feel foggy: why would I want to do that, again?

Everything comes back to me in bits and pieces, like a dream. I must have been in a daze. A kid named Mael, a meadow, glowing black surfaces, a line drawn on the ground.

Instead of starting a fire in my own bedroom, I shake off the impossible, dig into my pocket, and pull out my cell phone.

Only when I look at it do I realize that I made the whole trip back home from the bookstore without once checking my phone. I totally forgot it existed. No music, texts, or games, no checking TikTok, Twitter, or Instagram or doing any of the other things I do on my phone. I live on this thing, but even after I got home, I ignored it. So weird. I try to remember ever *not* listening to music on the subway.

Come to think of it, I can't really remember any of the trip home.

I shrug and call Logan, trying not to think of the book and the fog that I just came out of. That's something else I rarely do—use my phone to make a call. Who *talks* on their phone? It's a day for weirdness, I guess.

"Hello."

"Logan?" Obviously. I'm such a dweeb. Who else would answer his cell?

"Hey, Gaige. I thought you forgot about me. What the hell?"

"Sorry. I was out." *Don't think of the book. Don't think of where you went.* "Lost track of time."

"No duh, babe," he says. I wonder if I made the right decision, calling him. He sounds super pissed. "Clancy wanted *me* to tell him where you were during class today. You know he doesn't like it when his favorite student skips."

"Wait. What? It's Sunday. What do you mean?"

"Wow. You really *did* lose track of time, didn't you? Can I come over? My mom's being unreasonable again. I need to get out of here. What's the weather like at your place?"

"What do you mean?" At this point, I don't exactly care about his mom. Or my parents. "What are you talking about school for?"

"Gaige. It's Monday. Evening. You missed school. Clancy was pissed. It's not Sunday. Have you been smoking weed or something?"

"Logan, are you bullshitting me right now? This isn't funny. Tell me you're fucking with me and I'll forgive you."

"Why would I lie? Look at your phone."

I pull my hand back and look at the banner at the top of the screen.

6:13 PM

MONDAY, JUNE 13

"Holy shit." There's also a ton of missed notifications, like maybe everyone was trying to find out where I was.

"What? What's going on, Gaige?"

"I was just at this creepy little bookstore downtown. I bought this book. No. I didn't buy it. The creepy man who worked in the creepy bookstore *made* me take it home with me. He wouldn't let me leave without taking it. I took the subway back, walked home, came into my room, sat down, and looked at the book.

"Something happened then, but it's all a fog. There was someone in this place, and tall grass, but also this thick tar like substance. I *went* somewhere. I don't know what this book is doing to me. Then—then, I guess, I called you. But it was fucking Sunday when I left the bookstore."

"Funny. Real funny. Now stop trying to freak me out. Why do you always have to be so extra, Gaige? Isn't real life dramatic enough for you?"

"*Logan.* I'm not joking. I sat down on my bed, opened the book, and everything just… happened. These things… I don't know. That's all I did. I opened the book and looked inside, is all. What's happened to me? Where did I go?"

"You fell asleep and had a dream, probably. I'm coming over, babe. You better figure out how to tell me you're messing with my head in a way that makes me laugh, because I'm not laughing right now."

"You have to come. I need you to look at this book and tell me what you see. I really don't want it. I need to get rid of it. And, OK, what the hell is with my parents? Why didn't they come wake me up? But I wasn't sleeping. I just got here. I was just looking at the book, I swear. What the hell, Logan?"

"You're scaring me. This isn't funny."

"I know."

"I'll be right there."

I drop the phone on the bed beside me and stare down at the book. I want so much to open the cover and look inside, just one more time. There are all these things on the periphery of my memory, but none of them really make sense. Even as I consider opening the book, though, it's also the last thing I want to do.

My head feels light, like it has separated from the rest of me and is floating off into the distance. Only a thin thread anchors it to the rest of my body. It's a balloon, floating up to the ceiling, and its string is about to be pulled too taut and break.

Before I really work up the courage to open the book again, I hear the buzzer. Saved by the bell. Then I hear my mother walk to the front door and push the button that unlocks the door down in the lobby. I sit silently, waiting for the next sign that Logan is approaching. Soon, the unit doorbell chimes.

I hear Mom talking with Logan on the other side of the condo. After their short conversation, I hear footsteps, and then Logan opens my bedroom door, and I breathe a sigh of relief. I have never felt happier to see him. Ever.

I spring from my bed and aim myself directly at Logan. I hold him at arm's length and look into his large brown eyes, eyes that never cease to comfort me. I run my hands roughly through his thick black hair, testing to see if he's real and really in front of me. Then I grab him in a full-body hug, like I haven't seen him for a year or something.

"Baby," he says, after pulling back with a look of surprise. OK, so I'm not usually such a demonstrative boyfriend. Maybe I sometimes even forget to hug Logan. Maybe my idea of foreplay is removing clothing, so he might be shocked by this alternate show of affection otherwise known as a hug. You get the picture. "What is up with you? You're not usually this... *weird*. Even for you, this is..."

"Right?" I say. I place my hands on his stubbly cheeks and kiss him. I just want to grab him and pull him in for another hug, but I know I'm being crazy. The kiss will have to sustain me.

As I hold the kiss, though, my eyes tightly closed, someone else's face starts to float up out of the darkness in my head. I quickly open my eyes to stop the image from fully appearing. When I see Logan's face, the waves of jet-black hair in my mind's eye disappear. That hair would be a lot like Logan's, actually, if he were to let his grow out.

The kid from the place beyond the words. *Mael*. Their face comes back to me like it was part of a dream. They did say I was dreaming. I shake my head to get rid of the lingering images.

"It's just," I say, finally coming back to now, "I got this damn book. I didn't want it. I just wanted to, you know, look at it. You know I'm a book geek, right? The bookstore was so weird. And dark and gloomy. Everything in it was dark except for this one book. It was like the light shone on it differently. It glowed on the shelf like a beacon. And then Lurch was like, *Oh, not that one. Not. That. One.* And I was like, *Fuck you, buddy*. Because who even does that? Tells me I can't look at a certain book? He made me want it more, right? And then he calls me by my name. What the hell was that about? How the hell would this old stranger even know my name, Logan?! Tell me that, huh? It's not like I said my name out loud or was wearing a nametag or anything. How the hell?! And his fucking cat—"

"Whoa, whoa, whoa," Logan says. He places a comforting hand on my cheek, pets me. Inches closer. "I can't keep up. I have no idea what you're talking about, babe. What the hell happened to you?"

"I'm trying to tell you, Logan." But I know I'm not getting it out properly. Do I even know what happened? When did I lose the time? On my way home or after I got here? When I opened the book? Did the book steal my time? What happened when I opened it?

He takes my hand and leads me back to the bed. We lie down with our heads on my pillow and, for the longest time, we say nothing. We just stare up at the ceiling. I feel better already. Logan is a calming influence in my life, always. Even though we sometimes argue a bit too much, his presence soothes me. He's my person.

"OK. So you went to a bookstore? Which one? And why didn't you invite me to go with you? You know I want the new Julian Winters. I like bookstores too, you know."

I stare at the ceiling, stalling as I attempt to figure out how to answer him. Nothing comes to me. "Huh."

"Huh, what?"

"Huh, I don't know what it was called? I have no idea."

"Bull, Gaige. Now I know you're putting me on. You love bookstores. You have a photographic memory when it comes to books, even the stores that house them."

"Eidetic. Eidetic memory," I say. I'm such a douche. I always have to correct people. It's an annoying trait. "But I can't remember the name of this bookstore for the life of me. I don't know that it had a name. I didn't even know it was there."

"Where *is* there?"

"Elm. Off Yonge. Over by the Eaton Center. You know the part that's all cobbles and old-timey? I only went down there to cross over to Bay Street and walk through the park, I guess. I don't know, really. I just decided to go down that street. But I never got to the park. I saw the bookstore, and I had to go inside. You know me."

"I've never been down there. Doesn't ring a bell."

"Doesn't matter. I couldn't believe I found a new bookstore. I'm familiar with every single one in this city. I couldn't wait to get in there and look around. But it turned out to be an ancient pile of dust. I mean, you could *taste* this place, for real. Sometimes that's a good thing, like in Shakespeare and Company, you know? Not this time, though. It was stale. Gross. Like old man taint or something."

"Disgusting, Gaige. You're so weird. Don't say *old man taint* ever again. I beg you."

"Yeah. I think we've already established my weirdness. And sorry, but it *did* smell like old. Man. Taint. Anyway, this creepy old man worked there. And his vicious little cat. Bugger bit me."

"What? Where?"

It's the first time I've thought about the bite since I sucked blood from the wound whenever the thing bit me. Yesterday?

I lift my arm and hold my finger above us so Logan can see it. Seeing it myself, I'm instantly aware that it stings like hellfire.

"Holy shit. That's infected, babe."

I'm not gonna lie, I'm scared. I can almost hear the old man's words: *Clean that out before it gets infected. Cats are filthy creatures.* It actually starts throbbing as I look at it. The pain rises up like a balloon out of nowhere.

"Shit. The old man told me it would get infected."

"What old man? I can't follow whatever it is you're talking about."

"The dude at the bookstore. Keep up. It was his cat. But it hated him, clearly. When the cat bit me, the old man told me it would get infected. He also knew my name, Logan. What's happening?"

"He probably just knows your dad or something."

"Ew. Trust me, no."

"Well, there has to be a logical explanation."

"Yeah. He's a freakshow. And his cat bit me. And I'm stuck with this book that I don't want. And most probably rabies, too. I'm going to die of rabies."

He looks at the bedside table and turns back to me.

"What book? Where is it? Can I see?"

"Yeah," I say as I feel around on the bed beside me without really looking. "It's right here."

Only it's not where it should be at all. I paw at all the empty space beside me. No book. I sit up and look around. No book.

I lean over the edge of the bed to scan the floor. No book. I go down on my hands and knees and look under the bed. No book. Fucker's nowhere to be seen.

"This isn't funny. Where is it? Get up. Get up."

"The book?" Logan asks. He doesn't move, though. "Where did you have it last?"

"*On* the bed. The second before you came into the room. It was *on* the bed with me."

"Well, it's got to be around here somewhere. Trust me, it's not under me. I think I would feel it. Are you sure you didn't bring it into the washroom? Or the kitchen? Or something?"

"Logan. It was in my hand when you opened my door. It should be right here." I pound the bed with my fist.

"Check the closet."

"Why would it be in the closet? That's ridiculous."

"Don't call me ridiculous. I'm only trying to help." He pouts. I really don't feel like consoling him *and* losing my mind at the same time.

"I'm not calling you ridiculous. I'm sorry. I'm just really freaked out here. Where the hell is it?"

"Maybe I should go." He sits up, swings his legs around, and puts his feet on the floor.

Panic runs through me like a hot knife through butter.

"No. No. Stay." I sit up and hug him from behind to keep him on the bed. "I really don't want to be alone right now. Please. Stay."

"What is *with* you?" He turns to look at me.

"Just stay, baby. Please. I'll find it. I wanted to show it to you anyway. Sorry. I'm just feeling a bit freaked out, is all."

He sighs like it's a real inconvenience for him to stay, but then he kisses me and calms my fears. When he swings his feet back onto the bed, I take it as a good sign. I attempt to cuddle him and he allows it, but he's not convinced. I can feel a rigidity in his body.

I kiss him again, and he finally relaxes enough to kiss me back. I take solace in his thick lips and warm mouth. He gives me strength.

"Maybe it's under the covers? Under the pillow?" he suggests after we end the kiss.

I feel helpless, but eventually I leave his side and tear the bedroom apart, looking for the book. My behavior seems to make Logan nervous, but he stays put. He might even be afraid to move. To him, it must seem like I've gone from sane to unstable in seconds flat.

The book's *not* in my room. I feel even more off-kilter when I tell him I'll be right back, then leave the room to scour the rest of the condo for a book I know goddamned well was on my bed in my bedroom.

When I return to my bedroom, Logan's ass is high in the air, and his head appears to be stuck between the bed and the wall. If I wasn't in a one hundred percent, dead-on panic situation, I would take advantage of his position and smack his cute little ass. But here we are.

"*What* are you doing?"

"Just checking under the bed again. You have a lot of shit down here, babe. Look." He holds up a dust-covered shirt. "This is my favorite shirt of yours. You look so hot in this. No wonder you haven't worn it in so long. You frigging lost it in your own room. The book is probably somewhere under there with all the other lost artifacts." He resumes rummaging.

"I know it's not here, Logan. This isn't funny. I'm not gonna find it. And that old man was so ominous. Like, I opened myself up to something bad. I need to find that book. I need to find out what's inside of it. And how I can get rid of it. For good."

Logan comes up from behind the bed and gives me the weirdest look. "You mean you didn't even look at it?"

"Yeah. I did. Only, the pages were blank. Until."

"Until what?"

"Until they weren't." I look down, unable to meet his eyes when I hear just how ridiculous I sound. "Don't ask for an explanation. I don't have one. I swear, I looked, and it seemed to be nothing but empty pages, and then I looked again, and there were words gathering. Swirling around. I don't know how to explain it. I may have blacked out. Don't ask me."

But what did I see when I opened the book? It's all there—cloudy and fragmented, but definitely all there. I remember looking into its pages and falling through the words as they melted into a river of ink. And a kid named Mael. I keep going back to Mael, a gorgeous, androgynous kid with jet-black hair glowing in the darkness surrounding us. A kid who called themselves a Batcaver, whatever that is. Maybe the lost time disappeared into that gelatinous darkness that made up the Other Side. It's like the substance itself was alive.

"Stop scratching that. We should go to the clinic. You need antibiotics or something."

"I can't help it. It's so goddamned itchy."

"Yeah, but you'll just make it worse."

I glance down at the bite. It looks angrier than it did minutes ago, when I first remembered its existence and started scratching it maniacally.

"Can we talk about the missed day now?"

"You weren't joking, were you?" he says. "Listen, babe. Whatever happened, we can get through it together. We'll figure it out."

"I wasn't joking. Wish I was. I came home, sat on the bed, and opened the book. Then, I guess, I called you. When I came home, it was still Sunday. I think. Then, suddenly, it's Monday evening, and you're telling me I missed a whole day of school. Something happened when I looked at the book."

"You must have just fallen asleep. Didn't your parents say anything?"

I look at him like he just spontaneously grew a third head. "*Really?*"

"What?" he asks, looking insulted.

"Number one, you know what it's like around this place. They don't talk to me. They're too busy being angry pre-divorce *enthusiasts* to talk to me. I'm like a ghost on the battlefield here. Number two, I think I would know if I fell asleep. And it's not like it would have been a nodding off kind of thing. We're talking practically twenty-four hours here.

"My parents both leave for work before I get out of bed in the morning. Plus, they both come home after me at night. They wouldn't know that I didn't go to school today unless they got a call, which clearly they did not."

"Ah," he says. "Right."

I lie back down beside him. "Maybe we should go back to the bookstore."

"Sounds like a cheery place. You sure you *want* to go back?"

"If only to know what the hell the place was called. Why can't I remember the name of the place? It has to have a name, right?"

Logan jumps from the bed and yanks my arm. He pulls me up until I'm sitting, then leans in and kisses me. Logan kisses are pretty awesome. We've been going together for about six months, and I'm still not used to how good his kisses are. They're still pure magic. He probably has the biggest lips in all of Heydon Park Secondary. Like, lips you just want to latch onto and never let go of. And they're all mine.

This gets me up.

"OK," he says. "Let's go, Gaige. You know I'm here for you. Want me to beat this guy up for you? Let me at him."

"Yes! Ha. Please do. My knight in shining armor." I pull him closer, somehow laughing despite everything. "But before you go slaying my dragons for me, just one more kiss."

Chapter Four

As the subway approaches Darius Station, I stand up and take Logan's hand. "This is us."

He slowly rises to his feet. The train stops, and we get off and make our way through the station. I literally feel like I'm going to the guillotine or my last meal or something.

Coming up to street level, I'm surprised to see that it's already getting dark. I'm glad to have Logan's hand in mine. Mine might be shaking a little; I'm so totally freaked out.

We say nothing as we make our way to Elm Street. I don't know what Logan's thinking about, but I just want to remember the name of the bookstore before we get to it. I've made it a competition with myself. My mind's a complete and utter blank, though. The closer we get, the harder I think and the surer I am that I'll never come up with the name. Did it even *have* a sign outside?

I get more and more nervous as we approach the store. Once at the front door, I know something's wrong. And not just a little bit wrong, otherworldly wrong.

The phrase Outside World comes floating to the surface of my thoughts in a whisper, like a mist from my subconscious. As I play with the words in my head, remembering that Mael used them in the dark place, Logan taps my shoulder.

"Hello?" he asks, bringing me back to the present. "Why are we stopping?"

"Because this is it." I let go of his hand, put my own hands up to the glass of the door, and look inside. The huge bells that had hung from the inside doorknob (yesterday? The day before?) are gone.

Hell, everything's gone.

"But there's nothing here."

"Logan. I'm telling you. Yesterday, this was a bookstore. I know you probably don't believe me. But—right here. This was a bookstore. This place."

He cups his hands against the big front window and peers inside for the longest time. Then he steps back and looks at me. You know that feeling you get when someone you really like—no, *love*—looks at you like you've totally lost your mind? Like they would rather be anywhere else in the world than here with you? Like they're afraid you're going to take out your machete and start hacking them apart, limb by limb?

That's almost exactly how Logan looks at me.

"Gaige. This place is empty. And it's been that way for a very long time. What's happening?"

I look inside. A few sheets of newspaper are scattered in a corner, as if blown there by the force of some invisible wind. There's a Styrofoam cup in the center of the room, and an empty Coke bottle standing guard beside it.

But that's it. There's nothing else in the whole building besides dust. Caked dust. The kind of dust that tells you nobody's been inside for at least a year. Maybe longer.

Without warning, my eyes fill with tears. It's not like I'm actually crying, though. These tears are the kind that come when you're scared shitless and coming unstrung. Along with the tears comes a mile of gooseflesh. I'm thoroughly skeezed out. I'm stress-crying, that's it.

I don't want to pull away from the door and face Logan. That would mean I'd have to talk, and I'm not sure I can form words. Besides, this proves that I've come unhinged. What could I possibly say to Logan to justify anything at this point? My whole story has fallen apart.

"Are you sure this is the place? Maybe it's down the street more."

He's trying. Bless his sad little heart, he's trying.

I finally pull away from the door and walk out into the street, where there are no cars. Actually, no people either. The whole street's deserted. I can see down to Yonge Street, which we turned off of to get here. That street's still busy with life. It always is. Cars move up and down it. People walk by. It's a normal Monday-evening downtown street. But the one we're on? Suddenly empty. Dead.

I look back at the bookstore—or the long-abandoned building where there *should* be a bookstore. Where there was a bookstore yesterday, goddamn it. I need to get inside. I *need* to.

Might as well take advantage of the emptiness of the street. Before I can talk myself out of doing it—or allow Logan to stop me— I make an executive decision. I move back to the curb, pick up an old, dented garbage can, and return to the door. The big window beside it will be so much easier.

"Gaige. No! What the hell do you think you're—"

His words are cut off by the sounds of the impact and glass crashing to the sidewalk, and then a garbage can rolling across the floor of the empty store.

"Holy shit, Gaige. What the hell?"

"Sorry. I had to. Someone's messing with my head, Logan. I need to figure out who, and stop them."

I kick at the gaping mouth of the window, breaking away the teeth of glass along its bottom edge. As I lift my leg up and over the ledge, Logan grabs my shoulder.

"We *can't* go in there, baby. We just can't."

"*You* don't have to. Stay here and be my lookout." I shrug his hand from my shoulder and continue inside.

"No," he says, a little too shrilly. "Wait for me. I'm not standing out here alone."

The encroaching darkness may be getting to him. Or maybe he's worried about his unhinged boyfriend. *Something* is making him nervous. It's a good sign that he picks me and the bookstore over the empty street. He must not be completely terrified of my insanity just yet.

"I want to look around. There's a back room. I need to check it out. I'm telling you, Logan, this was a bookstore yesterday. It was filled with dust and bookshelves and books, and an old man and his cat. I haven't completely lost my mind."

"I didn't say you did, babe. I believe you. I do." He lifts a foot and steps up and over the ledge. I offer him my hand, and thankfully, he takes it. Once inside, we make our way to the back of the store together. There's a door on the back wall, slightly ajar. Whatever is behind it, I'm positive it'll hold a clue to whatever the hell's going on.

A cat comes scurrying out of the room before we even make it to the door. And it's not just some random old stray, either; it's the same white cat that bit me. Same almost pink eyes. Same bastard cat for sure. Proof that some of my sanity is still intact.

"That's it," I shout. I point frantically at the thing as relief washes over me in waves. "That's the cat that bit me. See, I wasn't imagining things. That fucking cat bit me."

The cat jumps through the busted window and takes off down the street, into the darkening night. My first thought is, *Shouldn't I have caught it so they can cut off its head and do that test they do for rabies? Don't they have to do a rabies test on the thing that bit you? Doesn't that test involve decapitation?*

I scratch at the bite. Logan reaches for the doorknob and pushes the door open all the way. It squeals like it hasn't been opened more than a crack for at least a millennium.

We see nothing, just an empty office or storage area or whatever—no books, no bookshelves. No old man. It's just another empty room, this one a little more pathetically strewn with garbage than the main room we walked through to get here. It has the added bonuses of cat shit in the corner and a heady stench of ammonia.

"Nothing," I say. This kills me. I'm dejected enough to melt into a puddle and disappear. "This place was a bookstore yesterday. Where's the old man?"

I can't keep the fear out of my voice. I hate the way it sounds.

"It's OK, Gaige. There's gotta be an explanation. I believe you."

"That was the cat. I swear."

Logan smiles and holds my hand. He leans in and kisses my cheek. As we're about to leave the room, I see something out of the corner of my eye. A black strip of material peeks from inside the nearly-closed door of a little closet in the corner. I let go of Logan's hand and go to the closet.

When I open the door and look inside, I nearly fall to my knees. It's a long black dress jacket, the kind a nearly dead, tall, skinny old man with greasy long hair would wear were he attempting to be a ghoulish, Lurch-like character running a rogue bookstore.

Before my brain sends the signal to my hand not to do it, I reach out and touch the jacket. I feel a slight shiver of an electric shock as my fingers make contact with the material. The shock travels up my arm and all the way to my spine, where it moves up and down that bony highway while the goose bumps burst out on my arms.

"This is his jacket," I mumble. My fingers still cling to the vile thing. Without thinking, I remove it from its hanger. The motion moves the dust around, and I catch a whiff of the same stink that came out of the book when I first opened it.

It smells like the black, inky tar place, I think. Memories of that place swirl in my head: the dark luminescence, the smell, the fear.

Logan grabs for the jacket, but I scream, startling him away from it. For some reason, I can't deal with it coming into contact with my boyfriend and fouling him with its skank. He's still untouched, and I'd like him to stay that way, thank you very much.

"Don't touch it," I say. Every second, I feel a little more unsettled. Logan steps back, and I do something that only someone on the brink of insanity would think to do: I swing the jacket up over my shoulders and slip into it.

As the jacket envelops me, the electric charge I felt a moment ago becomes an electric blanket of doom. What the hell am I even doing? Who the hell would put this disgustingly foul thing on? Lurch was inside this. I'm touching the thing that was touching him. I have finally snapped.

"Gaige," Logan says with a look of utter disgust on his face. "What did you just do? Take that off. It's disgusting. That thing could be filled with disease. It stinks. Take it off."

"I just wanted to make sure. This is the jacket the old man wore. That was the cat that bit me."

I say this like I'm taking stock of the things that will prove my sanity.

"So?" he says, looking at me quizzically.

"So? It means I haven't lost my mind. Someone really *is* fucking with me."

"But why? Why you? Why make a whole bookstore appear just for you and then dismantle it after you leave? This place is abandoned. Gaige, there's no way there was ever a bookstore here. Not yesterday, anyway. No way, no how."

"I thought you said you believed me. Besides, this jacket proves it," I say as I pull at the sleeves. I put my hands inside the pockets. There's something in the right pocket. Something wet. I almost don't want to bring my hand back out. I don't want to look at it. I'm pretty sure I just dipped my hand into a moist pool of coagulating blood.

I look at my hand. Nothing. I put it back inside the jacket pocket. No wetness. My mind's playing tricks on me. I pat around and find an inside breast pocket. The thing I find inside it *is* real. And not moist. I pull out a faded business card.

Chalek's Emporium.
Purveyors of All Things You Didn't Know You Wanted.
Buy, Sell, Trade.
Since 1875. Jack Chalek, Proprietor.

"This has got to be a joke."

Logan grabs the card out of my hand and reads it.

"Maybe that's what this place used to be, some sort of curio or antique shop or something?"

"Nice try, Logan. I don't even think this neighborhood was around back in eighteen-whatever."

"Seventy-five. Eighteen-seventy-five."

"Whatever," I say.

"Take that thing off. You're giving me the creeps. You should go home and shower. You don't know where it's been."

"I think I do. I think it was on an old, creepy dude just yesterday. He was right out of a black-and-white horror flick."

Another wave of goose bumps ripples over me. Why the hell did I put this thing on, knowing it was on that skeezy old man? I whip it off and throw it to the floor, the gross-out factor now overwhelming. Why do I even?

"We should leave. Are you done doing whatever it is you felt you needed to do here?"

"I guess?" I say, sounding as petulant as I feel.

"You're going through a lot of crap right now, babe. Your parents are imploding. Exams are coming up. You've been under a lot of stress."

"Please don't go there, Logan. You've been great with everything. You've saved my life a few times when I felt myself on the brink. Don't. Please don't tell me I've snapped. These things really happened. I didn't imagine them because I'm under stress. Look: that cat did this to me. I did *not* give myself a cat bite. I promise you, I didn't."

He raises his hands to stop me, then pulls me close and hugs me. He has a calming influence, just like I said.

"Deep breaths, babe," he says, obviously backing down from his *you've lost it but it's OK* theory. "OK. I'm here. You're OK. We got this. Let's just go."

To tell you the truth, I want to cry. But my fear is too raw. My throat's bone dry, so I know my tear ducts have nothing to offer.

"We can go home and look for the—"

"What? The book? Right. If there's no bookstore, there's no book. It just stands to reason, Logan. I imagined the whole thing. I've lost my mind. You don't have to go along with the fantasy. There is no book. There never was a fucking book. I lost my mind, and I'm such a goddamned bore that the thing I imagined in my breakdown was a fucking bookstore, of all things. A bookstore."

How's that for pulling a complete three-sixty? That's a sure sign of losing it, right there.

"Come on, Gaige. The place is real. The jacket's real. The cat's real. You're not imagining these things. Someone's messing with you. Clearly."

If you can't count on your soulmate, who *can* you count on?

"But who would do that? That's impossible," I say. "Let's just get out of here. I wanna go home now, if that's OK with you."

"Maybe that's a good idea. We could do the homework from Clancy's class. We finally started the *Hamlet* review today, and you missed it. I think I saw a tear in Clancy's eye. His little Gaige wasn't there to celebrate with him."

"Very funny."

I hold his hand as we make our way out of the hole where the window used to be. I step over the threshold, the crunch of glass under my feet. I already feel a bit better.

"We need to reread the first act."

"Actually, though, I meant alone," I say. "If that's OK."

"What?" Logan looks at me like I just stabbed him in the heart. Or maybe the back.

"I mean, I want to go home alone. I just want to go home and go to bed, if you don't mind. It's been a long… day."

"*Really*?" One thing all guys should know: when your boyfriend has his hands on his hips and his mouth is the shape of an O, it's never a good thing. It's a sign of trouble in your relationship. When accompanied by an exaggerated *really*, it's even more dire.

"I'm sorry, Logan. I'm just a little skeezed out. And tired. I just wanna go home, shower that oogie jacket off of me, clean this wound before it kills me, and go to sleep."

"Whatever," he says before stomping off in the direction of the subway station. "You do you, Gaige. You always do. It's not like I matter or anything anyway."

I run to catch up with him. "Come on, Logan. Don't be like this. Please."

Once I catch up, I reach to take his hand, but he pulls it away. That's also a bad sign.

"I'm sorry, Gaige." Logan says. We stop walking. He looks down at my hand and finally relents, taking it in his. "This is just a lot to take in. I love you. I'm going home. I know you're tired. We can talk about this tomorrow. OK? I'm not mad. Not really. Just a little overwhelmed."

I smile, relieved that he won't leave in anger.

"I just wanted some alone time with my boyfriend," he says. "But I totally understand."

"I love you," I say, not really knowing what else *to* say.

He starts to walk away but turns back, a big smile forming on his face. "Of all the boyfriends in all the world, leave it to me to find the most mysterious one. Always drama. You're a ride, Gaige. I love you, but you're definitely a ride."

"You love it, Logan Regan," I say as I give him my most winning smile. "You thrive on it."

He rolls his eyes but can't keep a straight face. "Go home, Gaige. See you tomorrow."

He turns and walks away, and I breathe a sigh of relief. Even in my new dumpster fire of an existence, all is still good with me and Logan. That's all I need. I watch him disappear around the corner onto Yonge Street before I make my next move.

Chapter Five

I DON'T EXACTLY LOVE BEING alone, in the dark, on the street where a phantom bookstore used to be. And I definitely don't like thinking about the book that isn't a book. But no matter how I think about it, I can't make what happened to me into a figment of my imagination. I have a cat bite. I smelled musty books and old man. I went somewhere when I opened that book. It happened. I know it all happened.

After Logan leaves my field of vision, I turn back to face the building where the bookstore used to be.

I can't even—oh, shit.

I close my eyes and slowly reopen them. I do it once more for good measure, but nothing changes. No matter how hard I try, I can't blink away what I'm looking at, what's right in front of my face.

The window I smashed with the garbage can is now intact.

The bells hang on the doorknob again. They rest against the glass on the other side of the door.

And there are books in the display window. Yep. Bookstore. It's back.

Sanity is something you take for granted, right up until the very moment you realize it has slipped away. Once you see it crack, you wish you could have it back—but you also understand that it's already too late.

What else could I possibly do right now? What would you do?

I open the door and step inside. The sign behind the counter tells me I'm in Chalek's New & Used Books. Every Book You Always Wanted. Buy, Sell, Trade.

He definitely has a brand. I swear, that sign was *not* there the last time. I think I would remember it.

The cat on the floor in front of me tells me I've made it all the way back to Crazytown, where the bells on the door jingle for me and me alone.

I make my way into the aisles of tall bookshelves. I don't remember the rolling ladder being here yesterday. These added touches of authenticity are pretty impressive.

I also can't imagine this place actually fitting into the empty space that was here just five minutes ago. In fact, I know this store is way bigger than that space was. My sanity slips a little further away as I make peace with this particular observation. The impossible square footage of the store is kind of the least of my problems, though.

Somewhere deep within the store, someone clears their throat. I'm beginning to think of the old man as a some*thing*, though. Something cleared *its* throat. It's the same *rocks-in-a-dryer, nails-in-a-blender* sound I remember from yesterday. I don't want to see him, but I obviously have questions. Questions only he can answer.

"Hello?"

Nothing. Just another throat-clearing. Talk about a buildup of anticipation. This old man's good at what he does. He knows how to build tension and fear.

"Hello?"

I walk to the end of an aisle and turn the corner only to bump into Lurch. Literally.

"Oof. Um. Oops. Sorry."

"Gaige. I didn't think I'd see you back so soon. What brings you back to the store, Sonny Jim?"

"Really? Is that how we're going to play this?"

"I'm not sure I understand. Did you enjoy the book?" He walks past me and heads toward the counter at the front of the store. "Did it *reveal* itself to you? Was it a good read? Did you go places? Woohee!"

"Number one," I say, following him through the store, "don't call me Sonny Jim. Number two, I don't know what that means. Number three, what the hell is going on? Number four, what the hell is going on?"

"It has, hasn't it? The book has begun to show itself to you. How lovely. That's why you're back. It's getting inside. How fun!"

"Dude. Lurch guy. The book disappeared. I tried to show it to my boyfriend, and then it wasn't there. I looked everywhere for it. It vanished into thin air."

He laughs, and the death rattle deep in his throat comes up to meet the laughter. Then he coughs the cough of an end-stage, two-pack-a-day cancer patient. He takes a handkerchief out of his jacket pocket—yeah, an actual handkerchief—and I can't be sure, but I think he spits into it.

In my mind's eye, I choose to see the hankie fill with a splotch of bloody phlegm. I'm not gonna lie, it kind of calms me down. But I don't see it with my eyes, so I can't confirm that it actually happened. It's just fantasy. Just wishing death on my enemies, I guess. I'm probably going to hell.

He places the soiled hankie back inside his jacket pocket, and I recall having my hand inside that same pocket just minutes ago, the wetness I felt there. My skin crawls with a million tiny bugs of fear and loathing. Oh. My. God.

"Son. That book is yours. Not your *boy*friend's." He says *boyfriend* with a sneer, as though he doesn't approve of our relationship. "I'm certain you'll find it where you last set it down, s'long as you don't bring your little boy toy baby boy with you to see it. That book's only for you, understand? Just like all the books you see here. They're each only for one person."

"Yeah, Lurch? I also tried to show him the bookstore. Only it wasn't there. Wasn't here. It wasn't here. Where the hell did the bookstore disappear to? What's your trick?"

He comes out from behind the counter and walks over to the cat, who is sprawled on the dust-encrusted floor. Dude bends down to pet the shaggy thing like he hasn't already figured out that it despises him. The cat hisses and tears away from the old man's touch, disappearing into the dark depths of the store.

"Jack."

"What, now?"

"I said *Jack*," he says. "You can call me Jack. We're gonna be spending some time together, I expect. You might as well call me by name. I don't much cotton to that moniker you've been throwing my way."

"I ain't spending another second with you. All I want is for you to explain what the hell is going on, and then I'll be on my way."

He coughs again. I have a feeling he coughs a lot. There's something teeming down inside him, something ugly and cancerous. A fist of something dark and horrid. Instinctively, I just know it.

And I also know that it can somehow come up from the darkness and crawl down inside of me if I get too close, if I let my guard down. The cancerous thing is looking for new hosts.

I recall a different darkness now, the one inside the book beyond the words. Somewhere impossibly dark and slick, inky and viscous. There's a line on the ground there, a line I'm not supposed to cross, made by Mael. The dream wasn't a dream at all.

"That's not the way it works, son. I can help you out along the way, but there's no telling you the big picture. You opened your book. After I suggested that maybe it wasn't the best thing for you to do, you opened it. That's what happens, usually. People don't listen to me. It's almost like telling them to leave something alone makes them want it more. It surprises me every time, the way people just don't have an ounce of willpower. I can't do anything about free will, now, can I? That's yours to do with what you will."

"Can you stop speaking in riddles, Lurch?"

"Jack, by god. Call me Jack."

"OK, *Jack*. You're wigging me out."

"I am who I am. Can't change that." He fondles an oversized ring on his left hand, rubbing it absently. The ring has a junk-store look to it and makes me think of the business card I saw. "Why don't you go home now and look at that book you wanted so badly? I'll be here when you need me again."

I approach him like I'm gonna hit him. Believe me, I consider it. I did not sign up for the shit he's dishing out. When I get in his face, though, I can *feel* his space. It prickles my skin like it'd burn if I got even a fraction of an inch closer. So I stop.

"Listen, dude. I just want my lost day back. I don't want your damn book. And I can promise you, I won't *need* you."

"It's already your book. Not mine."

"You're a real conversationalist. Anybody ever tell you that, *Jack*?"

"You best get home now, Gaige. It's getting late. About time for the sun to come up, don't you think?" He smiles a great big shit-eating grin of a smile. Then his mouth forms an O of surprise before he bursts into a peal of jagged laughter.

I pull out my phone, ready to call him out on that one. I know it's still early. But when I look at the screen, it reads 4:50 AM. Impossible. We got here around seven-thirty or eight at the latest. It should only be nine o'clock at night, tops.

I glance outside. The sky's lightening, which means that it's Tuesday morning, and I have to get ready for school.

"What the hell is happening?"

As I look at him, the store seems to shimmer. The shelves suddenly look far away, and a lot like a highway in a heat wave. They seem to shiver and blink in and out.

Then the shelves are gone. The bells are gone. The counter's gone. I stand alone in the abandoned building again—alone with Lurch. I feel a slight breeze and notice that, once again, the window is smashed. Lurch walks to the hole, examines my work, and winks.

"Nice job, Gaige." He laughs and makes his way out of the hole and onto the cobbled street beyond. And then he's gone, off into the early morning.

Chapter Six

I JUST KNOW THAT BOOK'S gonna be sitting on my bed when I get home, as if it didn't vanish into thin air last night when Logan arrived.

It's literally the last thing I want to see. And yet there it is, right out in the open, on my duvet.

I leave it sitting there as I get ready for school. I can't miss two days in a row. Monday was actually the first day I missed this year. And it's June. I know, right? I hate missing school. I'm kind of geeky that way.

As I brush my teeth, I see the cat bite on my finger reflected in the mirror. Seeing it makes it itch again. It's beyond red. I'll probably lose my finger or something. You do *not* want to be bitten by Satan's bitch cat. Only bad things can come of that, take my word for it. Lilith—Satan named his cat Lilith.

Before I leave my room, I grab my backpack and sling it over my shoulder. As an afterthought—not a forced thought that somehow creeps into my mind unwanted and of its own accord, no way, impossible—I grab the book off the bed and slip it into my pack.

Why I grab it, I will *never* know. I guess I just feel better if it's with me. I need to keep an eye on the thing. I'm not quite ready to explore its pages again, but I'm not ready to give it up, either. Something happened when those words appeared; I went somewhere. I might need to go back there to figure things out, and I'm guessing the book is the only way in.

I should just light a match and hold it to the book. But something tells me I wouldn't be able to bear the screaming as its flesh goes up in flames.

Maniacal, right?

…

Once at school, I feel a little disoriented. I bring my backpack to my locker, but I don't feel right about leaving the book there. What if something happens to it? What if it *does* something and I'm not around to stop it?

"Hey, Gaige." It's Noah and Sara. Ugh. I don't want any conversations right now. *I can't, people.*

They come to a stop at my locker while I'm deciding what to do with my backpack and the thing inside of it. I'm not getting out of this. Noah *is* my best friend, after all.

"*You* missed school?" Sara says, letting out a little laugh of victory. She puts a hand through her fire-engine-red-dyed hair and tucks it behind her ear to keep it out of her face. Then she pumps her fist for good measure. Her smile is made all the more shit-eating by her dark purple lipstick. Sara is the school's most dedicated punk. She always looks like she just stepped out of a Ramones concert at CBGB in 1975. "Yes! Man, it must have been some ugly twenty-four-hour bug for you to blow your streak like that! Guess I win."

Noah laughs. He has this massive head of frizzy brown hair that waves about his head whenever he bursts into laughter. He's the perfect partner to Sara's retro groove. Picture 1970s guitar-hero rocker Jimi Hendrix, only as a nerdy white guy. He knows about the competition between Sara and me, how we were both trying to make it to the end of the school year without missing any classes. Wow, we're such geeks.

"My bad," I say, turning to Sara. I feign disappointment in myself, but I honestly have no fucks left to give. I have too many other things on my mind. "Looks like you win."

"You OK, my dude?" Noah says. His facial expression turns stern, bordering on angry, but I know Noah and recognize the look. He thinks something's wrong. "You look a bit gray. You all right? What happened?"

"I'm good. Just running late," I say. "Gotta get ready for class."

"Lunch? In the caf?" Sara asks, fiddling with the stud in her nose. She doesn't pick up on the BFF check-in. "You can tell us all about the plague that kept you away from school yesterday. How about it?"

"Yeah, yeah. Sure. I'll see you there."

Sara turns to go, but Noah moves in closer. "Hey, dude. You sure you're OK?" Noah knows me like he knows himself. He can probably smell the waves of madness wafting from me right now. He also has a great bullshit detector. He knows something is wrong, something that's not a head cold. His angry look would be funny if I didn't know it was his worry mask. "You good, bud? For reals?"

"Sure, sure. Aces. Honestly," I say. Even I can tell that I'm lying. I don't even try.

"I gotta go, guys," Sara says. "I've got gym, and I'll be late if I don't go now."

She leans in and gives Noah a kiss on the cheek before waving to me and heading off in the direction of the gym.

"OK, be honest," Noah says after he watches his girlfriend walk away. He's clearly head over heels in love with her, clunky Doc Martens and all. "Did you and Logan have a fight or something? You can tell me, dude. I'll kick his ass. If you want me to, that is."

"Noooo. Down boy," I say. I can't help but laugh now. Noah has a way of breaking the ice and paving the way to normalcy without you knowing it's even happening. "We're good. Really. I think. Well, there was a little bit of a . . . no, we're good. Just not feeling a hundred percent. Didn't want to miss another day, but I still feel like crap. That's all. I swear."

"OK, dude," he says, sounding totally unconvinced—like a good friend should. "I'll believe you. For now. If it's something more, you better tell me later. I gotta go, too. Harrison loses his shit if you're a second late. Gotta run."

Noah puts his fist out, and I bump it with my own.

"Gotta get moving myself," I say. It totally feels like I'm brushing him off. I grab a textbook from a shelf in my locker and show it to him. "History."

"See you around, then. Lunch? OK?"

"Yeah, sure," I say. The four of us always have lunch together. It's a given at this point.

He turns and runs down the slowly emptying hallway, disappearing into the chaos of kids making their way to their classes. Electricity is in the air. Everyone can feel the impending end of the school year. I wish I could tap into that lightness.

I start to slip the book out of my backpack but think better of it. I don't want to take the chance that it will vanish again because there are other people around, so I decide I need to carry the pack around with me all day. I have unwittingly become the Keeper of the Book. Or maybe it has become *my* keeper.

I must look unstable, though. On my way to class, I keep reaching back to stick a hand deep inside the backpack and caress the book. I just want to make sure it isn't going anywhere this time. I also feel an insatiable desire to look at its pages again. I'm desperate to get back to it, to revisit those swirling words, fall into them, and go to that other place. I need to know more. I don't understand how it happened, but I'm desperate to get back inside.

I'm so desperate, in fact, that I excuse myself from my history class ten minutes after it begins so I can take the book into the bathroom with me.

I go into an empty stall, close the toilet lid, and sit down cross-legged with the backpack on my lap so nobody can see my feet. After I dig the book out of my bag, I hang the backpack on the hook on the back of the stall door and hold the book in my hands for the longest time. I feel like I'm about to turn a corner I can't un-turn, like I'm skating on the edge of no return.

As if I haven't already gone too far. I am, after all, the owner of an evil book that seems capable of blinking in and out of existence of its own accord, and of literally sucking me inside of it. I'm sure I already passed the point of no return long ago.

I crack the spine and hold the book flat in my lap. First page, nothing. Second page, nothing. But then it slowly begins to fill with words again. Their swirling movement immediately enchants me, mesmerizes me. I look deeper, beyond the words, through them and into the ink, and see word fragments, parts of sentences, hints. It all seems somehow familiar and yet somehow unknown. I can't quite put my finger on it. It's when I see the words *and now Logan's gone too* that I shriek and slam the book closed in my lap.

I am way not ready to read what the rest of that particular sentence says. I'm far too terrified. I'd be lying if I said I'm not shitting my pants—no washroom humor intended, even though I'm sitting on a toilet. I think I'm ready to check out of this nightmare now. I need to find the exit.

Instead of ditching the book and running, though, I open back up to a random page. I think we've already established that I'm a glutton for punishment; I mean, haven't we? I'm basically hardwired to do the wrong thing. That's me, Gaige Warrol, King of Bad Choices.

I catch the odd phrase as I scan the pages attempting not to focus enough to actually read. *Drenched in sweat… tore at its flesh… Lurch came back again last night… I have to save him. I have to save both of them.*

Those last lines scare me the most. Lurch is what I've been calling the old man. And the last one? I feel like it relates to the Logan comment. This fucker best not mess with my friend or my boyfriend. He won't be ready for the me he gets if he does.

The scrabbling. I remember the scrabbling now as it comes back. It's what I hear right before—

I slip into the words, slip through them and into the ink as they swirl about on the page. Once I'm on the other side, it all comes back to me. This is where I met Mael. Everything they said comes back to me, too. I take a step forward, and my foot sinks slightly in the rubbery black muck. Mael was here, in this place. They wanted to help me, I think. But how can I be sure? This looks like someplace you would go to die.

Just as I remember Mael's waves of black hair, moving like seaweed swaying with the tides, their face comes to me. It's a memory at first, but then, as though summoned by the memory itself, it forms out of the inky substance beside me.

"Mael," I whisper, forgetting their warning not to touch them. I reach out, but they flinch and move back.

"Don't touch. You said my name. You remember me," Mael says, stepping forward again. They're fully formed now, fully here. I can see all of them. And they seem surprised that I've said their name.

"Yes." Of course I remember Mael. It also occurs to me that I was going to Google some of the things they mentioned the last time, but totally forgot to do so. "I do, but how is any of this even poss—"

"Dreams are sometimes like this, Gaige. Sometimes they don't flow together, and sometimes they continue where we left off. And isn't everything possible in our dreams?"

"But you're real." I reach out to touch them again. Their swarthy skin glows in the luminescence, and I imagine it is softer than silk. It's so perfect, I can't even.

Again, Mael jumps back to avoid my touch.

"You can't touch me," they say. "If you do, it's all over."

"What's ov—"

"The Outside World. The moment you either touch me or go too far past the threshold, you'll no longer be able to go back to the Outside World. You'll be of the Other Side, like me. You'll melt into this place like all the others before you. Please, Gaige. You can't let Chalek win again. I have to save one person. Just one."

There are tears in their impossibly large brown eyes now.

"Why are *you* here?" I ask as another memory comes back to me. "You told me you didn't choose the book. So why are you here? You should have been able to walk away."

Instead of replying, they move forward a few paces and point to a line traced on the ground, the one they made last time I was here. Despite the opaque darkness all around me, I can still see things in the slight, luminescent glow.

"This is the line you can't cross. You have to remember that in case there comes a time when I'm not here to warn you."

"OK. I remember. You made that mark before. But you didn't tell me what was on the other side. You didn't tell me about the gorgeous meadow."

"This is a dream, Gaige. Chalek makes this place from the inky substance around us. He manipulates all of it. There is no meadow. The other kids didn't always remember all the details, but this one's *really* important. So say it out loud: *I won't cross this line on the ground.* Say it. Please."

They run their foot along the ground one more time and gouge the line just a little deeper. The rubbery surface doesn't give much, but enough for the line to become more noticeable.

"I won't cross this line on the ground." I stare at it as I repeat Mael's urgent warning, feeling a bit silly. "But you didn't tell me about what's beyond it. Why didn't you tell me?"

"You don't understand. The place beyond that line can be anything Chalek wants it to be. He can make it appear any way he wishes, draw it into being with his black goop. He can steal your thoughts. To him, you're an open book. What you saw, that's what he wanted you to see; it's not what's actually there. He took it from inside of you. Please don't fall for it. It's all just goop and darkness. Everything you see is made up of this substance."

"I don't understand." But I save that mystery for later. One at a time. "Why are *you* here? You're the one who said no to the book and walked away."

"My free will saved me from being stuck with my book," Mael says. "But Chalek is a liar, a charlatan. When people don't fall for his traps, it only makes him angry."

"But he told me only one kid walked away," I say. "He let you walk away. He even said."

"But did he? Is that what he said?"

Mael returns to my side, just out of reach. They've only given me two rules, and one of them is simple enough: don't cross the line. That rule's as old as time itself. Half the old fables and fairy tales contain some version of that threat. I'm trying to ignore the fact that most of their heroes and heroines eventually cross those lines in the sand, despite all warnings. Even Adam and Eve, in the biggest fairy tale of all time, crossed that line. But I won't cross it. I have that rule down pat.

It's Mael's second rule, though. Whoa. That's the one I'm desperate to break. It's right up there with telling a kid they can't have a book that's sitting right there on the shelf.

Don't touch me. You can never touch me.

The closer they get, the more desperate I become to reach out and touch them. There is something about this person—their beauty, their sun-kissed skin, their hair, all of it. I try not to think about how even contemplating these things is a betrayal of the worst kind. I try not to think about Logan, back in the Outside World. I feel way too guilty right now. I'm in hell, and I'm thinking about this gorgeous nonbinary person stuck in this place instead of my own survival. Instead of my own boyfriend.

A boy wants what a boy wants.

"Try to remember exactly what Chalek said," Mael says. Their words startle me. I was so busy imagining myself touching them that I completely forgot they were there. If that makes any sense. I have no idea what they're talking about. Until I do. I reluctantly shake my previous smarmy thoughts and daydreams away.

Chalek's words come back to me in a heartbeat. *I recall only one child ever taking heed of my words, putting that book back on the shelf, and scurrying out of here empty-handed with their tail between their legs. Just one.*

"He said you scurried away."

"Yes. Until he stopped me. When I wouldn't fall for his tricks or traps—when I broke away from his spell—it enraged him. He can still do the things he does without our help. It's only that it gives him more pleasure when we choose. Maybe more power? I don't know everything about how this world works, but he loves to manipulate free will."

I recall the business card I found in the jacket pocket. *All Things You Didn't Know You Wanted.* The card explains what Chalek does, what he feeds off of: he sells desire and somehow harnesses it. He gets his kicks from tempting people and having them fall into his trap. Somehow Mael resisted his dangling carrot, and it clearly pissed him off. And now Mael's been sent to this limbo, this purgatory. This threshold to a world that bends to Chalek's will.

I look at Mael again, closer this time. It only takes me a second to realize something. They're the person I would make just for me, if it were possible to do so. Everything about them, right down to their shimmering waves of jet-black hair, their rich skin tone, their nose, their petite frame, their femininity, and their dark brown eyes, is my idea of the perfect crush.

Even now Chalek is tempting me, pushing me to touch the thing it would kill me to touch. Mael is another prop, another book Chalek wants me to claim and open. Mael is my next carrot.

"How do I know *you're* not a trick? You're so gorgeous. You're literally perfect. I would choose you, Mael."

"Gaige," they begin. They sigh and drop their head. Looking down at their feet, they continue. "I can't help that. I'm sorry. You don't have to look at me, though. Just hear my words. I'm here to help. Honest. He can control matter here on this side, but he can't control my will. I only want to help you. I don't want any other kids to lose. I want to stop you from disappearing into this." They gesture toward the glistening gloop that surrounds us. Is it pulsating?

I look beyond the trench they dug with their foot. For an instant, I see the field of tall grass again, the lone, tall oak in the distance, the wildflowers. I'm so drawn to that idyllic place, and it's so familiar; I know I've been there before. I just can't pinpoint when, or where it is.

"It's pretty, though. I know that field." I hear my words, but they sound so far away.

"Stop, Gaige." Mael's voice startles me, and my feet stop moving. I hadn't even realized they were propelling me forward. "There is no field. And this is not really how I look. Chalek can control almost everything here, everything but free will.

"He can pull thoughts and desires from your mind, and he can use those things against you. That's why I look this way, and why you see what you see beyond the threshold. He keeps setting traps to keep you here. He draws them into existence to entice you to his side of the two."

"His side of the two?"

"It's just what I call them: the Outside World and this one, the Other Side. This one belongs to him, but he still hasn't figured it out. That's why he sends kids inside. He's trying to understand it better. He can change things here, manipulate matter, even though he can't seem to enter this place himself. Not in body, anyway.

"He makes you see what you want to see instead of what's actually there. He knows what you want. Because of the substance of this place, he can make it happen. He can change me too. I know why I change, Gaige. I change for the next kid who comes, and the next, and the next. I was not like this in the Outside World. I was a Batcaver."

There's that word again.

"Oh, my freaking god." The penny drops. "He changed the way you look to make me wanna—"

"He's trying to trick you into going into the Other Side. He'd do anything to make you do it. But he can't make me go along with it. I don't know why, but he can't manipulate me. Maybe because I refused the book."

"We have to get out, then," I say. "I mean, if I get to leave, you do too. You can come back with me. We can leave together."

"We talked about this last time. We need to figure out a way to save *you*, to keep you from coming back. I'm here to help you, but you can't help me, so stop asking. Please, try to remember. I'm already lost, of this place. Remember that so I don't have to explain it again. You only sleep for a few minutes of Other Side time."

I grab onto this clue and run with it.

"So time *is* different here?"

Mael merely nods. They must feel the weight of it every day, piling up against them.

"How much time am I losing while I'm here?"

"That doesn't matter," Mael says. "Don't you understand? The only reason you're getting out is because I'm here to stop you. Most kids, they only come back two or three times before I lose them. But if I wasn't here, you would have gone inside already. He makes you want to go in. He does this to try to get inside himself. There's something in there that Chalek wants. Needs. He tries to enter with his victims, to find a way to follow them. And he also wants to move between the two places. He doesn't care when people vanish, disappear into the beyond. Die. All of you are expendable. He only wants to travel between the two places, to get at whatever it is he's so desperate to retrieve."

"OK, but why? Why does he have to do that if it's his place? If he can control things? And what's in it for you if you help me?"

"I only want to stop Chalek. If we work together, I think we can. I've been here for a long time, Gaige. I don't want any more of you to fall. His experiment fails every time; there's no traveling between the two places. It's a one-way portal. And Chalek won't accept that."

I'm back to losing myself in Mael's face. Their hair. My focus keeps coming back to my attraction. It's laced with repulsion now that I know Chalek has somehow read me, that he's using me against myself. It's like the feeling I got when he was putting thoughts in my head. I try to stop focusing on Mael's face, try to focus only on their words.

"—and if we do that, he won't be able to torture anyone else," Mael is saying.

"Do what?" I missed crucial words.

"We need to find a way to close the space between here and there. The more kids he feeds to his failed science project, the stronger he becomes… and the closer he gets to controlling the Other Side. He's trying to bring the Other Side into the Outside World. Or at least, something from inside it. That's what he wants to do. But he has to find a way in himself, and I think he's figuring out that this is his only way."

I can definitely get behind closing the gap between this place and the Outside World. Between the stank and the darkness, I've already been here far too long and too many times. I am *so* into trashing that book forever.

"When I get out, I'll burn the book. I'll make sure there's nothing left of it. Clearly, the book is the problem."

"I tried that. I told one of the boys to burn his book, and it didn't work. It just came back. And there are many books, Gaige. Each kid gets their own book."

I was only tossing the idea around. I didn't really think it could be that easy. But the despair I feel when Mael shoots down the idea so quickly is real, and I let out an exaggerated sigh. I feel just about as dejected as someone can feel—not to mention how I feel about knowing that there are more books.

"I need to leave now. I'm in school. They're going to find me."

"When you come to the Other Side, they can't find you in the Outside World," they say. "You are there but not there. You're more here."

"But you said I was dreaming. That means I'm sleeping. If I'm sleeping and dreaming this, I'm on the can at school."

"It doesn't matter. You should go. It's not good to stay too long, anyway."

"I can agree with you on that."

"Try to remember the line. Don't cross it. When you come again, wait right here. I will come. You have to wait for me. Don't cross the line. Promise me."

"I will not cross the line."

Mael's smile completely destroys my resolve. Their face lights up with it, it's filled with dimples, and it's more than I can handle right now. As I step toward them, my hand outstretched to touch their cheek, they blink away into the darkness, and there is nothing left but the luminescent tar-like surfaces that always seem like they're attempting to swallow me alive.

Time to end this.

Chapter
Seven

As soon as the thought crosses my mind, the Other Side dissipates. For an instant, I'm falling—until I jolt awake back in the washroom stall. The book is on the floor in front of me. I pick it up and hold it in my lap while I try to bring my breathing back to normal.

When I'm ready to face the music for spending too much time away from class, I return the book to my backpack, leave the stall, splash some water on my face, and exit the washroom.

Once I hit the hall, I already know it's too quiet. I don't hear a sound, not a single one. It feels like the world has died.

The route from my history classroom to the washroom is down a hallway that is virtually all windows. It's kind of like a solarium. It's always as hot as hell in this hallway in the daytime because of all the windows, doesn't matter what time of year it is.

It takes me about three seconds to realize that the world outside the windows is actually pitch-black, not bright with the June sunlight I should see. I lost more time. Shit. Of course I did. Mael said I would.

It's only this quiet because I'm the only one here. Just as I clue in to this fact, I reach the end of the hallway. I also reach the conclusion that there's no point in going back to history class, as it obviously ended hours—or days—or weeks—or eons ago. Who knows?

I pull my out cell and look at the time. Almost eleven. Same day. Phew. Tuesday, almost Wednesday.

I thank my lucky stars that the hallway lights are kept on at night. At this point, darkness would be far too much. I'm also grateful for solid footing. I do enjoy a good, old-fashioned floor. It's so much better than squelchy tar-like goop.

In a surge of newfound anger, I take the book out of my backpack, turn around, and whip it back down the long hallway. It skips across the floor a couple times and then slides to a stop.

Fucking thing's literally robbing me.

I want to leave it where it lands. I mean, if I'm the only one who can see it, it's not like it's actually there anyway, right? I can just wash my hands of it and walk away. Nobody else will ever know it was there.

Then I see a shadow at the window. Immediately, I think of Mael and the way they seem to form out of the Other Side substance itself, the way they step out of it and become, right before my eyes. But I know this shadow, and I know it's not Mael's. This one somehow reminds me of a skittery praying mantis, all limbs and lunacy. Unfortunately, I know exactly who it belongs to. There's no mistaking Lurch.

I have no idea how he's found me, but there he is, larger than life and twice as ugly. He stands just outside the long bank of windows, only the panes of glass between us, and he looks pissed. His skeletal face is all hard angles and hatred.

After staring at each other for what seems like an eternity, I look away first. Of course I flinch and lose my staring contest with the devil. I know what it means to lose, too—just like I know what needs to happen next. Bastard doesn't have to spell it out for me. He remains a silent sentinel, waiting for me to make the next move.

I walk down to the end of the hallway, pick up the book, and return it to my backpack. When I look back to the place where Lurch was standing, I see that he's gone. I've done what he wanted of me. I've retrieved his precious demon book. His job here is done. For now.

Not knowing what to do next, I grab my cell and text Noah. Can't hurt to bring him into the mix. The jury's still out about how well it went with Logan; might as well give Noah a go. He's brilliant. He'll figure something out.

Gaige: Hey Noah. Whatcha doing? Can you come to the school?

Almost immediately, he responds.

Noah: Ummm...I'm watching TikTok. Why'd you ditch us at lunch, bro??????

Gaige: I can explain. I think??? Sorry, Noah. Really. Please come?

Noah: You totally piss me off sometimes, you know! ****PAUSE** It's so late! Ugh. Be right there. Whereabouts? Whatcha doing there anyway?**

I don't think I should mention I'm actually *inside* the school. Seems too weird a thing to divulge in a text. The explanation would take too much effort.

Gaige: Nice touch with the literally spelled out pause, there. **APPLAUSE** Just come to the front entrance. I'll meet you there. I'll explain when you get here.

Noah: You're exhausting, dude. You owe me friendship dues! KK be right there

Now I just have to get *myself* there. I estimate that it'll take Noah about five minutes to get to the school. I start for the foyer, not exactly thrilled about having to walk back down the glassed-in hallway. Nothing like being in a goldfish bowl with a hungry shark looking in, lurking, waiting for its opportunity. I try not to look outside. I hum to myself and pretend I'm not terrified of the darkness on the other side of the windows. I don't want to see Lurch again, standing there on the other side, silently judging me.

Other Side. The term makes the hair on my arms stand up. *The* Other Side *belongs to him.* The words, something Mael said, come to me like the recollection of a dream.

I'm only at the front doors for a couple of minutes before Noah approaches. I have a bad feeling that I know exactly what's about to happen, so I close my eyes and cringe in anticipation.

I press against the release bar on the door.

Sure enough, after an all-too-brief pause, all the alarms in the school begin to shriek at once. Of course the alarms are set. Of course they'll go off once a door is opened.

The look on Noah's face is worth everything, though. As I walk down the front steps toward him, I try to seem casual and nonchalant as can be. The alarms scream bloody murder behind me, but I do my best to keep my cool and ignore them. Noah has this priceless, fight-or-flight look on his face. It's just too funny. Before I totally lose it, though, I catch up to where he stands frozen on the lawn. I grab him by the arm and force him out of his panic trance.

"Let's go, dude," I say. "It's just an alarm. No biggie."

"No biggie?" he says. "Holy shit, Gaige! What the hell were you doing *inside* the school? You didn't tell me you were ins—"

"It's a long story," I say. I walk past him and look back. "But maybe we shouldn't stand here to discuss it. I'm guessing the cops are gonna show up any minute now."

"You think?" he says. He catches up to me, and we sprint away from the school. We aren't very far away before we hear sirens descending on the neighborhood. We don't slow down for at least three or four blocks.

Finally, I can't take it anymore. For a seventeen-year-old, I'm not exactly fit. I need to slow down. I grab Noah's arm. "Whoa. That's enough." Pant, pant, pant. "Dude. I'm dying."

"OK," he says. But he doesn't just slow down. He totally stops, drops, and sits his ass down on the curb. "You have to tell me what the hell's going on. What were you doing inside the school, Gaige? And where'd you go today? Why are you like this?"

I plop down beside him. "Dude. What's that supposed to mean?"

He just looks at me, expecting an actual answer. I take a moment to catch my breath before I continue. "OK, OK. It starts in a bookstore that's not there, and it ends with a book I couldn't possibly show you, even if I wanted to. So, yeah, it's a long story. It feels like an impossible story to tell, though. I can try."

Noah shakes his head, and his huge mane of frizzy hair shimmers in the glow from the streetlight. "*Try* is not enough, Gaige. I need more. Details, please. Facts."

"You know that bookstore on Elm? The old one on the part of the street that's cobbled?"

"Ha. Right. I know downtown like the back of my hand. There is no bookstore on Elm. Anywhere on Elm. So no, I don't know *that* bookstore. What the hell is it with you and bookstores, anyway? You're obsessed."

"Right? It's like I see one, and I can't pass it up. I think that's why I got in trouble this time around. I think the bookstore was intentional."

I stand up and start to walk. I think I might take Noah for a little walk to Elm Street. It's easier to show than tell. He gets up and falls into step beside me.

"What do you mean, though? What kind of trouble are you in? And why would it take you to the school?"

"I fell asleep on the can, man. Hours ago. I never even left school today. I went to the washroom during first period, and that's where I woke up a few minutes ago."

Noah bursts out laughing, so I join him. After we recompose ourselves, I look at him and shrug.

"Thank god it's still Tuesday," I say, after we calm down and a realization hits me. "I haven't missed an entire day this time, so there is that! It's hard to keep track of what's happening with time."

But did I fall asleep on the can? I don't recall falling asleep; I just recall looking into the book and falling. Time disappeared.

I was there, but not there. And there again in a different time. But wait—Mael told me I was dreaming. You only dream when you're sleeping. I just don't know.

"Wanna go for a walk? I can show you where this bookstore is. Or was."

"But I already know there's no bookstore on Elm."

"Yeah, but the important thing is that there *was* one there on Sunday afternoon. And there *was* one again on Monday night. Who knows? Maybe there'll be one now."

"Dude," Noah says. "Are you the Riddler? Are we in the Matrix? There is no spoon?"

I want to laugh, but I feel too close to my breaking point and don't know if I should laugh or cry. Sometimes the two reactions aren't too far apart, and right now there's only a hair's breadth between them.

"Logan's kind of pissed at me. Just promise me you're not going to get pissed at me too. If I can't show you anything, if I can't make you see what I've seen… you'll get frustrated, but try not to get pissed. OK?"

"Whatever, dude. I'm not gonna get all touchy-feely sad because you can't explain yourself properly. I'm not your boyfriend."

"Careful, buddy. Logan's my baby boy."

I stop and reach into my bag for the book. Of course, it doesn't matter how much I paw around in there trying to find it; the thing's not there. It knows. The book knows.

"See, there's a book in my backpack. I got it at the bookstore that isn't there. But when I reach in to take it out and show you, it's not there. I know it's there, because the last thing I did before

I texted you was return it to my backpack when I realized I can't chuck it away without the old man coming back into my life to make it a misery. To force me to keep the book."

"This is some deep doo-doo. This is Stephen King shit, bro. What are you *even*?"

"I'm glad you're seeing things my way. I don't know what to do. I'm getting tired, too, because every time I turn around, it's a different day. But I'm not sleeping, exactly. Or I guess I am sleeping, because I'm dreaming. You can't dream if you're not asleep, right? It doesn't *feel* like I'm sleeping. But it definitely feels like dreaming."

I exhale deeply, finally able to stop talking. I sound unstable even to myself.

Noah might not be able to figure out what I'm talking about, but at least we're walking in the right direction. I'm taking him to Elm Street. Even if I can't show him the bookstore, I might be able to explain my predicament more clearly once we get there. I don't know how to begin to explain the book to him, or Mael. But we can start at the bookstore, and having Noah's genius on my team feels like the boost I need right about now.

Chapter Eight

"OK, I GIVE. WHY CAN'T I see the book?"

"I really don't know." I wish I did. I usually like to solve life's little mysteries, not skate along their edges, but this is different. This is unexplained. I usually deal in mysteries that have everyday, run-of-the-mill solutions. I have never dealt with a supernatural one before. "When I tried to show the book to Logan, it vanished."

"As in, you couldn't find it?"

"As in, it was no longer there. It vanished, thin-air style. Poof."

"Tell me more about the bookstore."

At least he's trying to be helpful. Noah's like our city historian. Well, the teen version of our city historian. He's constantly pulling random facts out of his ass to impress people. Like, does anyone besides Noah know the exact date when our city's subway opened for business? The answer, ladies and gentlemen, is March 30, 1954. "It was a Tuesday, you know." No, Noah, I did not know.

Contemplating this, I wonder what he can tell me if I throw a name out there.

"Jack Chalek."

Instantaneous hork and spitball. OK, I did not anticipate this. As the name leaves my lips, the spit leaves his. I jump out of its path to avoid getting hit.

"Dude, take that back."

"Oh, man," I say. "You've *got* to tell me what you mean by that!"

I'm not surprised that the name means something to him, but I'm also *astonished* that it means something to him. Until this moment, it's only been a part of the new, make-believe reality I occasionally find myself stuck in. Now I know this Jack guy is real, even if I am the only one capable of seeing him. If Noah knows about him, he's real.

"Jack Chalek was a monster, Gaige. He was infamous and disgusting. Dude was notorious, with a capital NO. He had this emporium where he sold old crap that nobody wanted. Only, he had a way of convincing people they actually *did* want it. And some of the people he seduced into buying his shit ended up in a mass grave in the cellar of his store. Dude was featured on that *Crimes Against* TV show a few years ago. You know, as in crimes against humanity."

I stopped walking about ten paces ago, but Noah's been too busy regaling me with Chalek's story to notice. I'm frozen in place as I wait for him to realize that I'm no longer walking beside him.

"Hey," he says, still oblivious to the fact that he's walking alone. He's super-history-geeking right now. "His store was in that area. Downtown. Maybe even *on* Elm."

Noah looks over to where he thinks I should be and finally realizes I'm way behind him. He stands there looking back at me while I attempt to move, and I want to catch up with him, but I can't. My feet feel like they're wading in quick-drying cement, like they're sunk into a certain rubbery surface.

"I met Jack on Sunday." This comes out as a little more than a whisper.

"Dude," Noah says. "What did you just say?"

I'm thankful that he walks back to where I'm standing, because I still can't move.

"I said, I met Jack on Sunday."

"Jack Chalek has been dead for… gotta be close to a hundred years."

"I talked to him again last night."

"Dead. Like *in the ground* dead. They massacred him so bad, ain't no way he could even be a zombie, dude. I heard there was nothing recognizable left of Jack Chalek when the town was done with him."

"And I saw him a few minutes ago at school, right before I texted you. I was in the hallway. He was on the lawn outside, looking in, judging me."

"Dude. Do you hear anything I'm saying to you right now?"

"Dude," I say. "The eyes don't lie. Do *you* hear what *I'm* saying?"

"Let's go to this bookstore of yours. I'm guessing it's the emporium."

We begin to walk again. Miracle of miracles, my feet remember how to move.

"Why don't I know anything about this guy if he's so notorious?"

"I don't know, Gaige," Noah says. I can hear the mocking tone in his voice already. "When was the War of 1812?"

"How the hell am I supposed to know that? What's that got to do with anything?"

"I rest my case."

Takes me a second, but I get it. OK. He may have a point.

"I know it's the same place," I say, ignoring his shitty little callout. "When I was there with Logan, the place was empty and abandoned. I found an old jacket in a back closet. Let's see if I still have an eidetic memory. I'm feeling a bit shaky after the last forty-eight hours of hell I just lived through. I might have trouble spelling my name at the moment.

"Here goes. *Chalek's Emporium. Purveyors of All Things You Didn't Know You Wanted. Buy, Sell, Trade. Since 1875. Jack Chalek, Proprietor.* Nailed it."

"Shit. Yep. That's the place."

"That was from a business card I found in the breast pocket of the jacket."

Wait. Why didn't I think that business card through? That date should have been a red flag. Logan even repeated the date. Christ, everything about this should have been a red flag, beginning with finding the bookstore. I need help.

"Yeah, but that's pretty much impossible too, right?" he says. He's attempting to be delicate, but his voice is dripping with doubt and suspicion. "You realize that, don't you? That building probably changed hands a hundred times since it was the emporium. I think it's only been empty for ten, maybe fifteen years tops. The chances of a jacket owned by Jack Chalek being in a closet there are next to zero. In fact, I'm gonna go out on a limb and say they're literally zero. It just could not be real."

"But wait," I say as we finally turn onto Elm. The store's just a half a block up on the right. I can see its facade. "How could Logan have seen it, then? If the jacket wasn't real, that means I should have been the only one capable of seeing it. But I know Logan saw it. He told me to take a shower after I put it on. He was thoroughly skeezed out by it."

"Dude, no." He spits again. He's become a Russian grandmother. Or Sicilian? Whichever would spit to ward off evil spirits and curses. "You put on a jacket that possibly, maybe was owned by the infamous Jack Chalek? I hope you took Logan's advice. That would be some bad mojo to get on you."

"Actually," I say. I have to stop and think. "Yeah. No. I didn't take a shower, because see, I keep losing time. So even though it was a whole day ago that I wore the jacket, it's only been a few hours for me. I'm losing blocks of time. They're just gone. The trade-off for the book."

When we get to the storefront, I notice that someone has covered the smashed window with cardboard. Without saying anything, I begin the task of removing the cardboard so we can get inside. Once again, the street's pretty bare. And the darkness gives us cover in case anybody walking by on Yonge happens to looks down the street.

"Come on inside."

"Dude. I bet this is the spot where the emporium stood. Probably the same building, even. I know it was around here. It would have been renovated a few times, but it's probably the same old shell."

"Maybe the jacket's still here?" But as I step inside, I see that it's not where I flung it yesterday. Shit. "Nope. It's gone."

"How do you know?"

"Because I tossed it on the floor after I tried it on. It was giving me the creeps, so I whipped it off and threw it over there."

I point toward the back of the shop by the office, where it should be.

Other than the missing jacket, which somebody probably picked up and tossed into a bin somewhere, there seem to be no changes to the place since the night before.

"Wow. Just knowing what happened here gives me the creeps. People died here. That man was a monster. A monster without a motive, if I remember correctly."

It feels different in here, now that I know the truth. It's more oppressive. The air's thicker. It feels like my life is in greater peril than I imagined. I'm more of a drama llama now, to be honest.

"He was gay, you know," Noah says out of the blue. Random facts. Noah has them. "It was on the *Crimes Against* episode. Something about his 'life partner' or something. I can't remember what it was. But, yeah."

"This is information I did not need to hear, Noah. Thank you."

"Let's go down to the cellar, dude," Noah says, ignoring my words completely. He's become a kid in a candy shop. My boy's totally geeking out now. "Where's the door to the cellar?"

I laugh a nervous laugh that I regret the moment it leaves my throat, because it makes me feel more scared than I was before I let it out. "And why in the name of all the fucks would we want to do that, now?" I ask.

"This is history, Gaige. Let's find a way down there. There has to be one somewhere."

I think of that thing Chalek said to me a millennium ago: something about a broiled chicken not being able to escape back to its coop. I've a feeling we're about to be broiled.

I take Noah to the back office. Just for shits and giggles, I open the closet door, which is now firmly closed. Lo and behold, the jacket's back on its hanger. It's a harbinger, if ever I saw one. It practically screams in my face, *Don't go into the cellar!*

"Shiiiiiiit."

"What?" Noah asks. Then a gasp escapes him, and he's so close I feel his breath on the back of my neck. Had I not already been covered in goose bumps, his exhalation definitely would have caused them. "The jacket."

"Yeah, the jacket," I say. "Let's just get out of here, Noah. I don't feel right about this place."

"Umm. I'm looking in that pocket. Did you put the business card back?"

"Yeah."

He takes the jacket off the hanger and pretends he's going to put it on me. I shrink away from it so fast, I fall to the floor.

"Dude. Who's the coward now? Holy," he says. But I can tell his courage is more bravado than anything else. He puts his hand inside the jacket and comes out with the business card. "Whoa. Authentic shit."

"Can we leave now, please? Keep your ghoulish souvenir if you want, but we should just step off now."

"There's got to be a way to the cellar," he says, more to himself than to me. Like he didn't even hear my plea. "Did you go exploring when you were here with Logan?"

"Not really. I guess we didn't feel like taking a romantic stroll to our deaths in the cellar dungeon of doom. There's not much here, anyway. Just the main storefront and this office. I don't think there's much else."

"Gotta be at least a washroom. Maybe the access to the cellar is in the can, man?"

Sure enough, there's a washroom behind the office. And of course there's a false door in the floor of this room. Of fucking course there is. Like it or not, we're headed for the cellar. You know, the place where all the bodies were buried by my friend Lurch. In another century.

Noah walks inside the tiny washroom and tries the light switch. *Are you shitting me? Why?* No way would the power be on here.

Nothing is going my way.

Chapter Nine

As soon as we raise the door in the floor, we're hit with the preternatural stench of decades of undisturbed air. And earth—the rich, dank stink of earth. There's something else, too. Something hauntingly familiar that I would rather not recognize.

I choke to keep the contents of my stomach from rising into my throat. I guess standing next to a toilet is kind of handy right now, but I still don't want to lose my lunch.

There is something completely unsettling about the smell. It's like the book, like the Other Side. The other side of the words. Of course. That's what the smell is. The inky darkness.

"Man. Smells like maybe they didn't quite remove all the bodies," Noah says. He laughs, but I can tell by his expression that he immediately regrets the action because it causes him to inhale a gulp of air.

"Are you sure you want to do this?" I say. This comes out like a plea for him to change his mind, but I try to make it sound casual. "Isn't your curiosity piqued enough just looking down there into the darkness? It's not like we have a flashlight. We won't be able to see anything anyway."

Noah raises a finger in victory as he has an aha moment. Then he casually opens the cupboard under the sink, reaches in, rummages around, and comes up with a frigging flashlight. No bull.

"Of course," I say, dejected.

"If you mean of course they're going to have a flashlight nearby so they can put their hands on it whenever they want to go downstairs to the storage area, then yes. Of course. But to be fair, we both also have flashlight apps on our phones."

He flicks the switch on the flashlight, and it comes on. *Are you shitting me, universe?* The flashlight works? How, even? The batteries should have split open and leaked corrosives all over the inside of the flashlight by now. This is *not* fair.

"Shit. Guess we're set either way," I say. How about that. Just my luck. "I was kind of hoping the flashlight wouldn't work."

"Let's go." Before I can protest, Noah slithers down into the hole, searching blindly for a ladder with his feet. He smiles when his feet gain purchase. "Ready?"

"Dude," I say. "I will never be ready for this. Let's do it and get it over with. How many people did you say he killed and hid in the cellar?"

"I didn't, actually. Not sure," Noah says. His voice has faded, though, as he's already standing on the cellar floor. I know his answer's bullshit. He knows his history like a college professor. He has the exact number of bodies buried in that cellar in the instant-access history folder in his mind; he just doesn't want to freak me out by telling me the truth.

I look down to get an idea of the general direction of the ladder before swinging around and dropping my legs into the hole. I can no longer see Noah, but I can see the ray of light from the flashlight. I know his general location below me.

"Here I come," I whisper, more to myself than to him. My feet quickly find the rungs of the ladder, and I make my way down, staring up at the bathroom light I wish I wasn't leaving behind.

Just as my left foot hits floor, I see a shadow of movement above me. I look up in time to see the face of Chalek grinning down at me, the light behind him making a halo of brightness around his ghoulish face. He puts a finger to his lips to shush me and then slowly closes the door in the floor above us.

"No!" I whimper like a baby, halting the shrill scream that attempts to crawl out of my throat. I'd scare myself even more by screaming into this skanky space, so I force myself to swallow it. "You bastard," I whisper, defeated, as my connection with Chalek is cut off.

With both feet on the floor, I make my way toward Noah, grab at his shirt, and pull—maybe a little too roughly. He falls backward and knocks against me. The flashlight flies out of his hand and hits the floor, then rolls a couple of feet away from us.

Thank god the light doesn't shatter. It would definitely be the end of me, to be suddenly thrown into total darkness amid this stench. I would not be able to hold back my screams. The last thing I can handle right now is being locked inside a dead killer's cellar in pitch-blackness. The light flickers but stays on, so Noah's able to see and retrieve the flashlight.

Being locked inside a dead killer's cellar with a small beam of light guiding us? Totally fine. Infinitely better. I did say *dead* killer, right? That makes it all that much creepier, don't it?

With flashlight in hand, Noah is back in charge. "What the hell happened? Did you shut the door behind you? What if it latched? Are we stuck down here, Gaige? Why'd you do that?"

"*I* didn't do anything, Noah. I was down here when it closed. I'd love to tell you it was the wind or something, but dude. It was old man Chalek himself. I saw him smiling down at me just before he let the door slam closed. I'm guessing the latch is absolutely in place. We're going to die down here. I hope it was worth it for you. One last history project, eh, dude?"

I'm not as close to tears as I sound, but I do sound like a total baby. I don't want to climb up that ladder and test the latch, because in my heart I know it's locked solid. I can still hope it's unlatched, though. As long as I don't check, I'm fine-ish.

"Still insisting we're seeing the old guy, are we? He's dead, Gaige. It's got to be somebody who knows the history of this place. Maybe they're acting out their role-playing fantasies, and you're the sucker they chose to involve in their game."

"How likely do you think *that* is?"

"I'd say very. More likely than a dead killer coming back to life and choosing you to haunt. Some of these role-playing guys are crazy into their fantasies, Gaige. Even you would know that."

"I do. But I also *know* that the guy I keep seeing *is* this Chalek guy. I know it like I know my name. Besides, things are happening that are absolutely impossible. Like, otherworldly stuff. So you're wrong."

"Well, *I'm* trying the door." He retraces his steps, climbs the ladder, and pushes the door. Sure enough, it doesn't budge. He pushes it again, harder this time. Then, when it doesn't give at all, he begins erratically pounding it with his fists. "Help! Let us out!"

Noah's shrieks for help travel through me like a virus. They only serve to up my anxiety level by about a thousand. I almost join him in his cries and pleas for help, but I don't think it would matter. It's futile. We're here for the long haul.

Everybody knows what happens next in horror movies. The flashlight eventually goes out. Every-fucking-body knows the flashlight eventually goes out. And, clearly, that's also when all hell breaks loose. That one little beam of light keeps us on the brink of—but not directly in the path of—danger, calamity, and death.

Chapter Ten

"What now?" Noah asks as he finally gives up on the door above us and returns to the cellar floor.

"I don't know, Einstein." I hold up my hand and start folding down one finger after another as I count off my checklist of things we've done. "Get ourselves into a horror movie predicament from hell? *Check.* Get lost in the cellar where all the murder happens? *Check.* Bang repeatedly on the locked door we're trapped behind? *Check.* Scream at the top of our lungs for help though nobody can hear us? *Check.*

"Yeah. I'm at a loss. Not sure what to do next. Maybe Johnny Depp will pop up out of the Elm Street mattress of death and give us a hand? Oh, hey! We're literally on Elm Street. I never put two and two together before now. Back to Johnny. Logan is already aware that Johnny's my one and only free-cheat celebrity crush. I'm sure he'd be OK with it. Or maybe, just maybe, Scooby Doo can give us a tip, or—"

"Mind not sharing your fantasy porn games with me? And FYI, that dude's a horrible human being who should just be canceled already. And, also, he's old enough to be your grandfather. Your sarcasm isn't helping, thanks. Anyway, since we're down here, maybe we should just look around. You know, see what we can see."

"Listen, Dora the Explorer," I say, "haven't you had enough yet? A dead murderer just locked us into his cellar dungeon. Does it get any worse than that?"

"I don't know, I guess he could *kill* us."

"It was a rhetorical question, asswipe. You know, the kind that does not require a response."

"Come on. Let's go," Noah says. I don't want to look around, but since he's the one with the flashlight in his hand, I'm not going to lose sight of him. I'm terrified enough. The only thing keeping me from a total breakdown is that tiny beam of light Noah holds in his hand.

The cellar, obviously, should be the same size as the shop upstairs. But judging by its cavernous quality, it is much bigger. Does it also incorporate the space under the neighboring stores? There's no way this cellar is the same size as that one small store.

As I contemplate the impossible vastness of the cellar, Noah begins to explore it. This means that, inside of a few seconds, he has put quite a bit of distance between us.

"Hey," I stage-whisper as I pick up my pace. "Wait for me."

"I think this is the place right here," he says. He stands beside a wall that appears partially excavated. No way it's still in the same state they left it in after discovering the bodies. If it was almost a hundred years ago, as Noah says, someone must have used and renovated the cellar since then.

But the more I look around, the more certain I am that the cellar hasn't changed since the building went up. The floor's uneven and appears to have been excavated at different depths. The walls, or at least some of them, seem to be made of dirt.

Noah picks at one of the dirt walls, bringing the flashlight closer to the fissures there. No doubt he's hoping to find a trace of ancient blood, or something macabre like that. A fingernail, maybe? A tooth? The history buff is orgasming over the scene in front of him.

"Maybe we can get out through one of the other stores. It looks like they might all be connected by the cellar."

"Huh," he says. "Yeah right." But I can tell he's not really with me. He's rubbing some thick, sticky tar-like substance between the thumb and forefinger of his free hand. He might also be comparing the number of divots in the wall to the body count in his memory, or some shit.

He keeps playing with the inky goop in fascination. I recognize it. It's the same as the viscous tar substance I found inside the book, and that covered every surface in the Other Side. It's what Mael came through when they appeared.

"Mael called that stuff Dark Ichor," I say, before realizing I haven't yet explained Mael to him. Hopefully he doesn't ask. Mael can wait. "I don't know what that means, but I think it's just a name they gave it."

"It's so warm," Noah says offhandedly as he plays with it. "It feels like it's getting warmer in my fingers. Good name, though. Ichor is from Greek mythology, an ethereal fluid, the blood of the gods. Also, did you know it was toxic to humans?"

"No, Noah, I did not. I've never heard the word before. Of course you know what it is."

"When they first discovered this crime scene, they expected to find a lot more victims than they did. Some of the missing were never located. They were just gone forever," Noah says. He pauses unnecessarily for dramatic effect. "A lot of the victims they found down here, though, had traces of a tar-like substance all over them. It was just like this *ichor*, you know."

"No. Why would I know something like that?" I say, looking at him like he just grew a third head. "Why would I want to? Of course I didn't know that, Noah. I never heard of the man before this week. I wish you wouldn't tell me these details. Why do you have to remember everything?"

Instead of answering, he holds out his finger and thumb to show me the goop stuck to them. He pulls his finger up and away from his thumb to show me just how sticky it is. It stretches between his fingers.

"There was a gel-like substance seeping from the wall they excavated when they were looking for victims. They couldn't trace its origins but described it as being tar-like. Maybe it *is* blood of the gods."

"OK," I say, trying to ignore his new fascination while simultaneously knowing exactly where the substance comes from. "Well, let's try to find another way out, then. Like I said."

"Why go now? We're down here. We might as well make the most of it."

"Um, I think I've had enough fun for the day. For the week. For the year. The sooner we get out of here, the better. And you really shouldn't touch that stuff."

"Hey," Noah says, basically ignoring my comment. "That's

probably how the dude did it. We're dealing with someone who has access to the cellar through one of the other stores. He knows the story about this Chalek maniac, and he's putting you on. He's playing a game with you. I just can't figure out why he'd want to do it. Or why he would single you out. You don't seem particularly gullible. Maybe it was random? You were just walking by at the right time?"

"Nice. Wrap it up, please. And I told you, this isn't some dude. This is *the* dude. I know it's him. Do you believe in ghosts, Noah? Because before Sunday, I was staunchly in the camp of not-frigging-likely, but I'm pretty sure I've changed sides. This guy is the ghost of Jack Chalek. Trust me on this one. Either that, or the guy never died."

He sighs and attempts to smear the black crud from his hand onto the wall beside him. He traces a line down the crumbling wall with his finger, like he's writing. Then he caresses the wall one last time before he moves on.

"This looks just like the stuff they describe in the article I read on the body recovery. It's almost like a thick ink, isn't it?" He wipes whatever's left on his pants and absently smells his fingers. Gross.

He traces a path across the back wall of the cellar with the flashlight as we continue to walk farther away from where the bookstore would be. Before long, we come upon another ladder. Noah shines his light on the lowest rungs.

"See!" I say, victorious. "Ha."

"Go ahead, then," he says. "Go on up."

"Why do *I* have to do it?"

"I'm holding the flashlight."

"Shit," I say. I climb the short ladder and reach up to the door in the ceiling. It's the kind of door that's just a wood panel; there's nothing to grab on to. The only option is to push, so I push.

Nothing.

"It's probably locked. Or latched. Or painted shut."

"Put your body into it," Noah says. The flashlight's ray wavers as Noah begins to climb up the ladder behind me. "You do realize we might have to break into one of these stores to get out, right? I don't think any of the cellar doors will be unlocked. Especially since all the other cellars are attached."

I climb up another rung so that I'm scrunched against the door. I tuck my head in and brace my shoulders against it. I push and push, but nothing. No give whatsoever.

"It's not going to budge. We'll have to try another one."

Noah climbs up a little farther and somehow wedges himself beside me. Together, we push against the door for a few seconds. There's no sound of a shift in the door's position amid the moans and grunts of our combined labor, not even a dull creak. I'm guessing it's been permanently sealed somehow. Otherwise there should be *some* give. Something.

"Let's try the next one," Noah says.

"Well, gee," I say, making sure my voice drips with sarcasm. "There's a fine idea. Thank you for being such a valuable member of the team. We need forward thinkers like you."

"Nice."

We descend the ladder and make our way to the next door in the floor—or, in this case, I guess, door in the ceiling. Shit. My life takes some weird turns sometimes.

"Here," I say as we arrive at the next ladder. "Give me the flashlight. I'll hold it. You're bigger than me. I'm the original ninety-eight-pound weakling."

He looks at me with a trace of suspicion, but relents. Then he hands me the flashlight and takes to the ladder.

"I hope you appreciate the things I do for you, Gaige Warrol."

"But of course," I say. "Now get up there and pop us out of this taco stand."

He climbs to the top and gently nudges the door, which clearly gives a bit. I fill with hope. This is the one. Noah positions himself on the ladder in such a way that he'll be able to use maximum force on the next push. He's some kind of mathematical engineering genius too, by the way. He's probably making quick equations in his head for best-case scenario impact force.

He barrels against the door. There's a slight pop, and it moves upwards about a quarter of an inch. It's mocking us.

"There's a simple slider lock on the other side. We should be able to pop it off if we both push at the same time; those things are only kept in place with short little screws. Get up here."

The ray of hope grows as I make my way up the rungs. If Noah thinks we'll be able to snap the lock off, I have every confidence that we can. Noah knows everything. We're getting out!

I'm not as graceful on the ladder as Noah. It's harder for me to worm my way up when there's already someone else on it.

Once I get myself in position, Noah says, "OK. On my count. One, two, three…"

I don't even tell him he should count down, not up. Sometimes I actually can bite my tongue to keep from correcting people. That's how good I am.

We shoot our shoulders forward and crash into the door with all our might. We hear the snap of something breaking, but as much as it sounds like we've made our way through this obstacle, the door only goes up so far before it stops. No dice. Not yet.

"One more push should do it," Noah says. "Again, on my count."

"Are you sure? This isn't hopeless, is it?"

"No, dude," he says, exuding confidence. "On my count. One, two, three…"

We ram the door one more time, and this time it gives. Whatever was still holding on snaps off immediately, and the door shoots upwards. It must be on some sort of spring hinge or something, though, because it slams back down just as quickly, smacking both of us on the tops of our heads.

"Ouch."

"Motherfucker!" Noah yelps. I think he may have gotten a bigger smack than me. Still, his frizzed-out hair should have absorbed most of it, no? He pushes upward and raises his arms to force the door to stay open. "Go ahead. I got it."

I wiggle past him and come up through the hole in the floor. In the pitch-darkness of the space, I can still make out slight shapes. Looks like a storage room of some kind. I wait for my eyes to adjust.

"Hello?"

"Oops," I say, remembering Noah. "Sorry. Here." I hold the door up so he can let go and climb through. Then he turns the flashlight back on and starts to look around what is definitely a storage room. There are shelves on either side of us. It's a pretty narrow room, more like a closet; I can touch both side walls.

I let go of the door. It slams back into place, and I jump at the loud noise in this quiet, vacant shop.

Noah makes his way to the door and flicks a light switch. The room fills with fluorescent light, despite the fact that the store is clearly long abandoned.

"Huh? Power?" he says. "Who knew? And also, why? Let's get out of here."

"Shit. Something tells me I'm about to set off the second alarm of the night. This is not my life."

"Prophetic speak, dude," he says. He laughs as we leave the storeroom and come into the main room of the store.

Noah flicks another switch and half the store is illuminated. It's the abandoned store three doors down from the imaginary bookstore, obviously a greeting card shop at one time. A *long* time ago. The floor is strewn with cards, gift wrap, and all sorts of other crap. There are racks and shelves everywhere. It all looks like a 1970s stage set.

Even the front counter is covered with impulse-buy trinkets and doodads. There's stuff everywhere, like whoever ran this place left in a hurry.

"Ooh," Noah says. "Maybe I should get a birthday card for my mama. It's her birthday next week."

"Smart-ass. We're not touching a thing. It's probably swimming in rat and mouse shit."

"Chillax, dude. I was kidding. Who's gonna set off the alarm, then? Up for another one?"

Might as well. The vanishing bookstore didn't have an alarm

on it, though. Maybe this one doesn't either. I make my way to the double doors at the front of the store.

"Here goes nothing." I flick the bolt below the knob and push.

The whole store—hell, the whole block—fills with the loud, rebellious shriek of alarms. The sound shakes the insides of my body. I can feel it in my fillings. I take one look at Noah, and we seem to say the same thing without words. *RUN!* We bolt.

Chapter Eleven

WE'RE ON THE SUBWAY PLATFORM before we even speak again, two thieves running away through the night. This book is making me do the craziest things. It lies in wait in my backpack, taunting me with its there-not-there-ness.

"That was probably close. How far behind the alarm do you think the sirens kicked in?"

"About five minutes, give or take," Noah says. He lets out a burst of nervous laughter. "There were probably cops right on Darius or Yonge. They're often up there, just around the corner. We *were* right downtown."

"I gotta stop being so gangsta, dude."

"Gaige, man. You're about as *gangsta* as Peter Pan. Please don't even use that word. It's not *for* you."

The subway pulls in and we board.

"Wanna come to my place? It's getting late." I look at my phone and sure enough, it's just after midnight. Made it to Wednesday. "You can sleep over, if you want."

"Sure. Can we watch Gidget movies and do our nails, too?" Noah says. He punches my arm and laughs. "You're so very very."

"Ouch," I say. I rub the burn out of the spot where he punched me. That's gonna leave a bruise. "Douche. What the hell's a Gidget? If you don't want to, you can just say no. And PS, there's nothing wrong with doing our nails. Don't be homophobic. Also, it's late. It would just be to sleep."

"I'm good without nail polish, thanks. And, I forgot. You don't know about anything before about 2012. Gidget's this rocking girl from sixties movies. Never mind. I should have said *Love, Simon*. Yeah, I can come over. Why not? We have to leave for school early tomorrow, though. I have something to do in the lab before class."

"Sure, but I think you mean *this morning*. It's already past midnight." Talking about school makes me remember what happened earlier. "I wonder if we're going to hear about the alarm being set off."

"You got any pizza in your freezer?" That's another infamous thing about Noah. He's an eater. I mean, he's an *eater*. He wants to eat every moment of every day. "I'm starved. It's hard work breaking out of a murderer's cellar."

"A dead murderer's cellar."

"Right?! Even harder. I require sustenance."

"If we don't have pizza, we'll have something. No worries."

"Our stop, dude," Noah says. "We should have just walked. How lazy are you?"

"Lazy enough, yo."

"No. Just, no," he says, shaking his head. "Don't talk like that. I told you. No gangsta. No slang, either. You're not legit enough to pull it off. These words are not yours to use."

"What? And your afro gives you street cred, I'm guessing?"

"No, dude. Don't call it an afro, either, because it isn't one. I'm white. I've been blessed with these tight curls because only I can pull them off. That is all."

"Bahaha."

We get off the subway and start the ascent to the street. As soon as I'm close enough to street level for my cell service to kick in, my phone starts to buzz. I haul it out of my pocket to read the screen. Logan.

Logan: What's up, babe? I haven't heard from you.)-:

"I better respond to this one. He sounds sad, which is probably code for pissed. Uh-oh."

"Ktchoo!" Noah squeals, emulating the sound of a whip. Like Sara isn't exactly the same. I'm surprised she hasn't texted him yet, trying to find out where he is.

"Funny," I say. "And how long is the leash your girlfriend keeps you on?"

"Low blow, broseph." He keeps walking in the direction of my place once he gets to the top of the stairs. "Sara isn't like that, and you know it."

OK. Denial is a thing. I stop walking long enough to type a reply.

Gaige: Sorry, babe. I'm with Noah. Just hanging out. Thought you might need some time after the other day? Also, thought you'd be sleeping

Logan: That's why u thought it was a good idea NOT to text me or talk to me or call me?

Oh, shit. I'm right. He's mad. Of course he's mad. "He's freaking out. Oh, boy! Better try to calm him down a bit."

Gaige: I'm SORRY.

Logan: Are you still doing the bookstore thing? Looking for the book?

Gaige: I'll talk to you later, babe.

I know that last text is going to get me in trouble. Logan doesn't like when I dismiss him. Not one of his favorite things.

"Wait up," I say to Noah as I race to catch up with him. He's almost at the front door of my building.

"Dude. Are you whipped or what? You're always making some kind of misstep with Logan. Doesn't seem very chill. Do you even like the guy?"

He stops walking, and I manage to catch up.

"What's not to like? He's got a smoking hot bod, puppy dog eyes, and he's not afraid of pleasing his ma—"

"Whoa," Noah says, laughing. "TMI. I do not need to know your love life. Just seems he struggles with your eccentricities a bit. I don't blame him. But there's nothing wrong with you. Really."

I punch his arm and push him into some random guy passing by my building. I laugh my ass off as I watch him apologize to the guy.

"Dude," I say, putting on my serious face. I reach out and grab the handle on the entrance door, but don't yet open it. "I'm not eccentric. He just doesn't understand some of the predicaments I get myself into. And don't dis my boy. Also, don't worry about our sex life. It's exceptional."

"Whatever. Your phone's buzzing like mad. You gonna pretend you don't hear it, or what?"

"That's the plan for now, yes. I kind of blew him off." I hold the door open for Noah to enter. "Probably not gonna be love letters waiting for me on my phone."

"I'm voting for *that's not wise* right now. We'll see how this plays out. You know that drives him crazy."

"Yeah, well," I say as the door closes behind us and we make our way to the elevator across the lobby. "He wasn't happy about the whole disappearing book and invisible bookstore thing. I can't win this one."

I press the button for the elevator, the doors open, and we make our way upstairs. Thank god I have pizza in the freezer. Something's gone right for a change. Thanks, Mom.

After we eat pizza and get ready for bed, it's nearly two in the morning on a school night. I'm exhausted from the screwed-up, time-jumping crap going on and ready to sleep forever. I pull out the cot and make up Noah's bed.

It takes me about two seconds to fall asleep after my head hits the pillow, but I keep waking up whenever my phone buzzes. It buzzes a lot—Logan, trying to get my attention. I love him so much, but I just don't know how to make sense of any of this. I'll fix things in the morning. In person.

Sometime during the short night, I wake up enough to put my phone in silent mode. This only happens after Noah whips me on the side of the head with his pillow and tells me, "Control your bitch." How politically incorrect can one get? I forgive him because of his lack of sleep.

When we wake up to my phone alarm a few hours later, I realize I can't possibly go to school. I can't stop thinking about Mael and how they're trapped in that place. "Why don't you just go in to school alone, Noah? I think I have some things to do today."

"Gaige," Noah says. "You never miss school. You already

missed Monday, and most of yesterday. Basically all of yesterday. Eventually, your parents will find out. And you need to talk to Logan. Are you sure you want to skip again?"

"I'm sure as shit," I say. I lean over the side of my bed and look down at Noah on the cot beside me. "I have some stuff. Let me know if anybody mentions the alarm. Oh, and tell me how Logan is if you see him. I'm a little worried."

Noah feels around on the floor beside the cot for his T-shirt. Once he finds it, he springs off the cot and pulls it over his head.

"You have to talk to him yourself, dude." He grabs his jeans and squirms into them. I make no effort to get out of bed. Hell, I'm sure I could stay here for a week. But I wait for Noah to leave. It's time to read the book again.

"OK, dude, I'm out. I need the lab before class. I'll catch you tonight sometime. Maybe we can break into a bank or something."

"Yeah, right," I say. "Funny. Do you want me to walk you out?"

"Dude, stop with the creepy stuff. We're not dating. You don't need to walk me to the door. It's just down the hall. I think I remember the way. Get over yourself."

"Go to hell," I say. He merely laughs, turns, and walks away. He throws a wave over his shoulder as he leaves.

"Later."

Chapter Twelve

I CAN ONLY SIT STILL for a few minutes before I lean down over the side of the bed and struggle to reach for my backpack. I drag it up onto the bed beside me, open it, and pull out *My Book of Dreams*.

"So what's gonna happen today, dude?" I ask the book. I don't expect an answer, and I'm relieved when I don't get one, because who knows.

I flip the cover open and look at the inside flap. I think of Mael, the kid inside. This makes me remember the things they said, the thing they called themself. Before I do anything else, I set the book beside me on the bed and reach for my phone to Google *Batcavers*. The results stun me. I flop back on my bed, feeling for the very first time the despair that Mael must be feeling. Batcavers were like Goths, before they were called Goths. I Google Voodoo and Twilight Zone, but too many results. Klub Domino brings exact results. A club right here, downtown. Mael is from the early eighties. They've been trapped inside the Other Side for, like, forty years.

I think of the gelatinous darkness in which Mael is confined, and of the words I glimpse before falling into that world. It all makes its way back to me. I sit up, drop my phone, and pick up the book. I don't know if I have enough courage to begin this again, to turn pages and allow it all to happen to me again.

"Just what would you like that book to do or say, Gaige?"

I immediately throw the book across the room and pull the covers over my head, so complete is my terror. But covers aren't gonna help me when the monsters are real. A bedsheet doesn't make a great barrier between oneself and a murderer—especially a dead murderer.

"I know who you *really* are now," I say from under the covers, as though my newfound knowledge is somehow ammunition against him. I slowly poke my head out and see Chalek standing in the corner of my room. "I know you're dead. And I know that bookstore isn't real. And I know you killed people. Even your own boyfriend. My friend told me all about you."

"Look at you, so clever. Such a clever boy," he says. He laughs and moves almost imperceptibly closer. "But you're so very wrong about some of your intel, Sonny Jim. And we need to talk about you bringing your friends around to the store, boy. That's a no-no. You wouldn't want anything to happen to them, now, would you?"

"Kiss it," I say. Great comeback, Gaige. You showed him.

"Gaige, Gaige, Gaige," he says. "That's no way to talk to your new friend. You cut me to the quick, boy."

He stands at the foot of my bed now. A musty vapor begins to fill my nostrils and lungs. I imagine his stale exhalations traveling down my throat and living inside of me, and I want to scream, but I also don't want to move.

"I think it's about time you come with me."

"What do you mean?" I try really hard to sound casual, but I'm pretty sure my words leave me as a high-pitched, girly scream. I do not want to visit that place Mael calls Other Side with Lurch in tow. No way, no sir, no how. No! Even the thought of it makes me sweat and quake.

"We should go back to the bookstore now." He starts to walk toward me, and the thought of him touching me makes me ill enough to jump out of bed and make a dash for the bathroom. That is another place I would rather not visit with Mr. Chalek.

On the way to the bathroom, I glance at a photo of Logan on my bedside table. He's leaning in to give me a kiss on the front steps at school. Man, do I long to have that day of normalcy back. I can almost remember how ordinary it was, how insignificant and wonderful. I welcome the memory as it rushes through me.

Once inside the bathroom, I shut the door, lean back against it with a sigh of relief, and close my eyes.

When I open them again, though, I'm still in bed. I haven't moved at all. But I was sure I had. I remember the feel of the floor under my feet; I remember glancing at the photo and thinking about it while I slammed and locked the door. I heard the click as the lock slid into place. I remember feeling my back against the door. Yet the second my eyes open, here I am, back in bed. And Jack Chalek stands over me, glaring down at me with fire in his eyes.

"Get dressed, boy. I don't have time for your nonsense. We have some business to take care of now. You've been misbehaving." He tosses me my crumpled clothes from yesterday, which were in a pile on the floor beside my bed a moment ago.

"Why me? Why did you choose me? Why a bookstore? Please. Just let me be. I don't want your horrid book."

"The book is neither mine nor horrid. You chose *me*, son. You chose the bookstore. This is all your doing from moment one. I told you not to touch that book, now didn't I, boy? Seems to me the boy who sees a bookstore that isn't there and enters into it all willy-nilly is more the fool for doing so. You brought it all on yourself, you did."

He turns away from me, presumably to give me some privacy. I get out of bed, almost resolved to my fate. I dress while Jack Chalek waits patiently by the door.

When I finish and turn to him, he holds out the book in his left hand. I know I threw it across the room moments ago, and he hasn't made a move to retrieve it; he's been standing by the door. How is he able to do these things?

"I don't want to do this. Isn't there something I could do to get out of whatever it is you want from me in your sick little—"

I can't finish what I want to say, because in the blink of an eye—no, less than the blink of an eye—I find myself standing in the middle of the bookstore. Dust motes and all. I glance around, but I don't see the cat. Then I remember the infected bite. It's stopped itching long enough for me to forget about it, which is a good sign. I peek at it. It's still puffy and not too healthy looking, but at least it's better than the last time I looked at it.

"Where's Lilith?"

"Good memory for names, boy. Lilith is off on some business of her own right now." Jack's voice fills the air around me, but I don't see him. It sounds more like his voice *is* the air around me. "We're here for *you*, Gaige. Now open the book."

"But what if I don't want to? I never asked for any of this. I just walked into your messed-up fucking bookstore and saw something shiny. That doesn't mean you own me, Lurch. That doesn't make the book mine."

In a shimmer, he walks right through the front door of the store. The bells ring louder than they would if he actually opened the door and rattled them.

"It would well please me, son, if you would stop calling me Lurch."

"Well, Lurch, I'm not happy. I don't want to be here. Maybe you'll have to settle for what you get."

"Petulance does not become you, boy. It's a dangerous hill to die on."

He puts his hand up in front of my face and slowly makes a fist. At first I think he's trying to threaten me, but as the heat begins to fill my belly, I realize he's actually doing something to my insides. The more he tightens the fist in my face, the worse the pressure in my belly.

I fall to my knees as the heat turns into an unbearable pain. I can't stop the moans from coming out of my mouth. I'm sure he's crushing my intestines in his fist, I just don't understand how. On my knees isn't good enough. I slump down further and roll myself into a little ball of pain on the filthy floor. I can't stop squirming. It's impossible to get away from an ache this strong.

Just as I think I might die from the excruciating pain, Jack bends down, looks me in the eye, and says, "Enough?"

"Please," I say. OK, I beg. I plead. I may even promise him my firstborn.

"Call me Lurch again and I will squeeze the life right out of you, son. And I'll make you shit your drawers to boot, by the god."

"OK, OK. Please stop. I'm begging you. Please stop."

I lie on my side and sort of walk my feet along the floor, so I spin on the spot. I have to find a way to stop the pain. I can't take another second.

Then he unclenches his hand and drops it to his side. Immediate relief. The throbbing pain of my bruised intestines begins to fade. I think I may actually live, though I'm not sure I won't still shit myself. I struggle into a sitting position.

"Are we clear?"

"Yes." It's all I can say. "Yes." If he can do something like that, he can do anything. I don't stand a chance against him.

"Open the book."

"Do I have—"

He raises his fist. I immediately eat the rest of my words and open the book. He drops his fist.

"I don't understand," I say. I just want to know what the hell is going on.

"You don't need to. You just need to know you picked this, son. You picked the book. I told you not to touch it. That means you chose this. Not so cocky now, are you, Gaige? Where's your *boy*friend, now?"

"But you *made* me want the book."

"Can one really influence the wants of another? Desire's a tricky bitch, Gaige. I think you're being unreasonable now. It might be because you heard some… un*savory* things about me. I assure you, they're mostly untrue and inaccurate."

"So you *didn't* kill people and leave them here in your creepy-ass cellar?" I point below us. "Are you telling me you haven't been dead for, like, a hundred years or something?"

"I'm not a bad person."

"Good people always collect bodies in their cellars. Good people are always killed by the villagers when they riot because they've had enough murder."

"You don't have all the information, Gaige."

I know a trick when I see one. Chalek only wants to trap me. He wants another person for his book. *In* his book. I don't know what happens to his victims, but I do know they disappear. I know they can't come back. Mael told me that much.

I feel courageous, for some reason. It feels like he needs me to open the book and read it before he can get any real control over me. Maybe. I'm not certain, of course.

Chapter Thirteen

"READ THE FARKING BOOK."

Mental note: Lurch doesn't do swears well.

I clap it closed. But then my courage goes out the window instantly, because he clenches his fist, and the pain returns to the pit of my belly.

I flip open the book again and wait for the words to appear. As they materialize, I begin to read the first page and immediately hear screaming. I'm certain it's coming from the cellar below us. I attempt to block it out while I read on.

Things begin to get blurry. I look down at the pages, attempt to read them. Really, I do. I just can't concentrate on the words. The screams agitate me to distraction. Is it Mael? On the Other Side? The words are swirling too quickly. They become an ocean of eddying black ink.

The screams sound a bit like Logan, to be honest. It's definitely a screaming boy. I can't focus on anything. There's a scrabbling noise coming from everywhere around me.

The screams aren't coming from the cellar, but from the book itself. I'm reading the screams. The words are screams.

"Boy?"

The more pages I turn, the more discombobulated I become. I'm falling. Somebody calls out to me, but I don't recognize the voice. I don't like the voice. It rumbles and grates like a train running into a stalled car stuck on its tracks, or a terrible rash that eats at your skin and leaves poison pustules behind.

"Boy? Gaige?" Chalek. It's Chalek.

Something Mael said comes back to me like a dream. *He tries to enter with his victims, to find a way to follow you inside.* That must be what Chalek is trying to do now.

I know I can't outrun his voice. The voice is death, danger, dying. As much as it repulses me, though, there's something in its pitch that draws me nearer to it.

And the boy—Logan? Oh my god—has stopped screaming. I don't like that. The screaming scared me, but at least when he was screaming, I knew he was OK, still alive. The silence tells me something different, leaves too many questions.

As I enter the darkness, Mael immediately comes into focus in front of me.

"You're here." They say this with deep disappointment, like they don't want to see me. "Gaige. You brought him with you! You can't do this. He's winning."

I look behind me, baffled. There's no one there.

"No," I say. "I swear. I came alone."

And then I hear the voice again. The rattling voice of death that can only be Chalek. I've never heard him in this place before.

"Boy!" Chalek shouts. His voice comes from nowhere, from everywhere.

I recall Mael telling me that Chalek wanted me to go inside so I could find a way back. Chalek doesn't want the Other Side for himself. He only wants to figure out a way to bring something back *from* the Other Side. He thinks it can somehow be a two-way road, and he's using us as guinea pigs to figure it out. But what is Chalek so desperate to retrieve from this hellscape?

The Other Side isn't already Chalek's. This is all about him trying to conquer it, understand it. He needs others to help him because he's afraid of it, and for some reason, he can't even come this far. Not to where Mael is. Something is blocking him.

"Mael," I whisper, as though Chalek can somehow hear our conversation if I don't keep it down. "Can't he come here?"

Mael moves closer, and I'm immediately drawn to them, even as their many warnings about not touching them come back to me.

"Not yet, he can't," Mael says. This sounds more like a warning than anything else.

"Gaige." Chalek again. This time the word goes right through me, shakes my bones. It's almost impossible to ignore the voice. I see Mael flinch as Chalek's voice infiltrates everything around us, as though it literally causes them pain.

"I have to leave," Mael says. "I can't ignore him any longer."

"Be careful. He's angry because he's trying to come inside with you. He's close, but not here yet. Something's stopping him. He gets closer every time, Gaige. Yes. You should leave."

Chalek may be angry, but I feel somehow like I'm the one holding the cards here. We can hear his voice, yeah. But he isn't physically here. He can't move freely between the two places, and he gets angry when he can't come in with others. He'll do whatever it takes, even if it means destroying the Outside World.

"Gaige." I can't avoid the call anymore. As Mael retreats into the darkness and fades away, I open my eyes and flinch as Jack Chalek's face comes into focus in front of me. I'm back in the bookstore.

I jump from my seat and scurry backward across the room, away from him. Away from his smell. Away from his badness.

"What did you do to me?" I say, terrified that I have been asleep in his presence. "Stay away from me."

"You fell asleep. I merely tried to wake you."

He's lying, of course. His only goal was to dash inside when I opened the portal. He wants to use me to get inside, and I think he just came close. He can't get what he needs if he can't move freely between the two worlds, though. He needs me.

I look down at the book on the floor. That's it—I want nothing more to do with the vile thing, or the man who tricked me into wanting it. I kick it away from me.

Even as I consider escaping, I think of Mael's face and see it clearly, in all its perfection. I can't leave this nightmare behind just yet. Not without trying to figure out Mael and their role in all of this. They are, after all, trying to help me. And they have been trapped for *so* long. Shouldn't I at least *try* to help them?

As I continue to back away from Jack Chalek, fear boils up inside of me. First the fear that comes with self-preservation, and then the fear of something terrible happening not to me, but to someone else. To Mael. Or—

The memory of screams comes back to me like acid reflux. I suddenly know that Logan is in danger. I know that the screams I heard were somehow in my mind—or in the book—but they were also real. And they were his.

"Where's my boyfriend? What did you do with Logan?" I ask. My backward momentum has stopped, and against my better judgment, I find myself moving toward the man. "Where is he?"

"Now, why do you think I'd do anything to that lovely, fey little boy of yours?" he says. Or, I should say, he rattles. All the death in the world dwells within his throat, and every word he utters has to scrape by that festering death before it comes out of his mouth.

"Where is he?"

"Why don't you pick up your phone and call him, Gaige. Or text. That *is* what you kids do nowadays, isn't it? Text, text, text, no? Then again, you've been too busy avoiding and ignoring him to bother to check in with him, now haven't you?" The playfulness in his expression does not translate to his voice.

As much as I hate to admit it, his idea's a good one, easy to put into action. I hope desperately that it'll give me immediate reassurance.

I take out my phone and begin to text Logan. Before I finish, though, I change my mind. I don't want to have to wait an insufferable minute for him to reply. I once again do what I would never do in normal circumstances. I call him.

"Gaige! Gaige, is that you? Oh my god." He's full-on panic mode. Something's wrong.

"Logan," I say. "Are you OK? What did he do to you? Where are you, baby?"

"What did who do? Where am *I*? Where are *you*? Everybody's been worried sick about you. It's been almost two days, Gaige. Everyone's looking for you. We called the police."

Two days. Two days? How could I not know that two days have passed? I was with Mael for such a short time.

"I don't understand," I say, as I realize that I have yet again lost a large pocket of time to the Other Side. Somehow, it's even less possible to comprehend this time. Knowing that I was in this skanky bookstore with an old dead guy for almost two days makes me want to scream. He could have done anything to me while I was asleep.

Mael. They said something when it happened at school. That I can't be in two places. That when I'm in the Other Side, I'm only there. I'm sure they said this.

"Gaige, where were you? Where *are* you?"

His voice is a desperate plea. There's no anger about my ignoring his texts. I can tell from his tone that he's considered the possibility he might never see me again.

"I'm at the bookstore, Logan," I say, knowing the words could potentially cause an explosion on the other end of the phone. I look at Jack and want to wipe the ridiculous smirk off his face.

"Gaige."

"What? I know. I know. But that's where I am. I swear."

"I have to tell them, Gaige." His voice is filled with guilt now. There's a pause. "They hoped you would maybe contact me, so they've been checking in with me and my parents nonstop. I have to tell them you're OK. And I have to tell them where you are. How am I going to do that if you're somewhere that doesn't even exist?"

"I understand, babe. Just tell them where I am without mentioning the bookstore. I think I could probably use some rescuing right about now, anyway." I send a smirk across the room to Lurch. It feels good to give him a taste of his own fuck-you medicine. We both know what this means: the bookstore's going to disappear again. And soon.

I'm met with silence.

"It's OK, Logan. Really. Do what you have to do. I'll see you later. After I talk my way out of whatever it is I need to talk my way out of."

"But that doesn't change anything, Gaige. I'm still worried about you. Have you been in that filthy, abandoned building all this time? And, if you have, what the hell are you doing there?"

"Did you scream at all while I was gone?" Winner of the Weird Question of the Millennium Award. The trophy goes to Gaige Warrol. Thank you, thank you very much.

"No, I didn't scream. What kind of question is that? You don't get to ask the questions, Gaige. It's your turn to answer them. Everybody thought you guys might be dead or something. That you had met with foul play."

I can't help it. I burst out laughing at his use of that phrase. It seems more than a little silly. Detective-show worthy.

"I'm sorry. Sorry, Logan. Nothing about this is funny. I'm sorry. Really. I was just worried about you. I guess I had a dream that you were in trouble and screaming for help, if that makes any sense. I just wanted to ask so I'm sure it was only a dream. It seemed so real."

It's Lurch's turn to laugh. He giggles in my face. Repulsive.

"It's OK, Gaige. But you're gonna have to get some help. None of this makes sense. I was there. There's no bookstore. There's no man."

"I'm going to let you go now. Tell them where I am. I'll wait here."

"I love you, Gaige Warrol."

"I love you too, Logan Regan."

"OK. Bye. Don't be surprised if you hear a bunch of sirens soon."

"Oh boy. Wow."

"Yeah. Wow."

I wonder why he wouldn't direct them here in the first place. It would seem obvious to me, if I were him. But maybe he did. Maybe they came and simply saw nothing.

At any rate, I don't get the chance to ask him; he's hung up. I return my phone to my pocket and back a few more paces away from the cretin. I enjoy the fact that his little party is about to end. The smile on my face tells him everything I want to say. I feel oddly giddy.

And right on cue, a cacophony of sirens fills the neighborhood. I stand there smiling at Jack Chalek. There's nothing he can do.

The closer the sirens get to Elm Street, the more I wonder how this chapter's going to end. I don't even want to blink. I want to *see* the bookstore disappear. I want to see his cheap little parlor trick evaporate before my eyes.

"Did he mention your boy Noah at all, Gaige?" Jack says. For someone who should be pissed about this major kink in his plan, he's sure quick to put a big shit-eating grin on his face. "Or is he too jealous of your friendship to mention his name? Is that it? Is your boyfriend jealous of your best friend? Doesn't he even care about *Noah's* whereabouts?"

"What do you mean?" The acid in my belly climbs the short, gravelly road to my throat. "What the hell do you mean?"

"I just wonder if they think they found *both* of you? The boyfriend never mentioned poor ole Noah, did he? I wonder if he assumed he was with you. Or hoped he wasn't? What do you think, my boy?"

Only now do I realize that Logan said *you guys* a couple of times during our conversation.

"What did you do?" I grab the collar of his jacket. "What do you mean? Tell me. What did you do? Where's Noah?"

"*Where's Noah? Where's Noah?*" he mimics, all shrieky-panicky. Then he lets out a gross peal of laughter that makes my skin crawl.

The sirens reach a crescendo. I have essentially created Jack's opportunity to escape. With the screeching of tires on the cobbles outside, the bookstore blips out of existence—and Jack with it, questions unanswered. I'm left with the stench of his jacket, balled up in my fist as he vanishes.

He leaves behind a thin vapor of echoing laughter that bounces off the walls just enough to totally creep me out.

In a cloud of confusion, I walk out of the store and into the street. Still hearing the ghost of Chalek's fading cackle, I look behind me: there's nothing left of the bookstore, just dust, newspapers, and garbage in an empty storefront. The police see only an awkward teenaged boy, holding an ancient, crumpled jacket in his outstretched hand.

In the noise and chaos that ensues, I can only think of one thing. Where's Noah, and what happened to him?

Chapter Fourteen

"Son, you're not giving us much to go on. We need more."

"That is literally all I have."

After my ride in the back of the police car, I find myself in an interrogation room. Being interrogated, of all things. Apparently, until proven otherwise, one is presumed guilty of something when one vanishes without a trace on Wednesday morning and reappears on Thursday night. Especially when one comes back without their equally vanished friend. Who knew?

I *am* glad they're waiving the breaking-and-entering charge, though. They think it's sufficient that I get off with a warning, since I must have had a traumatic experience after all. Also, the door wasn't locked, so...

"I don't know anything. I wasn't even *with* Noah. He stayed at my place Tuesday night. He left for school on Wednesday morning. I didn't go with him. That's it. I swear. That's the last time I saw him. When he left my place for school on Wednesday. Yesterday."

"That makes you the last person to see him, Gaige," the officer says. He flashes me an accusatory look. I don't know how this guy could possibly be an effective cop. His red, bloated face has the angriest skin I've ever seen, and, if I had to guess, I'd say he's in his third trimester. Either that, or he drinks a lot of beer. I'd pay to watch this guy climb a fence in hot pursuit. "Noah did not arrive at school."

So this is where the shit hits the fan. If Jack planned this part, he's more brilliant than I've given him credit for. Sure, I already suspected that he was an evil genius, but this surpasses my imagination. Could he have had the whole thing planned? No. Impossible. It feels like I've been set up somehow, though.

I should have walked Noah to the door after all.

"That's impossible."

"I'm afraid it isn't. As we've repeatedly informed you, Noah never showed up for school. We've been through this." He's pissed, but he's trying not to show it. I can tell by his tone and the pulsing veins in his neck. His skin looks redder and angrier by the second, like it's gonna burst open. I don't think he knows what to make of me. Am I guilty of something or the victim of something? He probably just sees me as some little shit of a teenage dirtbag.

"Am I gonna get to see my parents now? My mom's probably pretty freaked out. And my boyfriend, too. I know Logan's out there. Can I see them now? Please."

"I'm afraid that's not going to happen any time—"

"Gaige," a second officer says as he breezes through the interrogation room door. This one is more TV show-worthy, a dark, pretty boy to counteract Mr. Potato Head. His dimpled smile makes me flush. "You're free to go. We can talk to you later if need be. You better go see your family now."

"I wasn't finished here, Officer Riley," the first cop says, attempting unsuccessfully to keep the annoyance out of his voice. The second officer's clearly higher in command, though, as he doesn't even bother to respond. He merely holds open the door for me and ushers me out with a nod.

He leads me to a waiting area at the front of the station, where my mom and dad wait with Logan.

"Gaige. Baby," Mom says. She runs over to me and envelops me in this crazy mother-bear hug that leaves me fearing for my life. So embarrassing. As she squeezes, Dad comes up behind her. They're so good at playing doting parents out here in the wild. I'm impressed.

"Where the hell did you get yourself to?" Dad says. The words sound hot, but his demeanor gives him away. He's glad to see me, relieved. In that awkward way we usually show affection with one another, he reaches over Mom and pats my back while Mom continues her death grip. It feels like a penguin smacking me with its flipper.

"Sorry, Dad. I didn't mean to." What a weird thing to say. I didn't mean to what? Mess with a dead serial killer? Leave this dimension? Travel through time?

"You know what," he says, his thick mitts pounding my back relentlessly. Now he's a bear pawing at a picnic basket. "It doesn't matter. You're home. You're OK."

I fight the natural teenage instinct to flee from parental affection—especially *their* parental affection—and allow them to embrace me a little longer. I thought I was their invisible son. I'm sure they had a sleepless night and a panicky day. Even though my disappearance probably gave them a respite from their marital wars, I should probably still allow them this moment. It's the least I can do.

As I lose myself in their embrace—yeah, as embarrassing as it is to admit, I kind of like it—I look past my dad and see Logan standing patiently behind him. He looks bashful and scared, sexy and sad and beautiful. How did I ever allow myself to think Mael was so perfect when I've had the perfect boy in front of me this whole time? *My* boy. How did I even end up with this boy?

I let go of Mom and wait for her to catch up to the fact that the family love-in has run its course.

"Oh, oh," Dad says, sounding totally embarrassed. He lets go, or rather stops penguin-slapping his hands on my back, and moves away so Mom can also fully break free. "Come on, Darla. These kids probably want to say hello."

"Oh my," Mom says as she lets go and kisses me on the cheek. "I'm sorry. You know me."

I actually don't know you, Mom. Not this Mom, anyway. Neither of them is ever very affectionate, especially lately, with their constant feuding. But obviously, I let it slide. One last squeeze and I'm free.

"Hey, baby," I say to Logan. Then I realize that I have never used a term of endearment for a boyfriend in front of my parents before. A molten lava of embarrassment flows up my neck and across my face.

We still hug it out, though. Embarrassed or not, I'm getting a hug from my boy. Hell, we even kiss. With tongue and everything. When we stop, I realize that Mom has turned her back to us, while Dad watches the whole thing with morbid fascination—or pride, or curiosity, or something I don't quite know how to describe. Whichever.

Awkward moment.

"Where's Noah?" Logan asks after our lip-lock ends. "I thought he'd be with you. Are they still questioning him?"

"No. He was never with me."

"What?" Mom says. "We thought they found *both* of you. You weren't together?"

"Shit and goddamn," Dad adds.

"Can we just go? I'm tired." My mind may not have lived through the hours of my disappearance, but my body certainly has. I'm still creeped out over being either asleep in that monster's presence for all those hours, or literally in another dimension. Also, I still haven't figured anything out. Do I believe Mael when they say I'm only in one place at a time? It's not like my body isn't in my own bed when I'm dreaming normally.

Did the time I missed blip by like a nanosecond for me? Was I in that bookstore that whole time, curled up on the floor, holding that book from hell and endlessly falling into it?

"Yes," Dad says. He's feeling useful, I can tell. I have to think to remember what he's responding to. He's telling me we can go. I'm guessing the last couple of days have been hard on him, too. He likes to control every situation. He's a lawyer. They're like that. "Come on. I'll bring the car around front. You guys can meet me at the front steps."

"OK, dear," Mom says. *Dear*, she says, like they weren't just at home dividing assets or something. I hear no taint of sarcasm, anger, or irony. No shits given here, though. I'm not falling for it. Ugh. They love to pretend our family isn't imploding when they're in public. Appearances, and all. Sickening. "I'm just going to check with Officer Farrell. Make sure we're done here."

"No. We're done here, Darla." Dad's one of those I-ain't-taking-shit-from-no-one guys. I guess that includes the cops. "They can't hold him."

This just makes him sound like a cop-show douche guy. But it's in my favor, so I'm OK with it.

One more "OK, dear," and Mom's good to go. I take Logan's hand, and we walk out front to wait for Dad. Dad heads for the parking lot behind the building to get the car.

Now that the police interrogation—as useless as it was—is behind me, I have a pretty good idea that the real interrogation will happen later. Eventually, the glow of having me back will fade, and my parents will want to know what the fuck's going on. Because I have no way to tell them, I'll be in an awkward, uncomfortable position—one I won't be able to squirm out of easily.

Chapter Fifteen

I AM A GREAT WAITER. I can out-wait anyone. So I bide my time and wait for the evening to be over. I listen to their rants about disappearing on a school night and making them worry about my whereabouts and wellbeing. I blush when they make me feel like a two-year-old in front of Logan throughout the entire inquisition. I nod and shake my head in appropriate places to make it appear as though I'm listening. And I promise never to scare them like that again. I have a mission, and I can't tell anyone what it is. So, I bide my time and allow them to get out their frustrations.

I know where Noah is, and I fully plan to make my way back and rescue him. I also know that Jack Chalek is going to make it very difficult for me to do so. But I'm feeling very stealthy, like a gay, Indiana Jones-esque teenage superhero. Waiting only gives me more time to strategize.

Like I'd ever have a chance of victory over a dead guy. What is even with me? When did I knock my head and wake up thinking I had superpowers?

But maybe I have something. I'm beginning to trust that Mael can help me, or at least they *want* to help me. They could have just let me walk into nowhere land, but they stopped me. That's something, right? And if Chalek can't come in without help, maybe I *do* hold some of the power.

Come eleven-thirty, Mom and Dad finally go to bed. Logan is long gone. Time for me to get lost again. I hope I don't misplace a pile of days this time.

I decide not to take the subway. I'll walk; I need the time to think. I hope the cops haven't sewn up the place too securely, but then wonder if that even matters. Let's face it, it'll be the bookstore again when I show up, and I don't think the bookstore operates on a plane where police tape matters all that much.

As I turn the corner at Yonge and Elm almost half an hour later, the irony of the timing is not lost on me. It's midnight. The witching hour.

Nor is it lost on me that it is now Friday, and I am officially all set to miss an entire week of school. School is just not in the cards at the moment.

I can see the light from the bookstore window on the cobbles before it. Of course. I knew it would be so. It looks so pretty, even idyllic. Ha. And before I even arrive at the door, I know that good ole Jack will be standing at his pulpit behind the counter.

When I arrive, the bells are already ringing. Seems they're eagerly anticipating my arrival. Nice touch, Jackie. Nice touch indeed.

I open the door amid the cacophony and step inside. Almost absently, I scratch the spot where Lilith the cat bit me so many days ago. It's almost fully healed. A supernatural cat can't kill this guy.

Maybe the cat bite gives me superhuman strength, like Spider-Man's spider bite. It's possible. That would make me Pussyboy. What? I don't make the rules.

"Hello, Gaige." Jack holds up the book. "I thought you might be back. You forgot something. You should never leave your dream-weaver behind."

"Dream what, now? Where is he?"

I don't wait for an answer. I make my way to the washroom at the back of the store, lift the trapdoor in the floor, and slide down the rungs of the ladder as quickly as I can. I know that I cannot think about the steps I'm taking, or I'll freeze in terror. Just. Move. Forward.

Of course, the dead guy is at the bottom of the ladder waiting for me. You have no idea how discombobulating it is to see the impossible made possible. Jack Chalek is a master of the impossible. What's worse, I'm getting used to it. We're becoming old friends, he and I.

"You might be getting warmer." He's toying with me. He rubs his upper arms with his hands in the international sign for *it's-fucking-cold-in-here*. "Woo! Warmer, but still cold as a witch's tit in February."

This time, I remember that the flashlight app on my phone will suffice for illumination. I take my phone out, turn on the app, and prepare to explore.

"Bro, I'm losing interest. The least you can do is tell me what this is all about. There's got to be a reason why you're doing this, and why you chose me to do it to."

I know exactly where to start looking: the dirt wall that Noah told me was probably where Chalek buried the bodies. The one where he found the tar-like goop that fascinated him so much. The goop that also makes up the Other Side. I walk toward the wall, hoping beyond hope that there isn't a new hole dug into it—like, a Noah-sized one.

Chalek keeps right at my heels. I can see him out of the corner of my eye, feigning interest.

"Do you remember the boy screaming?" he asks, taunting me. "Did you hear that in that book of yours? In your dreams? Or was that just me?"

"It's not my book, dude. I didn't buy it. It's not mine."

He pats me on the back, and I experience a whole new chill. These goose bumps are beyond anything I have ever felt before.

"You don't buy the Book of Dreams, Gaige. You pick it. No. Let me rephrase that. The Book of Dreams picks you. And then— oh wonder of wonders—it invites you in. That, dear boy, is the delicious part."

"Whatever, dude. I'm not gonna want the book just because you need me to. Why don't you tell me where he is so we can get out of here?"

I look around and realize, for the first time, that it's a different cellar than the one Noah and I were in when we were last here. That one was dark and required a flashlight. I look at my phone and realize I don't even need the flashlight app.

This cellar is lit with bare bulbs hanging from the ceiling, but other than that one modern convenience, it appears older than the other cellar. This one has more dirt floors. It smells of wet earth, moss, and must, and—dare I say it—old man taint. It smells like the bleak dark world beyond the ink of the words, too.

The dirt's hiding something. This is the before-renovations cellar, the cellar where, no doubt, the bodies were found.

"You didn't answer my question, Gaige," Chalek says. "Please. Do you remember the boy screaming?"

"What about him?"

"It might just happen tonight."

I stop poking around to look at him. "What do you mean?"

"I mean, you were reading the book. In it, you find your dreams. Old ones, new ones, and ones you haven't had yet. The book knows all your dreams, Gaige. All your dreams. Past. Present. Future. When you sleep, you tell it everything. Don't you? All the things. You whisper them all, and it keeps them for you. Traps them for you."

"What are you even talking ab—" I stop in my tracks. "Wait, so I only read about the boy screaming? But I felt it; I heard it. It happened."

He giggles and playfully puts a hand over his mouth to muffle it, feigning shyness. He's fucking with me.

"Just tell me. What about the boy I heard screaming yesterday?"

"We should concentrate on the first boy first, maybe. No? The boy who's missing today? Noah, is it? The troublesome one who brought you to my cellar in the first place."

"Please stop fucking with me?" I say. "Just tell me."

"Noah. He does like you lots. I guess he just wants to fix things for you, right? What other reason could he have for poking his nose in here, all on his lonesome? With us wolves. He's a brave one, ain't he?"

Shit.

"Now that's not a very good look for you, Gaige. You look a little green, young man."

I grab at the crumbling dirt wall beside me and hold tight for balance. I'd throw up, but I'm pretty sure there's nothing in my stomach. What is food in Jack Chalek's world, anyway? I can't remember the last time I ate. Frozen pizza? With Noah. Tuesday?

"So many kiddies, I just can't keep track. Let's go back to today's boy, though, OK?" Chalek says. He rubs his hands together. He's having a field day. "Because Noah is missing, and Logan isn't screaming quite yet, is he?

"Your *loooover*, Logan," he teases. "Your dirty boy toy. He doesn't scream until about the end of act two or so. Give or take. We have some time for that. Have you been wondering why *this* boy isn't screaming, Gaige? Noah. Have you found *him* inside your Book of Dreams yet? Or just that *other* one?"

He's clearly seething with unspeakable anger just thinking about Mael, the kid who defeated him even though he trapped them. No mistake about it: Mael defeated him.

"Noah!" I scream it so loudly, I swear the dirt walls shift. "Noah!"

The bastard laughs. Like, a belly laugh. He actually leans forward and holds his belly like a grotesque version of Santa Claus, holding his *bowlful of jelly* belly. He's a tall, skeletal, hideous Lurch of a Santa Claus.

I'm more ballerina than football player, but I run at Chalek with such force that the tackle is pure perfection. I have him pinned to the dirt floor in a second flat.

I don't stop there, though. I sit on him, pin his arms under my knees, and whale on his old-man face. Punch after punch connects. And through the whole attack, he laughs. And laughs. And laughs some more. Spitting out blood, he laughs. Coughing, he laughs. Such a hideous, wet laugh, too.

"Where is he, you monster?" But I don't give him an opportunity to speak. I know he's not going to tell me, anyway. I just keep punching. After a few more fists to the face, he probably decides that I've had enough fun. The last fist I swing lands on the dirt floor below me with a thud. Chalek has vanished.

I shriek and grab my hand. Instant pain. I shake it out.

As I stumble to my feet, I see Chalek farther down the cellar with not a scratch on his face. He looks like a maniacal clown or something out of a horror movie, all limbs and madness. As I approach, I see that he's standing in a doorway. His palm rests on the center of the door; his smile threatens to rip his face open.

When I arrive at the door, he raps it lightly with his knuckles. And then he vanishes, his laughter filling the cellar. The sound echoes for what feels like an eternity, though I'm sure it only lasts a few seconds.

In a panic, I start slamming my fists into the door. Then I realize how much I shredded them on Chalek's face. Every knuckle feels white-hot.

The door is made from extremely thick wood. It doesn't give.

"Noah!" I call. "Noah!"

What if he isn't in there? What if Chalek just wants me to think he's in there so I'll waste my time? Could Noah even be in the cellar if it's not the actual, present-day cellar? When the bookstore's here, he can't see it. So how could he see or be held captive in a cellar that isn't really here?

"If you're in there and you can hear me, bang on the door!" I shout.

Nothing. I try to calm my breathing so I can hear, but I'm panting with fear. My heart threatens to beat beyond the confines of my chest.

"Bang on the door!"

I hold my breath for a fraction of a second, but it's no use. I sound like an asthmatic horse who just ran the Kentucky Derby.

Then I hear something. I can't decide what it is at first, if it's even anything at all. Then the sound comes again. It's a voice, but heavily muffled. The room has thicker walls than I thought, and the door's a fortress unto itself.

"Noah?"

I put my ear up to the door. I can hear him. He's *definitely* in there. His voice sounds like it's coming from a tin can wrapped inside a metric ton of insulation.

"I'll get you out," I shout, as loud as I can shout. "I'll figure something out, bud!"

I look around the cellar for something I can use to break down the door, but there's nothing here. Nobody uses this space; it's utterly abandoned, like the stores above. And I'm still in the old cellar, not the one that's actually here. This place must have something to do with the puzzle, but I can't figure out how it's connected. I'm still wrestling with the idea that Noah is, essentially, locked inside a cellar that he shouldn't even be able to see.

What if I left, got someone else, and brought them down here? The bookstore would vanish. The old cellar would vanish. Right? Maybe then, Noah would be released from this trap. We'd be back in the other cellar. Maybe that's where he *actually* is. It makes sense. In my addled, exhausted mind, it actually makes more sense than anything has in a very long time. Noah is in the cellar that I can't see right now, the real one. It's me that's trapped in the old cellar, unable to get to *him*.

"Noah. If you can hear me. I'll be back. I'm going to go get Logan. We'll come back and get you out of there."

I didn't know I could shout so loudly. The whole neighborhood probably heard me. Or nobody, seeing as I'm in Chalek's void.

I run to the ladder and clamber back up into the washroom. I guess Chalek has left me to my own devices, because he didn't close the latch on the door in the floor. He doesn't even poke his head out from behind a bookshelf or anything. He just lets me go.

I walk through the quiet bookstore, brushing by the rows and rows of dull, monochromatic books. Most of them have no titles. Now more than ever, I see them as props. The only book that truly exists in Chalek's make-believe world is *My Book of Dreams*, and I'm not completely convinced that it's not just another prop.

A portal, maybe? It's definitely a portal to Mael, and Chalek's own little nightmare world.

I leave the store, flinching at the peal of the bells as I walk away.

Chapter Sixteen

FOUR PEBBLES HIT LOGAN'S WINDOW before his bedroom light finally comes on. *Finally.* I was beginning to think I'd have to climb up and break in.

Seconds after he turns on the light, I see him at the window. He presses his face to it and looks out into the yard below. I wave like a raving gymnast, mid-floor routine. He waves back and opens the window.

"What are you doing out there, baby? It's the middle of the night."

"You have to come down." Nothing like stage-whispering. I'll be his Romeo any day. I think of Romeo's lines now: *But, soft! What light through yonder window breaks? It is the east, and Juliet is the sun.* Logan might just be my sun, but now is not the time for fun and games. Focus, Gaige. "Please."

He drops his shoulders in one of those slumps that says a thousand words, and I wonder if my Juliet even gives a shit about his Romeo. Clearly, he doesn't want to do it.

But he's going to relent. I can see it in his body language. He raises a finger in the international sign for *just a sec.* Then he shakes his head in either real or mock disgust. He closes the window and disappears.

When the light goes out again, I pray that there was truth in his *just a sec* gesture. If not, it means he just ignored me and went back to bed, which is also a possibility. But a minute later, the sliding glass door in the walkout basement screeches open, and I run toward him.

As he slowly slides the door closed with one hand, he puts up the other hand to stop me from giving him the hug I was just about to lay on him. The hug I need more than water right now.

"Whoa. Wait a sec. What's going on?" I'm sensing frustration. Poor Logan. I don't blame him. I sometimes wish I wasn't so extra.

"Can I explain on the way?" I say. He turns away from the door, and I take hold of his hands and hold them down by his sides. "Kiss?"

Of course he relents. His boyfriend's a hunk. He's gonna kiss him every chance he gets.

After a sloppy make-out session while we stand on the dew-wet grass of his backyard, I take his hand and begin to lead him away from the house and through Bellevue Square Park.

"So," Logan says, plopping down on a bench and bringing me down beside him. Looking over at the Al Waxman statue, I can't help but think of Mael and how much they miss Kensington Market. And how long they've been trapped on the Other Side. "Where are we going? And why is it so urgent?"

"Urgent? Nah. It's not urg—"

"Huh. Yeah. Not at all," Logan says. "You were walking on your tippy-toes just now, babe. You only do that when you're being held back from doing something you want to do. When you're anxious about something. Tippy-toes are a sign that you're not quite saving the world in the manner you would like. Why do you always get into these predicaments? And why do you always find a way to drag me in with you?"

"Suspension of disbelief brings a lot of action into one's life, babe." I laugh as I say it, but I also believe it. Only someone skating shakily on the edge of reason would have entered that bookstore. I get up from the bench, and since I'm still holding his hand he joins me. We start walking and make our way through Kensington Market. "Besides, you love me. You thrive on me dragging you in."

"Tell me the whole story, and I'll try my best to believe it."

I squeeze his hand. I'm thankful for his cooperation, even if he gives it a bit reluctantly. As we make our way to Spadina, I consider how I should tackle this.

"You know I can't, right? You know it's about the whole bookstore that's not there and whatnot, right?"

"How about I just take a leap of faith and pretend you have some supernatural connection with something otherworldly?" I know he's mocking me, but I don't care. He's also going along for the ride. Also, creepy that he said *otherworldly*. It's basically Mael's name for the place they're trapped in.

"Noah is still missing. You can at least agree with me on that inarguable fact, right? That's an actual thing, right?"

As we approach Baldwin Street, he stops walking, causing me to skid to a halt.

"Gaige, you know I'm only joking. I don't know how to deal with this, but I know you're not bullshitting me. Why would you make something like this up?"

"Maybe because I'm unstable and you're just finding out about it now? And maybe that makes you slightly nervous, because you don't know what to do about it. And you don't know what to do about *me*."

"I'm here, aren't I? I'm with you. We're going to that bookstore, aren't we? I can tell," he says. We start walking again, going east on Baldwin. "Does that place have something to do with Noah going missing?"

"I can't tell you what happened, because I don't know. But if you give me a few minutes, I can explain what I *think* might have happened."

"Hit me," he says. "I can take it."

We walk in silence for a few minutes while I gather my thoughts. I know what I'm thinking, but it's hard to put it into words.

"First, I need another kiss." I stop us in our tracks again and turn to face him, giving him a little *how-about-it* grin and a shrug. Diversionary tactic. I hope I'm too irresistible for him to ignore my request.

Turns out I am. Have I mentioned how good Logan kisses are? Like, phenomenal. They give me wavy-gravy legs. His tongue melts me like water over sugar.

"Better," I say, after he annihilates me with his mouth and leaves me to wobble back to reality. "Much, much better."

Logan offers a big grin, and I can see some of the hesitation leave his body as his shoulders relax and we begin to walk again.

He likes that I love and compliment his kisses. He always acts all peacock-proud and accomplished afterwards.

"Well," I begin as we walk, "I went back to the store because the dead guy who runs it wanted me to read that book again. Only, when I opened it, I heard screams. *Your* screams. Apparently, it was one of my future dreams. Which also might come to pass. Like, very soon. But that's a different story. That's why I asked if you screamed when I was away.

"Anyway, I got lost inside the book, and suddenly I woke up, and it was almost two days later. That's when I called you and you told me how much time had passed. For me, it felt like ten minutes. No. Five. Two, even.

"I think Noah must have realized I was missing. Like, maybe he went back to my house before he got to school. He couldn't find me, so he went to the bookstore instead of school that morning. If he couldn't find me, I'm pretty positive Noah would eventually have gone to the bookstore to look. And I'm guessing that's how he got dragged into this. He injected himself into the nightmare to try to find me."

"But why would he go to a place he can't even see if—"

"He's been there with me. We went down to the cellar, and we got trapped in there. We had to break out through another store."

"You what, now?" I look at Logan, and he has this *oh my god* expression on his face. I just nod.

"Right? He knew there were weird things happening, even if the bookstore wasn't there for him either. So when I went missing, he would have gone to the most likely place. And he wouldn't have just gone to the bookstore—or where the bookstore sometimes exists for me. He would've gone right to the source. He must have figured I was in the cellar again."

I stop talking, and we just walk for a couple minutes.

"I waited until my parents went to sleep tonight, and then I went back to see if my theory was correct." I look over to see if Logan is listening, because he doesn't say anything. "And, sure enough, I found him. Trapped in the cellar. Just as I suspected."

"So that's where we're going? To the cellar of the bookstore?"

"No. See, I figure that if you come with me, the bookstore will disappear. That means the old cellar will disappear, too. He'll probably still be in a locked room, but maybe it will be easier to break him out of it. Because where he is now, there's no way I can get to him. The door sounds about two feet thick or some shit. But, stay with me here, I think he's in the cellar inside the cellar. And with you there, the one cellar will disappear, and he'll just be... you know, in the cellar."

"Well," he says, squeezing my hand, "that's the most confusing thing I've ever tried to wrap my head around. We'll soon find out. We're almost there."

We get to Elm Street, walk past Sick Kids, and soon approach the bookstore from the opposite direction.

"I don't know how we're going to get past all *that* shit," Logan says as we arrive at the abandoned storefront.

He's talking about the stuff the police put up after I went missing. Ah. That stuff wasn't there when I was here last. Of course—it was a bookstore again at the time. Not like police tape and a few pieces of cardboard can stop me.

"We can do this," I say as we get to the door. "It just *looks* impenetrable."

Without waiting to listen to my reasoning, Logan picks up a nearby, snapped-off street sign and hurls it at the thick cardboard like a javelin. After a half a dozen well-aimed jabs and a few angry shoves, he's in. OK, then. I have an awesome boyfriend. He might even be a badass superhero.

"I was going to do that myself, you know."

"Come on," he says, "no reason you should have *all* the fun." He drops the sign and shoves one last piece of cardboard out of the way. "Let's go."

Logan to the rescue. So hot.

For the second time in a week, we find ourselves crawling through the smashed storefront window and into the unknown.

Chapter Seventeen

THIS IS THE PART WHERE I want to say I'm a mad-ass genius. I want to say we walk into the abandoned building, go downstairs, open the door, and free Noah because my brilliant theory was correct.

That would be so awesome.

But it's not that simple. I mean, I guess *technically* my theory's sorta right. But saving Noah isn't the piece of cake I imagined it would be.

The unexpected also happens: Logan begins to see the tear in the fabric between Jack Chalek's world and our own. I imagine that this is because Jack's trying to keep Noah trapped as long as possible.

At any rate, when we step through the window, there are remnants of the bookstore everywhere. It's not here, don't get me wrong, but hints of its existence are.

"Why can I see those books over there, babe?"

I start in surprise. "You see those? What else can you see?"

"The books, the knocked-over shelf, the cat."

"Holy shit. You can see everything I can see? You see the cat!"

Logan seeing the cat again actually gives me more relief than I've felt since this madness began. I'm on the brink of tears. Both he and Noah have seen the cat, now. Logan, twice. It's real, and so is the bite it gave me.

Logan walks toward the back of the store as I contemplate the implications. Is Chalek letting him in on this alternate reality, like he did with Noah? Is it intentional?

"Wait," I say, as I race to join him and fling my arm out in front of him. I practically clothesline him. A shadow moves across the threshold of the back room. And if I can see it...

"What? Jesus, Gaige. You scared the shit out of—"

I put my finger to my lips to silence him. He gives me a dirty look; he's not at all pleased to be cut off so forcefully.

"There's someone back there," I whisper. I point to the room, get in front of Logan, and walk toward the door, which is slightly ajar.

I reach out and push the door open all the way. Nothing. I'm beginning to think I imagined a shadow when a burst of laughter comes from somewhere below us.

"What the hell was that?" Logan asks from half an inch behind me, as he attempts to invade my space completely. "I mean, what *was* that?"

"*That* was Chalek."

"But I thought I couldn't see him. Or hear him. What's going on, Gaige? I'm scared. I don't like this. Can we leave now?"

"No way. That's exactly what he's hoping for," I say. I shake my head, take Logan's hand, and lead him to the trapdoor in the washroom. "We can't give him what he wants. Ever. We have to think of Noah."

As I let go of his hand and reach down to pull the door open, Logan squeals. "I am *not* going down there. No way. Uh-uh."

I know the obvious and easiest way to get him downstairs, so I don't even bother to argue with him.

"Suit yourself." I prop open the door. It looks like an angry maw in the floor, ready to devour everything within its reach. "I'll just be downstairs, then."

"Over my dead body," Logan says. "I'm coming with you."

Like shooting fish in a barrel. I drop down onto the ladder without saying anything. No need to rub it in.

"Wait. Don't go all the way down. I don't want to be up here alone. Even for a second."

I stop to allow him to catch up. Awkwardly, he makes his way onto the ladder, and we go down together—as much as two people on the same ladder *can* go down it together, that is. That's my boy.

"This is the most unsavory thing I have ever done in my entire life. That includes the time I held your head over the toilet and pulled your hair back at Shea Simpson's house party while you puked nacho cheese Doritos and strawberry milkshake all in, over, and around the toilet. And *I* cleaned up the mess."

"Sick, Logan," I say, remembering all too vividly my poor choice of snacks before said night of excess. To this day, I still can't eat nacho cheese Doritos, and I never will again. "Dead murderers are nowhere *near* that disgusting. I guess, thanks for looking out for me?"

"I always do."

At the bottom of the ladder, we stand waiting for our eyes to adjust to the darkness.

"Shit," I say. "I forgot to grab the flashlight. I'll be right back. There's one just upstairs."

He grabs my arm, and his fingernails dig in deep enough to leave marks. There's gonna be blood.

"Ow. Jesus, Logan. You took flesh, there."

"You're not going anywhere," he says as he lets go of my arm and reaches into his pocket for his phone. He pulls it out and turns on his flashlight app. "Turn on your phone's flashlight, genius."

"Oh," I say. "Sure. Yeah."

I turn my light on.

Chapter Eighteen

FEET ON THE GROUND, WE'RE ready to search for Noah—but yet again, everything looks different. It's not quite right. Just as there are remnants of the bookstore upstairs, there are remnants of the old cellar here, intermingling with the new one. It's like an amalgamation of both cellars. Every time I think I have Chalek's world figured out, he throws me a curveball. We're in trouble.

"What's next?" Logan asks. I so totally don't know. With Logan here to force reality back into the picture, I had planned to walk into the *now* cellar, find where Noah was trapped, and get him out. Now, wherever Noah is being held will be less accessible than I'd hoped.

Maybe Chalek has difficulty manifesting his alternate reality when more than one other person is involved. This looks like he tried to summon up the old cellar to keep me away from Noah, but his magic only served up half of it—clearly, cheap magic for a cheap thug. He can't fully bring the old cellar to life because he's letting three of us into his world, and he's just not strong enough. Amateur.

"I have no frigging clue. Dude, I've been in this cellar a few times now. But it's usually either the old one or the new one. This place is neither. It's both. It's a mix of the two." I point farther into the dark cellar with the light of my phone. "Noah's down there."

"Well, if you were already here, where he was, why didn't you just save him then?"

He looks at me like he thinks I've lost it—not a look you want to get from your own boyfriend. Thanks for the vote of confidence, Logan.

"Nothing is ever that simple here, babe. Trust me, OK? I need that from you. Plus, I kinda sorta already explained it to you."

He shrugs. I can tell he feels bad. I turn to face him, reach out to touch his cheek, and force him to look me in the eye. He offers me a vague smile.

"You know I love you, right?" I whisper.

Even with nothing but our little flashlight apps doing their best to chase the darkness away, I can see him blush. I lean in to kiss him and he kisses me back, forgetting his frustration for a second.

When I pull away, I think I recognize the new expression on Logan's face. I've seen it often, on many people: the exhaustion of being in my unpredictable company. But just behind that, maybe love. Or something close to it, acceptance maybe. Please, god, don't be resignation. It might be resignation. I couldn't bear that.

I swear, I never set out to be a difficult person; it often just turns out that way. Trouble has a way of finding me, and staying with me.

"Let's go," I say, before he has an opportunity to come to his senses and realize that he should get as far away from me as humanly possible. I start to walk toward where I last heard Noah's muffled voice through the door. "This isn't the same cellar it was the last time I was here, but the layout stays pretty much the same."

"I'm totally lost," Logan says. I turn back and give him a look of total exasperation. "Relax, Gaige. I'm coming with you. I just don't get it."

"I don't get it either, babe," I admit. "I'm just making everything up as I go. Nothing about this place makes sense. It completely defies logic. And physics. And reality. He can change everything on a dime. I mean, everything. But if I'm right, he's making himself weaker by letting you in. There's a crack in his magic."

As we draw closer to the corner of the cellar where I know Noah is holed up, I hear a quiet moaning through the earthen wall where I had hoped a door would appear this time around. Beneath the moaning, I hear scratching, a desperate scratching that sends chills up my spine.

It's all very *Cask of Amontillado*, if you ask me—that Poe story where this guy brings this other guy into his wine cellars, lures him into this little niche, chains him up, and builds a wall with brick and mortar to seal him in. Buries the poor bastard alive. I've read way too many old books, and this is far too close to that story. I can't let Noah die that way, closed up in his own little dirt mausoleum.

There's no telling what or how he's doing in there; I'm just glad to hear he's still making noise. I'm trying not to lose track of the days altogether. I think he's been trapped in his dungeon for over two days now. Unless—who knows? We could have lost a day or two since we came through the bookstore window.

"I can hear something," Logan whispers, grabbing my arm with his nails as he slinks up against me. I'm going to have a mess of cuts and scratches on my arms when this is over, if he keeps this up. "What is that noise, Gaige? It sounds like rats."

I shine the light on his face, and I can see that he's terrified. The fact that rats would be worse to him than knowing his friend—his boyfriend's best friend—is trapped inside a wall with no means of escape is not lost on me. It does make me realize, though, that Noah might just die in there if I can't figure out a way to get him out.

I wish it were rats.

Just as I'm about to explain to Logan that the noise he hears is Noah trying to dig himself out of his burial plot with his bare hands, a shriek of old man laughter explodes from the dark depths of the cellar.

I look in the direction I think the laughter is coming from, even though it kinda feels like it comes from all directions at once.

"Do you see that man standing down there?" I ask Logan, pointing to the end of the long cellar with my cell phone. I hope he does and simultaneously hope he doesn't.

"Yes," he says. "But why? I thought I couldn't see him. Why, Gaige? Why do I see him? I'm not supposed to be able to see him."

"That's why the cellar is messed up, Logan," I say, trying to make sense. "Because he's letting you in. He can't quite bring the old one back because he's letting you see him and his little world of tricks. It's like we're between channels on a bad TV set."

Another burst of death-rattle laughter rings out through the cellar, but Lurch makes no move to approach us. He just stands there, keeping his distance. Obviously, he's screwing with us. He knows how to build the tension like a boss.

"What's up, Lurch?" I call out. I don't like the way it makes me feel to hear my own voice raised so loud in these dungeon-like acoustics.

"You know I don't like that moniker, Gaige. And yet you continue to use it. You provoke me so, dear boy."

He says this into my left ear. In the split second since I taunted him, he has somehow moved from the opposite end of the cellar to close enough behind me that a few of his words were delivered while his mouth literally touched my ear. I can feel the wetness of his old man skank on my earlobe.

I jump back and wipe wildly at my ear to rid it of the poison dust of his dank, dead breath. I squeal a bit as I do this. Not my proudest moment, but you try not to squirm when a dead guy tongues your ear.

"Don't do that," I say. "Ugh. Ew, Lurch."

"*Mister Chalek*. Give it a try, Gaige. I know you can do it."

"Why should I give a shit what your name—"

"I said, give it a try, boy," he says again. His fist comes up, and as he squeezes it, I feel that hot, excruciating pain in my abdomen again. This is by far his best trick. Works like a charm. I fall from a standing position to my knees while holding my belly and slowly slither to the gross dirt floor, trying to somehow escape the inescapable pain.

"What's happening?" Logan screams. But he sounds so far away. The pain is so all-encompassing, it seems to build layers of distance between us. "Stop it! Stop it! You're killing him."

"I assure you, I am not."

"Please stop," Logan says as he comes down to the floor with me and rubs my shoulder, attempting to soothe me. "He's in pain. Please, Mister."

"Young lad, I promise you your little boyfriend here will survive this lesson. Gaige, what was that you were going to call me, now? Please, remind me again. I'm *liiiiiiiiiiiissssssssstening*."

The last word comes out long and lispy, like Chalek is mimicking a snake or something.

Logan rises to his feet as Chalek bends down and smiles in my face, poisoning the air around me with his foul breath.

"What's that, Gaige? I didn't quite catch that. Did you say something?" *That's because I didn't say anything, asshole.* Logan retreats behind Chalek. He wants no part of his monstrous orbit.

I stay still, feeling more defiant than is probably wise. I'm already down, already balled up and dying from the pain, but I'm not ready to relent.

He clamps down harder, and his smile twists from the exertion of making his fist even tighter.

"Mister," I squeal. But I can't get it all out in one breath. I need to stop for air. I can't even say it properly because of the increasing pain in my belly.

"You're killing him, Mister," Logan says. He's pleading for mercy.

"Chalek," I finally manage. It comes out like a bomb from the pit of my stomach. "Mister Chalek."

The pain ends instantly as his fist unclenches. His laughter grates throughout the cellar one more time.

"It seems I have distracted you a titch, Mister Gaige," Chalek says as I struggle to my feet. He offers me his hand to help me up, as though I would actually take it. "You should not play games with me, boy. I will always win."

"What are you even talking about?"

"I wonder where that lovely, soft little boy of yours has gotten himself to. He's a real looker, Gaige. He's yummy, ain't he? You two do some pretty nasty stuff together, I imagine, no? It's a shame how nobody ever stays put down here, though, ain't it? Where *is* that cute boy of yours now?"

I look around, but the spot Logan occupied a moment ago, when he pleaded for Chalek to stop torturing me, is now empty.

"No. What did you do? Where is he? Logan?"

I run back and forth across the length of the cellar, shouting Logan's name, flashing my phone light into every nook and cranny. He's gone. There's no sign of Logan anywhere, and I'm down here alone with this old man. Beyond my own breathless cries of desperation, Chalek's laughter is the only sound.

Chapter Nineteen

Do you remember the boy screaming... it might just happen tonight.

Chalek's prophetic words come back to me, and I can't believe I literally delivered Logan here, to this cellar, when I should have known better. I offered him up to the monster. And the monster took him, just like he promised.

After I finish scouring the cellar, running around like a lunatic and shouting into every dark corner, I come back to where Chalek stands, chuckling, arms patiently folded across his chest. He's overly amused by my terror and sense of defeat. As I stand before him, panting like I might drop dead any second, his face lights in a huge, greasy grin.

"Well, well," he says. "You certainly gave that your very best effort, Gaige, didn't ya? Well done. You just ran and ran and ran. But you look a mess, dear boy. All this running around for naught, it's gonna spend you, boy. You need a good hosing down, now, to rid yourself of all the dirt and sweat. Did you find your boy lover, you bad, naughty boy? Don't look like you did."

"Why. Are. You. Doing. This?" I want to kill him. But there's no killing the dead. I feel so helpless, all I do is scream. "Where is he?"

"It's such a shame that I do not know, Gaige. Because chances are, I would tell you if I did. Yep… chances are real good I would tell ya. That's for sure."

"Bastard."

"Now, let's not throw word bricks at each other. You know I don't like nicknames, boy. I'm thinking maybe your girly boyfriend—what was his name again, now? Logan? I don't know why your boy Logan ain't screaming to let you know where he's hiding. I'd say it's disconcerting, am I right? Isn't he supposed to scream round about now?"

The bastard bursts into another stretched-out, maniacal peal of laughter for good measure.

"What did you do to him?"

As if on cue, Logan's sudden screams tell me what I already knew. They come from behind the wall. Within the wall. He's with Noah, only, I can hear him better than I've been able to hear Noah. It sounds almost as though there's an opening between their space and ours, now. Logan's screams pierce me.

"Logan!" I scream, so loudly I hurt my own ears. Even Chalek flinches. "Logan, can you hear me?"

"Gaige, get us out of here! Please. I'm begging you. Get us out of here."

"Is Noah OK?"

The time it takes for him to respond is endless. Chalek seizes the opportunity to nudge my anxiety up a notch.

"Are they even together, Gaige? Maybe they each have their own little berth in the earth, so to speak." Chalek laughs like the maniac he is. He's gotta stop that laughter. It's fraying whatever sanity I still cling to.

"He's weak, Gaige," Logan finally says. "I'm with him. Don't listen to the asshole. I'm with Noah. He needs water. Like, now. But he's OK."

Chalek chuckles some more, this time a little quieter. I turn away from the wall to yell at him, but he contorts his face and moves closer to the wall. It's as if he hears something odd and is investigating the sound, or is pantomiming it.

"What's that? What in the world is that insufferable background noise?" Chalek says, scrunching his face up exaggeratedly. "Reminds me of the constant drip, drip, drip of the old plumbing I hear sometimes when I'm upstairs trying to shelve books in peace. Just nonstop, it is, Gaige boy. Drip. Drip. Drip. Such an intrusion on my silent reveries, it is. Downright annoying. I wish I knew where it comes from. Can't never find it, though."

He knocks on the wall a few times, like he's testing it or something.

"Such an insufferable noise. Can't never find the source, mind you. Somewhere, deep in the bones of this old building, there's an annoying old leak. I aim to find it, but I never seem quite able. I'm an old man, now, Gaige. Hard to root around in the underbelly to find the plumbing when you're old and frail like myself."

"What are you even talking ab—"

"Gaige!" Logan yells through the wall. "Gaige. There's water dripping down the wall."

"What did you do?" I ask Chalek. "What's happening?"

"It's not me, son," he says. "I swear, these old pipes. They just drip when they wanna. Ain't no stopping them. You can't reason with old pipes, Gaige. They'll drip if and when they want to, come what may. Nasty things, old pipes."

"Gaige, it's starting to pool on the floor. It's coming in faster now. It's dripping all over the place. What's happening?"

"Seems to me your little sweetie boy there said something or other about the other boy needing water, did he not? Seems to me they're about to get enough for a little sip or two. I suppose the old adage *ask and you shall receive* has a little something to do with this blessed miracle. Isn't that just a jim-dandy of a hallelujah? Gaige, I'm giddy with excitement for this amazing event. This old building, it cares in its own ways, don't it?"

"Please," I say. I grab onto his bony arm, and it's like rawhide with a pulse, sickly, translucent rawhide. My first reaction is to let go, but I push through it and grip harder. "Please. I'm begging you. What do you want from me? Anything."

Chalek laughs again. He brushes my hand away from his arm like it's a fruit fly. I'm little more than an annoyance to him, and he holds my friends' lives in his hands.

"Gaige. You silly boy. What could I possibly want?"

"Gaige, it's up to our ankles," Logan says. "It's coming in faster, coming in from everywhere. Please do something."

I hear moaning, and I know from the timbre of the voice that it's Noah. It's almost like he's trying to speak but is no longer capable of doing so.

"It's a shame. I never did find that leak, try as I might. Plumbing is a tricky bitch for the layman, Gaige."

"Please. I'll do whatever you want. Just let them out. Tell me how to get them out."

"Where's that book of yours, boy?" Chalek says. "Do you even remember where you last had it? You kids these days, you have so many possessions you just don't care anymore. You're so irresponsible."

Try as I may, I can't for the life of me remember when it was I last saw the book. Here? In my backpack? I just can't recall.

"I don't—"

"*I don't know*," he taunts sulkily, in something eerily similar to my own voice. "*I don't remember.*"

Just as I'm about to beg for mercy one more time for good measure, Chalek brings the book out from behind his back.

"Ta-da. You are irresponsible, Gaige. You should be ashamed of yourself."

He's good at what he does: I don't know if I should feel relief or even more terror. I'm definitely confused. I slump against the nearest wall and put my head down. I really don't know how much more I can take.

"Please. Just let them out." I look up into his face, pleading. As the tears begin to fall, I say in almost a whisper, "They didn't choose the book. That was all on me. They didn't choose this. Please."

Instead of using his words, Chalek holds out the book.

I can't believe my hand betrays me by reaching for the book. Even as I see it happening, I can't believe I'm doing it.

"You have some reading to do, don't you Gaige. You've been trying, you really have. But you're not doing a good job. You keep failing, you farking little boy. Focus. You can't come back out if you don't go inside."

This damn book is what this whole nightmare is about. I wish I could figure out a way to walk away from all of this. I can't decide if Chalek is playing a game with me, or killing me slowly and taunting me mercilessly along the way. What the fuck is his endgame? He needs me to enter so he can wiggle in with me, but he also wants me to come back out?

"Please, Mister," I say. "Just let me see my friends."

God help me. God help Logan. God help Noah. God help Mael, if it isn't too late.

I take the fucking book back.

Chapter Twenty

Of all the things to happen next, I did not expect this. As Chalek releases his hold on the book and allows me to take it from him, I blip out. This time, I don't even have a chance to open the book before I'm falling inside.

I realize almost instantly, however, that that's not actually what happens. I'm not in Mael's Other Side world at all, and Mael is nowhere in sight. This is a different kind of darkness. I still smell earth and musty cellar, not the much more horrible, all-consuming stench of the Other Side where Mael is.

It doesn't take me long to figure out where I am. Between the earthy stink and my wet feet, I quickly place it. I'm standing in a mausoleum of my own, book in hand.

I wanted them out, not me in. Fuck.

It's so dark, I can't see a thing. And tight. I can reach out and touch wall on both sides. The dripping water is all around me, running down the walls, dripping onto my head from above. At least, I hope it's water. I'm trapped, like them. But I'm not with them.

"Gaige," Logan says. I can hear him so clearly, almost as though he's standing beside me. I dig in my pocket for my phone, scraping my arm on the wall while doing so. I can feel the panic of claustrophobia building up inside me. I try to soothe myself by breathing steadily, even as I pull out my phone and scrape my arm again for good measure.

"Gaige," Logan says again. "We're trapped."

I turn on my flashlight app, and everything comes into focus. Everything including the book from hell. The way its gold cover glints in the light serves only to piss me off. It's mocking me.

The walls in here, though running with water, look mysteriously like the walls of the Other Side. The inky goo is everywhere. I look down and see that it's stuck to me wherever I leaned or fell or scraped myself against the wall.

The water drips from several different places, and the pool I'm standing in is almost up to my ankles now. It looks vile, but it's definitely water, not the goop. It flows too fast to be anything but water.

I guess I should be grateful that Chalek allowed me to keep my phone. Maybe he just wants to ensure that I'll see what's about to happen to me if I don't find a way to stop it.

"There's gotta be a way out," I say, leaning toward the wall closest to where Logan's voice came from. I look at my hands. A phone in one and an irritating book of madness in the other. What would MacGyver do? I'm guessing, get the hell out of the mess long before he found himself locked inside his own watery grave, watching his impending death. "Let me think. Let me think."

"Is Noah OK?" I ask, remembering how bad he sounded moments ago, when I was still on the outside.

"I'm fine," he says. I can tell he's anything but. His voice is gravelly and weak, but it's reassuring that I can hear him through the wall between us.

"We need to get him some water," I say. As the words leave my mouth, there's an almost imperceptible increase in the dripping. I imagine it's the same for them. The water flows in just a little bit quicker. It's up past my ankles now.

Chalek's attempt at humor? I'm not laughing.

"I'm OK, Gaige. Honest." He does his best to convince me, raising his voice to show he still has the strength to do so.

"What happens when you read the book?" Logan asks, out of the blue.

"I'm not going to do this again, babe," I reply. I try to keep the anger out of my voice, but it's impossible. "Now is not the time to argue about this. I've already explained things to you. If you want to tell me how it's all impossible, fine. Just not right now. Save it for when we get out of here. I don't need your condescension at the moment."

"Are you done?" Logan says. Even with a wall of dirt between us, I can still see the eye roll. I imagine it, anyway.

I pretend to consider his question for a moment. "Um, yeah. I guess so. No lectures needed about how all of this is impossible, Logan. I can't deal with another—"

"I thought you said you were done?" he says, interrupting me mid-rant. "That doesn't sound like done to me."

"Guys," Noah says, "can we *not* have a lover's quarrel right now? You two are literally the worst. We're kind of trapped in our own tombs at the moment. And I'm not exactly thrilled that I have to share mine. Now is not the time."

Despite the fact that Noah just used most of his remaining energy to make his point, I can't help but laugh a little. His point is, like, so on point.

"No. You're right, Noah," I say. "You're right. We have to work togeth—"

"Just stop talking," Logan says. "I wasn't going to say it's impossible. I'm here. I'm in it. I'm sorry, OK! I'm sorry I didn't believe you, Gaige. I believe you, *now*. We have to get out of here. It was an honest-to-god real question. What happens when you read the book? Tell me like you're telling someone who's not going to laugh in your face and call bullshit. What actually happens?"

"Oh. Why didn't you just say so?"

"Because you didn't give me a chance. You were too—"

"Guys," Noah interrupts again. "The *water*. Focus. It's not going down. We need to figure this out."

"Oh, shit." He's right. It's halfway up my shins now. And it's bloody cold. And murky. And gross.

"Yeah."

"OK, let me think."

"Remember when you helped me come out?" Logan says. Nothing like a wild turn in the conversation. I wish I could see him. I'd give him so much side-eye right now.

"What does that have to do with anything? Like, literally."

"You told me I always had the power to do it, that it was inside me the whole time. Remember how you talked about the Emerald City and the Wizard? How they were just distractions? Pretty props? That Dorothy didn't actually need them."

"Baby," I begin. I move closer to the wall, even though I'm

kind of terrified to touch it. "You were *always* strong enough to do it on your own. You just needed help to realize it. A push to the first step. You had it all by yourself."

"OK, settle down." He chuckles. "Yeah, yeah. I don't need a cheerleader right now. My point, and I do have one, is that you have what it takes to get us out of here. I know you do. You don't need the Wizard. You don't need to go to the Emerald City. What happens when you read the book, Gaige? Focus."

"Oh. Wait… I think I follow. Is the book like the ruby slippers in this scenario?"

"Yes. My distraction was the wall I kept up to protect myself. I just needed to let it go, to walk through it. That's what you told me. *Just walk through the wall. Put on those fabulous ruby slippers and walk on through to the other side.* My analogy may fall apart a little here, but—you can get us out of here, Gaige. That book, it's a key. The ruby slippers. It has to be. What does it do?"

"I see words. Words I somehow recognize, like they're mine. Chalek says the book is my dreams, that the words are my own dreams. Mael said, *It's imprinting you; you're imprinting it.*"

Oops. I can't believe I just talked about Mael. I can feel the blush rise in my face, my neck, and my ears. And the guilt. Lots of guilt, too. I suddenly feel like I've betrayed Logan by speaking about Mael. Christ, every time I think about Mael I betray Logan. Let's face it, they're literally my wet dream.

"Who said what, now?" Logan says. Of course he detected my slipup. Of course he did.

Oh boy.

Chapter Twenty-One

I WAIT IN THE DARKNESS to see if the tension will go away on its own. Like that ever happens.

"Who's Mael?"

Oh, you know, just this kid. They live inside the book. As one would.

"This stuff is just like the stuff I found in the wall the other night, Gaige."

I don't know if he's intentionally trying to save the day or if he's just absentmindedly talking because he's entered the delirium stage, but Noah inserts himself into the conversation just in time.

The goopy stuff. Of course he remembers. He had it all over his fingers, like a baby playing in his own shit.

"It is. I know." I move closer to the wall and shine the beam of my phone flashlight on the cover of the book as I prepare to open it. "It's also inside the book. If that makes any sense. Which it probably doesn't, but you kind of have to experience it to *get* it."

"Who's Mael?"

He's good. I thought *I* was the jealous one, yet here we are. Maybe I can weave Mael in with the goopy substance.

"Whenever I try to read the book, I fall into it. First it's just a big swirl of words, and I only catch glimpses of phrases, never enough to fully make sense of what I'm reading. Then the swirling gets more and more intense until I melt through the ink, and I'm on the other side of the words."

"And?" Logan says, impatient. "Then what happens?"

"Then I'm in a dark, dank space filled with tar-like slop. The same stuff that's all over the walls in here. The stuff that Noah played with the other day. This stuff…"

"It's a weird substance, Gaige," Noah says. "I still can't place it. I should be able to place it. It's thicker in here than it was the other day. Did you try to push against it?"

"Why the hell would I want to do that?" I make a face of disgust that is totally lost to the darkness. But ew. Gross. Why would he even do that?

"Well," Noah says, "because I've been stuck inside this tomb for a couple of days now, I'm guessing, and I'm inquisitive. I touch things. That's what one does when one is curious."

I think of my own need to touch the one shiny, sparkly book amidst all the dull ones the other day and have no argument to give. He's right.

"Gotcha," I say.

"Do me a favor and push against it now."

"I'd rather not. Can you maybe just tell me what happens?"

"I think it would be better if you just gave it a shot on your own."

Oh, shit. I so do not want to do this. I look for a way to put the book down or hold it without using a hand. It's too big for a pocket, and I don't want to try to pinch it between my legs or in an underarm in case I drop it in the encroaching water. Why the fuck I should care, I don't know, but I do.

I'm going to have to put my phone in my pocket to do what Noah is asking me to do.

"Did you try it?"

"Give me a sec," I say as I reluctantly give in to my fate and stuff my phone back into my pocket. Fearing total darkness again, I'm a bit relieved to find it's not as complete as I thought it would be. It's more luminescent, like the Other Side. There's a little bit of a glow to keep the total darkness at bay.

I look at the walls around me and see that the goop is more concentrated in some places than in others. I remember something Mael told me about it, about moving between the Outside World and the Other Side. This must be Chalek's attempt to do that. I don't know how he got this stuff down here in his cellar. Maybe this is where he originally found it?

I might as well go big. I make my way to the other end of the narrow space, where the entire wall is thick with the stuff. I slosh through nearly knee-deep, freezing water as I go.

"OK," I say. "Here goes nothing."

Chapter Twenty-Two

STILL HOLDING THE BOOK IN my left hand, I place the palm of my right hand against the wall. The warm, sticky substance gives slightly with my touch. It's the same stuff that covers the place inside the book, beyond the words. The stuff Mael traveled through. "Ugh."

I give it a little push. My hand breaks through the wall's soft membrane and disappears. It looks, in the luminescent darkness, like my hand has been cut off at the wrist.

I panic and pull my hand out. Of course it's still there. I rest it gently against the wall and try once more, pushing a little and then a little more, until my hand disappears again. I watch as the goop moves in and fills the space in as I go, like I'm immersing myself in Jell-O. Only, I'd be able to see my hand if it were simply stuck inside a wall of Jell-O.

"Gaige," Noah says. I hear him, but I don't answer. "What's happening? Did you see how much it gives?"

I want to answer him, I do, but I'm fascinated by this and far too invested in it. My arm is only visible above the elbow, now. The rest is buried inside the wall of goop. Instead of answering him, I push deeper. I'm enthralled, now. I can't look away. I can't stop pushing my arm in to see where it goes. Even as I feel a heat swell about my hand and forearm, I keep pushing deeper. Dude, I'm such a glutton for punishment.

"Gaige," Noah says from the other side. "Gaige, say something."

As I get in up to my shoulder, the intensity of the heat on everything from my elbow down is almost unbearable. It's also oddly soothing. It's like when you first get into a hot tub—unbearable in a good way. I keep pushing.

"Gaige," Logan finally shouts. "For shit's sake, say something! Answer him."

Just as my right side begins to disappear into the warm black muck, I feel the pressure on my fingers give. I've broken through something.

Other Side is my first thought. I just found another way into Chalek's nightmare place.

Rattling laughter fills the room, the cellar, the world. It's so gravelly, it's unmistakably Chalek. And it fills me with dread.

"Oh, Gaige, you naughty so-and-so." His voice is everywhere. I hate when he does that. It's only when I feel his breath on my neck that I realize he's in here with me. Oh god. I push against the wall to get away from his breath and proximity. A wall I was afraid to touch only moments ago now becomes my escape. I lean against it, still pushing through, but Chalek just crowds in behind me.

"You discovered something here, now didn't you?"

"Get away from me."

I try to ignore him. I wriggle my fingers. They're completely free of the viscous goop. I've somehow worked my way through to the other side. But the other side of what? Of where? The queasy feeling that fills me is so sudden, I panic. I was right. It *is* Mael's Other Side. I picture my hand sticking out of a wall, my fingers flailing about, and feel nauseous. It's the exact same feeling I get when I have to reach down under my bed at night, like something unseen is going to grab my fingers and rip them off. Or eat them.

I pull my arm back so fast, and with such force, that I fall back against Chalek's chest.

"Oof," he squeals as I knock the wind out of him. "That was not your cleverest moment, now, was it, Gaige?"

I move sideways to pull away from him and scrape against the wall again.

"You found the door—the literal way out—and yet you chose not to use it. What is wrong with kids these days? What is wrong with you?"

"Noah?" I call through the wall, ignoring Chalek as much as I can. There's almost no way to not be in physical contact with him; the space is so small. "Can you hear me?"

"Yeah," he says. "Loud and clear. Just like before. Is Chalek in there with you? What happened? Why didn't you answer us? What did it do when you pushed against it?"

"What did it do for you?"

"It gave. I mean, my hand just kept going deeper inside it. My hand was literally inside the wall."

"How far did you go?"

"Far enough to know that it was disgusting."

"We have to go farther," I say. I look over at Chalek, who hovers behind me. In the faint, eerie light, I can see his face light up with that jagged, creepy little old man smile.

"You tell them, Gaige," Chalek whispers. He giggles and holds his fingers up to his lips like a shy little kid. "Let's see where all this takes us, shall we? I'm so curious, I could shit a frog just to watch it croak! Aren't you?"

This guy really likes to put on a show. Too bad he's such a killer-y, murder-y villain. And also dead. He could have been a good entertainer.

"Guys, I pushed my hand in, and it came out the other side. I think it's a way out, but..."

"But we have to go through it?" Logan says. I can hear the pleading in his voice. "Like, our whole bodies? Oh, shit, Gaige. I don't even want to touch it. I can't. I just—"

I can hear the fear and disgust in Logan's voice. He's coming undone.

"Mael is a kid I met inside the book, Logan," I say as an offering.

"Why didn't you tell me?"

"What chance did I have?" I say, even though I know I had lots of opportunities. Like, I could have told him when we made our way over here. "And would you have believed me?"

"So there's two of them?" Noah says. I'm sure he wants no part of an argument at this point. Best to get out of danger first and argue later. Practical Noah is being practical again.

"No. Just Chalek." I turn back and look at my cellmate. He's got a strange expression on his face. It pains me to do it, but I take out my phone with my goop-caked hand, hold up the flashlight, and examine Chalek's face more closely. Definitely anger there, just under the surface. "Chalek's the only bad guy. Trust me."

"So," Chalek whispers. "You've met my friend Mael, have you?"

He knows full well I have. His anger dissipates, and he gets a skeezy look on his face.

"What?" I ask him.

"I made Mael just for you, don't you know? They're so your type, don't you think?"

Before I can reply, he's gone. He adds a little laughter for good measure, to fill the space in his sudden absence.

"Is he in there with you, Gaige?" Logan asks.

"Not anymore."

"What are we going to do?"

"Well, Logan," I begin. "It's kind of like what I said about your coming out. Like, exactly, actually. We're gonna *put on those fabulous ruby slippers and walk on through to the other side.* Summon your courage, guys. We need to step inside the muck, make our way through to the other side, and hope to hell it's the cellar and not a deeper circle of Chalek's hell, because this goopy shit is the same goopy shit that makes up the other place, the place inside the book. This is what the words dissolve into."

The room fills with Chalek's laughter one more time, for good measure.

"OK," Noah says. "Damn."

I move to face the wall I pushed my hand through. I can tell by their voices that Noah and Logan are right beside me, just on the other side of the wall dividing us.

"I'm right here beside you," I say, getting as close to the wall as I can. I imagine them huddled up close together, just on the other side.

"OK, OK," Logan says. "You're right there. So we're going to do this, then? I don't have any ruby slippers, Gaige."

"Just pretend. You're diva enough to pretend; I know you are."

"Fair enough," he says. "So, we're gonna put our actual faces into this substance none of us can name to walk through the other side of our literal tombs to a location none of us can identify ahead of time, in the hopes of it being a way out? That's it, right? Just so we're clear."

"Exactly. If it's any consolation, I already had my hand out there and nothing happened to it. Nothing ate it. I still have all my digits." I hold my hand up and look at it. My entire arm is caked with the black goop, but it's still intact. All good. I say we take a chance.

"Well," Noah chimes in, "my balls are about to be floating in this skank sewer water that's going to eventually drown us anyhow, so I'm game. If we trade one monster for another, I'm good with it. If we do nothing, we'll die swallowing the rankest water I've ever smelled in my life. So, there's that."

He has a point. A solid point. And the water *is* up to my knees now.

"OK," Logan says. "I guess you're right. Can we all do this at the same time? Noah and I have just enough room to go side by side. If we start on three and go slowly, maybe?"

"I'm good with that," I say. "Outstretched arm first, though, OK?"

"Once all three of us have one hand through to the other side," Noah says, "we'll count it out again and go the rest of the way together."

Noah is the best planner. Like, literally the best.

"I'm so on board with that plan, Noah."

I turn off my flashlight app, return my phone to my pocket, and pray that whatever it is I'm about to walk through doesn't absolutely murder its guts. Why is telling my parents I busted my phone practically my biggest fear in this scenario? What is wrong with me?

"OK then, so on three, we start with one hand," Noah says.

"Holy shit, holy shit."

"Take a breath, Logan. Come on, baby, you can do this. It's OK. At least, this part is. I already put my hand through. You heard me. It was just intense heat. But it was also OK. It didn't hurt. I got my hand back. So, there's that."

"So reassuring."

I look at my hand, caked in goo but still in one piece.

"On three, then?" asks Noah.

"On three," I say. I quickly add, "only one arm, up to our armpits, though, OK? And count backward, not forward. Then we stop to take a breather."

"Three, two, one—go."

Chapter Twenty-Three

ON ONE, I PUSH MY hand through the wall, and it sinks inside and disappears. I push all the way through to my armpit in one fell swoop this time. I think this is the way to go, because the heat is less intense than when I did it slowly, gradually.

"Are you thinking what I'm thinking, Noah?"

"I have no idea what you're thinking, Gaige. I just want to forget the fact that my arm is somewhere else, and I can't see it. But I can feel that my fingers are free on the other side."

"I'm thinking that the quicker you send yourself through the goop, the better. I put my arm through superfast, and it wasn't as intense. I think maybe on three we should just totally burst through to the other side and see what's waiting out there for us. I mean, it's going to be out there waiting for us anyway. No time like the present."

"I'm not looking forward to this," Logan says. "What if we drown in this shit, Gaige? I don't want to drown in an unknown poisonous substance."

"Just hold your breath and move through it as fast as you can. Push with everything you have. Ruby slippers this bitch."

There are a few seconds of silence, and in them, I can feel the seriousness and weight of what we're about to do.

"Hey," I say. "Is Noah OK? I mean, really OK? Is he strong enough to do this?"

"I can answer for myself. I'm aces. Really. Completely wiped, dehydrated, done in… and ready to go."

"Ooh," comes a voice, seemingly from somewhere far away. Chalek. "I can't wait to see what happens. So exciting." He laughs. I can't help but feel that all of this is a testing ground for Chalek. Maybe this is his way to figure out how to travel between both places, like Mael said. *There's something in there that Chalek wants. Needs.* The last thing I want to do is help Chalek, but also, I don't want to die inside this tomb.

"Didn't need to hear your friend again, Gaige," Logan says.

"On three," Noah says. "Three, two, one—"

I push myself into the wall as hard as I can. When it hits my face, I'm immediately reminded of Mael, of seeing their face form out of the tar. We're doing what Mael does, I'm sure of it. When they come to see me, this is what they break through to do it. They're trapped, like us. *Mael's not formed from it.*

I try not to think about the fact that Mael can never be un-trapped. Or so they say.

Walking through the almost solid mass of goo is harder than I thought it would be. It's nothing like shoving my arm through it. Moving my legs becomes almost impossible. I'm going to die, frozen forever in this impossibly thick black Jell-O.

I push my left arm forward, book first; I'm Bob the drag queen, entering the room purse first. As I feel my hand break through the other side, I also lose my grasp on the book and hear a thud somewhere far away as the book falls. The good thing is, it falls to the ground. That means we come out somewhere, in some place.

The heat in my face as the goop swallows it whole and tries to get inside all its orifices is almost excruciating, but in a weirdly good way. It's like putting a steaming hot washcloth on my face, only more intense—then like someone is holding it tightly to my face, attempting to smother me. I can't fight against it; I can only keep pushing on through. I hold my breath.

With a little pressure pop, my face bursts out on the other side. I gasp for air, relieved. I try to reach up to swipe the goop away from my eyes, but my right arm still isn't free. One last push and I squeeze out completely, a juicy sploosh of noise bursting my eardrums as the space behind me fills back in.

I fall to the ground and take several long breaths. Even though the air down here is stagnant and dank, it's still a miracle to be breathing it. I look back in time to see the last of the goop retreating into the crevices and eventually disappearing back into the wall.

I'm in the cellar. Jesus fuck, I'm in the cellar! Thank god.

I turn to my right and see one leg, knee to foot, another knee by itself, and four hands protruding from the wall. I scramble up off the floor and reach to grab the hand I recognize as Logan's. It's the one I always hold. It's definitely his.

Before I grab it, though, I realize that it would probably terrorize him if I were to even touch it; he wouldn't know it was me. There's no telling what would happen if I grabbed his hand and started pulling. Visualizing Logan opening his mouth to scream while trapped inside the sludge like a fossil in amber, I jump back right before making contact. His lungs would fill in an instant, and he'd surely be dead.

Slack-jawed, I watch as they slowly make their way through. Like, it should not be possible for this to occur. What the hell even *is* this place where solid walls turn into viscous inky goo?

Logan's face appears first, like he's swimming up from the deep end of a pool. As soon as his head is all the way out, he gags, and inky goop spews from his mouth. This helps to propel him forward until he's almost totally free. How disgusting that he got it in his mouth. Also, terrifying.

Then he falls forward, and I'm finally able to reach out and grab on to him.

We fall to the ground in a ball of sludge and cling together like we thought we'd never see each other again. Like we almost didn't.

After a few seconds of clumsy clinging and hugging, I reach up with my own sludge-caked hand and wipe a swath of tar away from Logan's face until I can see most of it.

"I'd kiss you so hard right now if you hadn't swallowed that shit and weren't so damn disgusting-looking," I say. I try to laugh, but I honestly don't have the energy. I let go of him and lie back down on the ground.

"Trust me," Logan says, coughing and choking with each word, "kissing you is the last thing I want to do right now. You haven't seen yourself, have you?"

"I can imagine, though. If I look even half as bad as you, that is."

Oh, damn. Noah. I look up at the wall. He still hasn't made his way out. Shit.

Not caring if I scare the crap out of him by grabbing his hand, I throw caution to the wind this time.

"Grab a hand, Logan," I shout as I stand up. Logan scrabbles to his feet and sees Noah's hands hanging out of the wall. He's stalled.

We each take hold of a hand. Nothing happens. Noah's hand is limp in my grip.

Chapter Twenty-Four

"PULL!" I SCREAM. "PULL, LOGAN. He's not grabbing back. Pull!"

We begin to pull and, inch by inch, Noah's seemingly lifeless body slowly emerges from the wall. When he's fully released, the muck begins to retreat, sucking itself back into the pores of the wall until it's virtually gone. Noah slumps forward and falls to the floor before either of us can catch him.

"Noah!" I yell as I join him on the floor. Just as I turn him over, he spews a mouthful of sludge and vomit. I quickly sit him up so he doesn't choke on it. I slam my hand across his back a few times for good measure. Finally, he sits on his butt and can hold himself up.

"Holy shit, dude," I say. "You seriously looked dead there for a minute. I thought we lost you."

Clearly not ready for talk, Noah pulls his knees up and puts his head between his legs. He takes a series of deep breaths and swipes the goop from his face and his big head of hair, which is totally squashed down. As he slowly calms himself, he raises a finger for me to give him a sec.

"Let him breathe," Logan says, as though that isn't exactly what I'm trying to do. "He needs to catch his breath."

Noah brings his head back up and starts coughing violently. He spits, and phlegmy strings of the disgusting substance fly out of his mouth.

When he's done spitting, a string is still hanging from the corner of his mouth. He begins to swipe it away, then glances at me with an expression of sheer terror.

Noah grabs the goop at the corner of his mouth and begins to pull.

"Oh my fucking god," Logan says as he watches Noah pull an impossibly long, thick rope of sludge from his mouth. He pulls and pulls.

Logan turns away, gagging, as Noah tosses aside the black rope. He begins to dry-heave and then vomit, and more goo spews out.

There's no way that stuff didn't come up from deep inside Noah's belly. That gross goop was inside of him. So disgusting. Mind blown.

"Are you OK, man?" I ask.

He has another fit of coughing before he answers. After he clears his throat, he says, "I am now." His voice is shredded, absolutely destroyed. "Oh my god, what happened? That was horrendous. I'm never *not* going to have this taste in my mouth, Gaige. Never. Kill me now."

"Come on," I say. I stand up and reach down to him. "I'll pull you up. We gotta get you out of here. I'm guessing you need water. Maybe food. Maybe, I don't know, mouthwash?"

"Oh, man, Gaige," He takes my hand, and I help him to his feet. He moves to rest his hand against the wall for support, but immediately reconsiders and pulls away from it. Good choice.

I'm kind of afraid of walls myself, now. "We gotta get out of this place. Like, yesterday."

"I'm with Noah," Logan says. He's still spitting himself, since he also swallowed some of the stuff. "Let's get out of here before that old man comes back and decides to put us somewhere else, maybe permanently."

"And, like, I could also eat," Noah says. We all chuckle. So Noah.

Logan heads for the ladder that leads up to the bookstore washroom, and Noah starts to follow.

As I turn to join them, I see the book in my peripheral vision. It's sitting there on the floor, near where I emerged from the wall. It's waiting for me. I can feel it judging me, hating me, demanding something from me. Shit.

Reluctantly, I retrieve it. Then I head down the hall to join Logan and Noah.

I look down at my clothes, which are covered in what looks like a thick, hardening black tar. I'm also soaked up to my knees. I still don't know what this shit is. And if Noah doesn't know what it is, no one will.

We're downtown. No way are we going to get out of this area without being seen by at least a hundred people. And where the hell are we going to go, anyway, looking like this? We need to get cleaned up before we do anything else.

"We're not going anywhere with this shit all over us," I say in response to Noah's comment about eating.

"Let's just get out of here before we worry about how we look, shall we?" Noah says. The grogginess is slowly leaving his voice. Still, I can tell he needs water, sustenance.

Logan's already pushing on the door above the ladder. I'm surprised when it actually opens. Looks like Chalek is going to let us go this time. I guess he thinks we've been through enough for one day. Or however many days it's been since we got trapped down here.

Noah takes to the ladder, and I stay close behind him in case he needs help. He's looking a bit like a walking zombie. I reach out with my free hand and place it on the back of his leg as he makes his way up. He turns and smiles at me.

When Noah gets to the top of the ladder, Logan helps pull him up. Soon we're all standing in the tiny washroom and ready to go.

Chapter Twenty-Five

Once outside, we know we've lost time. It's daytime. Looks like morning.

For several reasons, I'm almost afraid to pull out my phone. I don't want to find out we've missed multiple days, I don't want to see a string of messages from my parents, and I don't want to discover that my phone is trashed. It did move through a wall of tar, after all.

Logan and Noah stand on the sidewalk outside the store, trying to scrape off as much of the black goop as they can. As they do that, I take my phone from my pocket and try to get into it. It doesn't look damaged, but it won't unlock for me. My hand is so dirty, the phone doesn't recognize my fingerprint. But I can see the display. It's Friday.

Miracle of miracles! We didn't lose much time at all, only a few hours. We left at night, and now it's morning. The very next morning. There is no rhyme or reason to this.

"We can go to my place," I say as I pocket my phone. "By the time we get there, my parents'll be at work and we can clean up."

"That would be oh-so-awesome," Noah says. "I need to get this pudding off of me before I die from disgust. I feel like baked shit."

Apropos, Noah. So apropos. We definitely *smell* like shit, too. Baked or otherwise. And he has the special added bonus of tasting it.

"Agreed," Logan says. "I've never wanted a shower so badly in my life."

We start to walk back to my condo. No one even has to suggest that we walk instead of taking the subway. The way we look, there's no way in hell they'd even let us into the station.

Judging by the looks we get from people, most of them are afraid of us. Walking side by side down the sidewalk is like parting the Red Sea. Everyone makes way for the three rejects. Nobody wants to chance touching us.

When we finally arrive at my building, we enter through the side door and walk up seventeen flights of stairs to avoid the concierge. No way would they let us walk past them into the building. And even if they did, there's no way we'd be allowed to go into the elevator looking like the creatures from the black lagoon.

As hard as it is to climb all the stairs, we all have the motivators of shower and food to push us through the struggle. Even Noah makes it in one piece.

"I'm first," Noah squeals as I unlock the unit door and push it open. He shoves past me, takes off his shoes and socks, and makes a run for the bathroom.

"You jerkoff," I say, as I watch the bathroom door slam shut and hear the lock click. "Damn."

"Let him go, baby," Logan says, smirking just enough to show me his killer dimples. "We can wash up together."

I am *on* board. Despite everything we've just been through, I am so on board with that. I toss the book to the floor and kick off my shoes and socks.

From the bathroom, we hear Noah run the tap and drink, joking all the while that it's the best water he's ever tasted. He's playing it up for our benefit. We both laugh.

We pretty much have to stand still in the hallway as we wait for our turn in the bathroom. As it is, we've written off the floor just by walking in. I'll have to do some heavy-duty cleaning once we're showered.

As I contemplate the mess between the front door and the bathroom, Logan crosses the hall and stands in front of me.

"What happened last night, babe?" he asks. Loaded question, or what? "I mean, I was there. I saw it all happen. But like, what happened?"

"I know, right?"

He puts a hand on my shoulder and pulls me in. I think the embrace will end in a kiss, but he pulls me closer, rests his chin on my shoulder, and squeezes me tightly.

"I'm sorry I doubted you. Really, I am. But what am I supposed to do with all this shit? I can't make it make sense."

"I know, baby," I say. I squeeze him back. Like, seriously. I feel like we haven't hugged like this, ever. "I don't know why I ever went inside that bookstore. I should have known—"

"No. Don't do that. Any one of us would probably have done the same thing you did. It's not like anyone would even think anything like this could ever happen."

"I know," I whisper. "I guess I just wish I didn't go jumping into shit the way I do. I could have just walked by, left it be. You know?"

"Yeah. But it was literally the one place you couldn't allow yourself to pass by. And that asshole knew it."

He has a point.

From where we stand, hugging, I can see the book. I guess the facade has dropped, because both Logan and Noah can see it now, too. I guess the veil between them and what's been happening to me has now fully lifted. We're all in this together now.

I think of Mael and wonder if all of us could go to that place, now. If we did, would Mael come out of the darkness to see us? Or are they just for me? What would they look like? How would that work?

As I find myself thinking about Mael, though, I feel a wave of guilt. Here I am, literally hugging Logan. We just survived an impossible situation together, and I'm thinking about a kid named Mael who is no longer of this world. A kid who has been stuck in their nightmare world for forty years.

I pull away from the hug, but before I let go of Logan, I move back in for a kiss. Then I let him go and bend down to retrieve the book.

I flip it open, but now is not the time. We need to wash off this stuff before it kills us. It smells like death itself. I close the book and hold it up to Logan. "This fucking thing is going to kill me."

"There must be a way to kill *it* before it does."

"I wish I knew," I say. But I'm beginning to think it might be too big for us. Like, this book opens onto a whole other world. We're just us. It's an uneven match.

"We'll figure something out, Gaige," Logan assures me. "We both know Noah is wicked smart. If anyone can find the way out of this labyrinth, it's gonna be Noah."

"Did I hear my name?"

We both turn at the sound of his voice. Noah stands at the end of the hall, naked except for the white towel wrapped around his waist. It's especially good to see him because I now know the answer to a question that's been eating away at me since we started walking home: *Does this stuff even come off?*

Turns out, it does. Noah is sparkling clean, like he was never covered from head to toe in an impossibly sticky, tar-like pudding from hell. Even his humungous head of hair, which was caked to his head with the shit, is back to its regular, explosive self.

He smiles. I don't know what he used to brush his teeth, and I don't care, but it's obvious that he did. As he walks toward us, Logan whistles a catcall at him, and I laugh. So much fun to tease the scantily-clad straight boy. Why are we gays so cruel?

"Shut up, asshole," Noah says to Logan, straight-faced, like he's totally disgusted by Logan's attentions. But he walks past us and lets out a shrill laugh as he makes his way to the kitchen. Before he turns the corner, he flashes his ass. "Don't mind me, Gaige. I'm just gonna make myself at home in your kitchen and make all the food. And then, if you two kiddies aren't out here in time, I'm going to eat every last crumb all by my lonesome. Then I think I'll check in with my girl, who probably thinks I'm dead. Don't tell her I chose the food first."

"Huh," I say to dismiss Noah. "Nice. Knock yourself out, buddy."

I place the book on a nearby table and grab Logan's hand.

We hear the crashing of pots and pans and the opening and closing of cupboard doors before we even get to the bathroom. Logan walks in ahead of me, and I close and lock the door behind us.

I have lots of plans for the next little while, and they mostly involve scraping this crud off our bodies. But they're not entirely, exclusively about cleaning ourselves. It's been too long, and we almost died. We deserve to blow off some steam together.

Chapter Twenty-Six

LOGAN STEPS OUT OF THE shower after me and stands waiting for me to pass him a towel. I toss one at his head and grab one for myself.

"We'll have to go to my room to find some clothes."

"I think that might be an issue," he says as he rubs the towel through his thick mass of wet black hair. "I don't think your pants are gonna fit me, Gaige. Floods, much?"

"Maybe you should have thought about that before you waded through that skanky shit and got all dirty."

"Ha ha. But you know your pants won't fit me. Damn. I did not think this through. Why didn't I find myself a normal-sized boyfriend, like everyone else?"

"Watch your mouth. Sorry I'm not a giant. You could always just wear a towel around all day. I mean, personally, I think it works well. I would not complain." I look hungrily at his exposed body to drive my message home.

"Stop being a perv. You've had enough. I'm hungry. Let's get out there before your friend eats all your food."

He flicks me with his towel, opens the bathroom door, and walks out naked and proud to my bedroom at the end of the hall.

By the time we finally get to the kitchen, Noah is sitting at the breakfast bar, talking on the phone with Sara. He's trying to calm her down.

I guess a full-on search for him is still going on. Probably something he'll have to deal with right away.

"What's for supper, Ma?" I say, interrupting his call.

"Sorry, Sara, the brats are home from daycare. I'll have to feed them their snacks. Gotta go."

Noah holds the phone away from his ear to avoid the yelling coming from the other end. And also, apparently, to show us what he has to put up with. With a flourish of his free hand, he presents us with the phone in his other hand, as if to say, *See?*

He puts the phone back to his ear. "I'm sorry, baby. You're right. It's not the time for jokes. I'm sorry. I'm just a little punch-drunk right now. Please don't tell anyone I called. Please. I'll deal with everything as soon as I finish eating. I promise."

He holds the phone away from his ear again. This time, he talks loudly in its direction. "I know, I know. I will. I'm sorry. Gotta go." He reaches over and taps *End Call*.

"You're a dead man," Logan says, shaking his head and holding in his laughter.

I laugh, but like, I'd be pissed too. Relieved, but pissed.

I'm not sure how one human being was able to make such a mess of this kitchen in the time it took Logan and me to clean up, get nasty together, and clean up again. It's a literal write-off, from one end to the other.

There's half a plate of spaghetti in front of Noah. Sauce is splattered all over the counter and his bare chest. He's still wearing only the towel. It's like a two-year-old tried to feed him, and not a very intelligent two-year-old.

"What the hell, dude," I finally say as I survey the rest of the damage. "Looks like the scrambled eggs and bacon weren't enough for you?"

He looks over at his second plate, the plate in question. There's a small clump of egg left on it, a few bacon crumbs, and a tiny piece of toast crust.

"I almost died, Gaige. Don't be an asshole. I just wanted to reacquaint myself with food, is all."

"Ffffffff." I shake my head in frustration. "All the major food groups and then some. Did you at least make anything we could share?"

"Open your eyes, dude! There's half a tray of french fries right in front of you. And chicken nuggets."

Sure enough, they're sitting on a tray on the stove.

I just—I don't know what to say. Wow! Either we were in that bathroom for a very long time, or Noah has figured out a way to harness this time-skipping shit. Recalling what Logan and I did in there, though, I suspect that Noah had a lot of time to create this disaster zone.

Logan stands in the middle of the kitchen, just taking it all in. He walks over to the french fries, picks one up, and takes a bite. "Only warm." He finishes it anyway. "Mmmmm. Good. Like, amazing."

"I know, right," Noah says, a huge smile on his face. He picks up a coffee cup and takes a drink. Then he picks up the can of Coke beside it and takes a sip from that. "Let's hear it for food, dude!"

Logan picks up another french fry and raises it like he's cheersing Noah. "Hear, hear!" he says. He tosses the fry in his mouth.

"I have the strangest friends." I shake my head, but decide it's easier to join them than bitch about the state of the kitchen. I'm hungry, dude. Food does seem like an amazing invention right now. "My mom's gonna flip. There's no food left in our house."

"I'm not your friend," Logan says, rolling his eyes. "I'm your lovvvvvvvah!"

I laugh and they both join me. I guess we can get serious later. Clearly, we're all exhausted and punchy. I sit down on the stool beside Noah's and dig in to the huge bowl of cheese popcorn sitting in front of me. It's literally the best fucking popcorn I've ever tasted. Chalek can wait.

Chapter Twenty-Seven

A COUPLE OF HOURS LATER, Logan and I lie on my bed staring up at the ceiling. We know what we *should* do next; we're just preparing ourselves for it.

Noah went home in my ill-fitting clothes to face the music and put his life back in order about half an hour ago. I'm sure he'll have to speak with the police and make up a convoluted story that they won't believe, but pretend they do. Everyone will be relieved that he's back. There will be unanswered questions, but the adults will just have to live with that and be grateful for his return.

Before he left, I made him help me and Logan clean up after the cyclone that hit my kitchen. I've never seen a bigger mess in my life. I don't even know how one person could destroy a kitchen at that magnitude on their own.

Logan and I hold hands and breathe calmly. It's almost like we're not going to do the thing we plan to do. Only the presence of the book, sitting in the space between us, gives our plan away.

The last thing I want to do is break the silence. Once that happens, we set our plan into action. And after that, anything can happen.

Believe it or not, this was all my idea. At least, I think it was. It came to me after I closed the door on Noah and turned around to see the book sitting there, looking all forlorn and neglected.

Before I knew what was happening, I opened my mouth to speak.

"We should read the book now. Together. See what happens."

At first, Logan wasn't totally sure. But we've been lying here like this for some time now, and I've explained every single detail I can remember about falling into the book. Judging from Logan's demeanor, I think I painted a clear enough picture for him. I even told him about Mael parts, about how pretty they are and how I'm certain they are nonbinary. The Mael parts were difficult to tell, but necessary. I *think* he got it.

Now, Logan interrupts the silence.

"So, essentially, being inside the book is kind of like being inside the wall that we walked through. Like, instead of just passing through, literally stopping to spend time inside the stuff that nearly killed Noah… that nearly killed all of us."

"Basically," I say. At least, I think so. "But!" I let go of his hand and raise a finger, victorious. "We won't get covered in muck. I mean, I was in the place, but not in the goop. The ground was made up of it; the walls were made up of it. But I never sank into it. I didn't bring it back with me like we did when we walked through those walls in the cellar. It's the same, but different. It's like the words on the page begin to bleed and swirl, and you go inside them. But it doesn't stick."

"Well, there's that. I guess I can be grateful for that."

Small wonders, am I right?

"Look, we don't have to do this. I just thought—"

"No. We should. We have to figure out how to end this, Gaige. We can't just keep going through this shit forever. This Chalek guy chose you. I don't know if he wants to kill you, play with you, or have, like, an epic battle with you. But we're all in this now. There must be a way to defeat this guy. He can't just keep torturing and haunting kids for his own kicks forever. Right?"

"I don't know. Clearly, I'm one in a long line. Who's to say I'm the last?"

"Me, Gaige," Logan says. "I say. We're gonna get this guy. We'll get him where he lives. You're not going to be one of his conquests. That'll happen over my dead body."

"I wish you wouldn't say stuff like that. You're tempting fate."

"Nah. He just chose to mess with the wrong kid this time."

I turn onto my side, and Logan does the same. Now that we're facing each other, I kiss him. He leans in to the kiss, and I allow myself to get lost in it for a few seconds.

When I pull back, he fights me at first. He wants more.

"And about Mael," I say. Logan tries really hard not to get a certain look on his face. "They tried to help me every time. I don't know for sure, but they may have saved my life. I think so, anyway. Mael made a line in the blackness and insisted that I never cross it. They said I would be stuck inside that world forever if I did."

"And you think this Chalek guy changed the way Mael looks so they would appeal to you. So, like, they look nothing like me, then. So Mael's kind of like the bookstore, an obstacle you can't resist. But if you touch *them*, you also stay forever."

"You don't need to have that edge of jealousy in your tone, Logan. I told you because you need to know. I don't know what's going to happen when you see Mael. You have to be prepared."

"I'm not going to get all googly-eyed for them, Gaige." Logan springs from the bed, clearly upset. He begins to rant and pace my bedroom. "You're the boy I choose. Not some ghoul from the house of hellfire you step into by opening some fucking book and jumping inside."

"Wow, Logan," I say. "We don't have to do this. Jealousy doesn't really become you."

"I'm not jealous. I told you that." He returns to the bed and sits on its edge. I sit up, slide behind him with my legs sandwiching his body, and lean my belly against his back. When I try to wrap my arms around him, he's reluctant at first and tries to shrug them away. But he finally relents and allows me to hold him from behind.

Sitting like this, I can imagine us forgetting all these crazy plans and just taking advantage of our time alone together. Feeling Logan's back against my chest, I just want to forget everything else and climb inside him.

But this needs to be done. We need to bring this nightmare to a conclusion, even if it means that Chalek wins. We can't go on forever. It's so hard to even keep track of the days since this madness began.

I squeeze hard, signaling the end of our embrace, before pulling myself away from the heat of Logan's body.

When I crawl farther up on the bed and lie back down, Logan reluctantly joins me. Then I paw around between us, hoping not to find the book.

But I do, of course. We move closer together, both of our heads on the same pillow, and cuddle closer as I open the book. Logan takes one cover flap while I hold the other. I turn a page with my free hand. Logan holds it in place with his thumb.

We look at each other, but all the words between us are gone. This is it. This is the moment we do or die.

I turn two pages at once and tuck them under Logan's thumb. Then I watch as the words begin to swirl. *Through the wall… Noah fell to his knees… it was past our ankles…* I'm reading what happened to us earlier, like it was just a dream, like Noah didn't almost choke to death on a string of sludge. Could it be that I dreamed all of that? The walls, the sludge, the water? We dreamed those things together? Impossible.

I try to drag myself away from the swirling words. It's one of the hardest things I've ever done. It's like there's a cyclone between me and where Logan should be on the bed beside me, a cyclone of melting ink formed by the dissolving words. He's there, but not there. I get just a glimpse of the terror on his face before I'm forced to turn away and refocus on the words.

The scrabbling starts. I don't know if it's me trying to get in or something else trying to get out. It's there every time, an ominous warning of what is about to happen. Chalek?

The words dissolve, and I blip away.

Chapter Twenty-Eight

SOMETHING'S WRONG. "LOGAN!" NO ANSWER. Just as I begin to panic, though, he appears at my side.

"What the actual fu—"

"Two boys never came together before, Gaige," Mael whispers, interrupting Logan's outburst and startling both of us. They slowly make their way out of the blackness and emerge in front of us.

"I wanted to see if we could enter together. I wasn't even sure it would work."

Logan squeezes closer to me and takes my hand with a monster grip. He stares slack-jawed at Mael, like he can't quite believe what he's seeing.

"Your boy is pretty," Mael says, surprising me. They look Logan over with wonder. "But I don't know if this was wise. You could have made it easier for Chalek to get in."

"He wasn't there. It was just the two of us. I was home. In my bedroom."

"Gaige," Mael says, shaking their head, "every time you enter the book, Chalek is there. He's with you always, now. He knows when you enter."

"That's super creepy," Logan says as he comes out of his stupor. He's looking around now, taking stock of everything. Taking stock of the kid in front of us. "You mean he watches Gaige?"

"Chalek wants only to find a way in, so he can bring *him* back with him. He'll stop at nothing." Mael says this to Logan, but then turns to me. "Chalek tries to claw his way inside with the kids. He uses us as pawns. We're his way to figure out how to move back and forth between the two places. Chalek lost someone in here, and his biggest goal is to bring him back from the Other Side. And you just brought another boy with you. It could have made it easier for him."

A burst of laughter fills the entire world, and I recognize it immediately.

"It's Chalek," Mael says. "He's getting stronger. He must have entered the threshold with you somehow. This is how he'll beat me this time. He must be closer to bringing the Other Side into the Outside World. He's closing the gap. He wants to get inside, to the part we can't enter without being lost forever. There's someone in there that he wants. And he'll stop at nothing to get him, Gaige. And you! You're helping him. You're getting him closer."

"Shit! I didn't do anything," I shriek unconvincingly. I do remember Mael saying this before, during another visit. They already warned me that this is what Chalek wants to do. "He wasn't with us when we opened the book. It was just Logan and me, I swear."

"Like I said, he's always with you now. He was watching. Waiting. This is not good," Mael says. They're staring at Logan and shaking their head. "What did you do, Gaige? You should not have brought this boy with you."

I turn to Logan, who's now frozen in place, staring at Mael like he can't take his eyes off the kid.

"Chalek will be angry," Mael says.

"Chalek *is* angry." He's nowhere to be seen, just a disembodied voice coming from all around us. There's no mistaking his death rattle. "Chalek is very angry. You've been mighty naughty, Mael. You've all been very naughty. I just don't know what to do with you. This is my playground. I found it first."

To my surprise, Mael comes over to where I stand and squeezes in behind me. Though they're careful not to touch me, they're also clearly seeking my protection. But from what? Chalek is nowhere to be seen.

I slap Logan's arm to get his attention. Still slack-jawed, he stands there like a statue. And not a very elegant one. I don't think he's coping well in here.

A dull roar comes out of the darkness from somewhere deep inside Chalek's being and gradually builds to a deafening pitch. Despite all the alarm bells in my head telling me to get the hell out of this particular dream, I step forward, into it. Anything to get Logan behind me, where Chalek can't touch him.

As the roar gets louder and more menacing, I put my hands to my ears to muffle it. Mael does the same. Eventually, even Logan reanimates and brings his hands to his ears.

I stand my ground, and Chalek finally winds down and goes silent. Mael cowers behind me, Logan at their side. I've come this far—there's no point in backing down now. Even if I never get out of here, I at least want to give it my best shot. I don't want to die giving up.

As if reading my thoughts, Chalek says, "All I have to do to keep you here is summon the book inside."

"Then do it. I'm not afraid of you, old man. People like you never have your own strength. You just spend your life stealing it from other people. I'm not afraid."

I stand sentinel against him. I will *not* let him get to Logan.

"I think I've already proven that to be untrue, boy," Chalek says. "Do we need another lesson on listening?"

"Everything he does, he can only do because of the dark magic in the Other Side, Gaige." I turn back to Mael. Even as they say these words, they're already stumbling to the ground in agony. But they're also desperate to get more out before Chalek silences them. "It's the substance of this place he uses, not that book. He rewrites this world with that ink. All those books— each one is a different kid he tricked to feed the darkness. He's experimenting. I don't know what he's trying to do, but I do know he just keeps repeating the same experiment over and over. He's a failed scientist who's in over his head. The books are just a way in to our deaths."

"I will end you, Mael," Chalek says. His voice reverberates, pulsates all around us, but he hasn't shown himself yet. I don't think he can get inside. Something is stopping him. "You have gone too far, said too much this time. Don't you speak another word, you little heathen witch. You shut your farking mouth."

Mael couldn't speak any more words if they wanted to. They're rolled up in a ball on the ground, squirming and yelling. I recognize that pose. Chalek must be squeezing the life out of their internal organs. It's his favorite parlor trick.

Chapter Twenty-Nine

I SQUAT DOWN ON THE ground to comfort Mael.

"No!" they shout. "Don't touch me, Gaige. Don't touch me."

I almost forgot.

"Are you OK?" I whisper. The only thing in the universe I want to do is touch and comfort them. My feelings for them are definitely complicated, even as Logan stands beside us, looking on.

"I'm OK," Mael says through moans and groans of agony. "He can't hurt me. Not really."

I know this isn't true. Pain is written all over their face. Chalek is definitely hurting them.

"What's that, child?" Chalek says. His voice is louder. He sounds closer. "I can't hurt you? Really? That what you said, is it?"

Mael flinches from the sound of Chalek's voice so quickly, they almost bump into me.

I scramble to get away and back up on my feet as Mael forces themself to a standing position. There's no mistaking the fact that Chalek is hurting them, but Mael perseveres.

"I know how long you've been here, Mael," I say, maybe to distract them. "I'm so sorry."

"I don't know if I want to know," Mael says."

"I looked up the places you mentioned. And I know what a Batcaver is. They're still here, Mael. We call them Goths now, but they're still here."

Mael smiles. "Thank you."

Logan still stands in a trance. He's sneaking glimpses at Mael whenever he can but seems otherwise incapable of speech or thought. My boyfriend is literally dumbfounded. What is up with that?

"Logan," I say. I'm right in his face now. "Logan. Earth to Logan. Come in! Hello."

"Huh," he finally mumbles. He looks me up and down, like he's trying to remember when I got here. "Oh. Where was I just now? Daydreaming."

"Now's not the time."

Chalek explodes into laughter. "Your pretty boy seems a mite broken, Gaige. You should not have brought him here. This Chapter was meant for you alone, dear boy."

Mael goes sprawling across my field of vision like they're nothing more than a rag doll in the wind. The kid is flung several feet before they hit the blackness and slowly dissolve into it. I watch the space they disappear into for several seconds, wondering how it happened.

"You've become a burden, Gaige," Chalek roars after somehow finishing with Mael. It's terrifying that he can hurt us without even being here. "I don't think I have to tell you that, boy. You've been nothing but trouble, you have. You're too mischievous for your own good."

"Sorry, Lurch. Looks like I didn't get a copy of the script. My bad."

"Don't you push me, boy. I'm on my last nerve with you and your little pretty boy here. You're not doing what you're supposed to do."

Logan flings me such a wild *what did I do?* expression that I can't help but crack up for a second. Comedic relief from the cutie at my side. What more could I ask for?

Before anyone has a chance to say anything else, Mael comes crawling back out of the goop on their hands and knees. I just want to go to them, help them up. But I know I can't.

"This," Chalek shouts as Mael emerges and gets to their feet. "This is the insolent child who refused to play my game."

"Let them be," I plead, moving closer to Mael. "Please, just let them be."

"Now why would I go and do that, my boy?" Chalek says, even as Mael grabs their stomach and folds over in pain again. "When I could do so much more."

"Please, Mister," Logan pleads. "You have to stop hurting them. You have to—"

Chalek meets Logan's plea with more cancerous laughter. It bounces off every surface until it spreads out all around us like an infection.

Logan begins to back away. Chalek only laughs harder.

I turn to Mael. They have a pleading look on their face. I don't know what to do. I don't know how to end their suffering.

"I'm sorry, Gaige," Mael says. "I can't help you. He can write this whole world any way he wants with his magic. I know that the book is nothing but a portal, though. If only there was a way to bring it inside, we could—"

"Shut your mouth," Chalek says. "You've said more than enough. I don't know why I keep you here. I thought it was a hoot at first, the way you try your damnedest, desperate best to help these selfish, silly, hapless kids. You may have outlived the fun, though. I think I may have had enough of this whole Mael business."

"Just let them go, then, Lurch," I say. I go back and forth between trying to make sure that Logan is OK behind me and worrying that Chalek is going to do something even more horrible to Mael. "Let them come back with us. Please. They've been here long enough."

He bursts into another crusty, throaty laugh. It's so vile, I just want to run away from it.

"You want to take this, this *thing* back with you, Gaige?" Mael straightens back up as Chalek says this. "You want this *thing* out there in the real world with you, do you? You sure about that? This child is spoiled rotten now, Gaige. They're nothing but poison now. They'd infect ya as sure as look atcha."

I look at Mael, desperate to help them but knowing I am powerless to do so. They've been given a temporary reprieve by Chalek, but their face still pleads for something. I don't know what? Help? Sympathy? Release from their constant nightmare?

"Be careful what you wish for, boy," Chalek says. "I may just give it to you. You'd be unleashing a fury putting this *thing* out there in the, what do they call it now, the Outside World? Mael'd spoil it something awful, and quick, too. They no longer belong in that world."

The beautiful being with the mesmerizing waves of gorgeous black hair comes stumbling toward me as though pushed from behind. I jump back to avoid their touch.

As though my aversion to their touch has just proven his theory about Mael's corruption, Chalek becomes a cacophony of laughter that grates harder and harder on my sanity.

Mael stands before me, their eyes burning into mine, pleading. I can't help but feel guilty about the predicament I've put them in by bringing Logan with me.

"It's. The. Dark Ichor. The Ichor is the thing that gives him power." Mael blurts this like they're running out of time, getting everything in before it's too late. "He won't summon one of his books to this place because he can't. They can't be here without a disaster happening. He's close, Gaige. Close to figuring things out. Don't let him take this world back there with him."

"You shut your mouth, Mael," Chalek yells. Mael's face crumples into a hideous mask of pain once again. "Be gone with you, farking fool child."

Mael appears to crumple. They slowly fall to their knees before sinking into the ground beneath them. They look up at me with a pained, twisted expression and melt into the shiny, tar-slick ground until there is nothing left of them but flailing arms, and then hands reaching out for help. Help I can't even begin to give them.

Amid Chalek's hideous laughter, I watch helplessly as Mael disappears completely into the ground in front of me.

"*That* was satisfying," Chalek says. He must die. "And look at me. I've made it inside. Time to bring the inside out, as it were, don't you think? We just need to get you to go all the way in."

But I know he hasn't really made it inside. If he had, we'd be able to see him. He's still outside. Just barely, but he's out there, somewhere in between.

"I'm never going to cross that line, Chalek," I yell. "And you're *not* inside. What's holding you back, old man? Something's stopping you, and it's making you furious. Ha. Funny."

"You best not mock me, boy," Chalek says. I struck a nerve. A big one.

"Gaige, we have to go," Logan says. I look at the ground, where Mael disappeared. There is nothing I can do. They're gone.

"Might be a good idea to listen to your little boy toy, there, Gaige. Who knows how much patience I have left? I am fraying at the ends, and your toy there looks like an interesting candidate for the next keeper of the gate, now doesn't he. I recently lost an employee here at the emporium. I could use all the help I can get."

Before I'm subjected to another outburst of laughter, I decide we've had enough. It's time to wake up. I turn to Logan, grab him in my arms, and do my best to shove us out of this mad world.

Chapter Thirty

"OK," I SAY AFTER A few minutes of heavy breathing and silence pass. "So, I guess we know what we have to do now."

"Oh, man," Logan says. He's sitting on the bed beside me, attempting unsuccessfully to regain his composure. He rubs his eyes with the palms of his hands, like he's trying to rub away the truth of what just happened. "I don't know if I can take any more. That was—that was too much. Mael—did they die? Did we watch that monster kill someone? Was it our fault?"

"I don't know," I say matter-of-factly. "I don't think so. I think Mael'll be OK. I hope."

"Wait. What do you mean, *We know what we have to do now*? Because I don't. Destroy the book? That sounds like an obvious solution to me. It opens the portal to Chalek's own private hellhole. Close the book forever and the problem goes away, no? Mael said to close the portal."

I stand up and go over to my dresser to grab my phone from its charger. I'm almost too afraid to look at the screen. I've no idea what time or day it is; I only know that it's dark outside. I look at the screen. It's late at night, but it *is* still the same day.

Still Friday, even though it's almost over now. More hours lost to Chalek's game.

"I don't think that's what he meant. Mael told me once that they already tried to get one of the boys to destroy his book. It survived fire. What we have to do now is go back to the bookstore."

Logan rolls his eyes. His frustration is palpable. "That's, like, the last place in the universe I want to go right now. Strike that. The book is the last place. The bookstore is a close second."

"But don't you see?" I ask. "Mael gave us a hint. They told us about the sludge. What do they call it? Dark Ichor. They said it's the Ichor Chalek uses. The book isn't the most important thing, Logan. The Ichor is. The goop. Chalek can literally rewrite matter with the shit. I don't know how the book works as a portal, but I think the cellar might be the real portal. The cellar is where everything begins. Chalek must have stumbled on something otherworldly all those years ago, and he's been using it ever since to mess with people's lives. And he feeds it. If he feeds it, it must grow, right? And what did Mael mean when they said there's something or someone inside that Chalek wants? We're missing parts of this story. Important parts."

"So you're telling me he found an alternate reality in his cellar, and it basically made him immortal? And he can manipulate matter with it? And we're running *toward* this fuckery?"

I give him the side-eye, return to the bed, and plop down beside him. "Nobody's immortal. Immortality doesn't exist. He just hasn't died yet. I don't think."

"Didn't one of you tell me that he was killed by an angry mob? Get your stories straight, Gaige. What's it gonna be? Is your friend a ghost or just super old? The biggest point I'm trying to make is, we're actually running toward this."

"I don't know what he is," I say. I don't know anything, and it's driving me crazy. "But we need to run toward it, Logan. We need to figure out what that stuff is and how he manipulates it to change matter. We need to go to the bookstore. Yes."

Logan sighs and lies back on the bed. He doesn't exactly look like he wants to move anytime soon. I lie down beside him.

It would be so easy to just doze off here beside him, just lean in and cuddle with him until we both fall into a deep sleep. I could definitely use it. I don't remember the last time I actually slept, like *slept* slept instead of falling into the book and dreaming fitful nightmares with my eyes wide open.

I'm just nuzzling into the soft skin of Logan's neck when he shrugs his shoulder, forcing me away. "No. We can't. Dude, if we fall asleep, we're finished. We need to figure this out. I'll go, OK. I'll go. But not without Noah."

"What?" I ask. "Why Noah?"

"Because three's better than two, and he's the brainiac. No offense. He thinks on his toes better and faster than either of us... than both of us combined."

He has a point. And Noah is the one who knew who Chalek was in the first place. I wonder how hard it will be to get him out of his house tonight, though. His parents have probably chained him to his bed. They must have been scared shitless about his whereabouts.

If they haven't chained him up, there's a good chance that Sara has. She's a chill girlfriend, but nobody's *that* chill. He was gone for days.

Before I even have a chance to tell Logan it's worth a shot to stop at Noah's to see if we can convince him to come with us, there's a buzz in the foyer. Speak of the devil? And shit, I hope it doesn't wake my parents. Thank god they usually sleep through everything.

I kiss Logan's shoulder, give him a light, playful slap on the cheek, and jump off the bed to run down the hall to the intercom. When I get there, I buzz the caller in without asking who it is. Fingers crossed, it's Noah. I mean, who else would it be?

After an excruciatingly long wait at the door, I hear the elevator stop on our floor. I peek through the peephole and sure enough, it's Noah on the other side of the door. He looks all goofy and smiley, like he knows I'm looking through the peephole.

Then I see a second face. He's not alone. Sara stands beside him, fixing her hair while they wait for the door to open. Holy shit. Well, there goes that plan. *Thanks a lot, Noah.* Damn.

"Who is it?" Logan asks as he joins me in the foyer. I slowly open the door.

Chapter Thirty-One

"Bro," Noah whispers. As if to suggest that it's too late for raised voices, he puts a finger to his lips to shush us and then points to an invisible watch on his wrist. "It's a door. Just open it and get it over with. What's your problem?" He mimes laughter, barges past me, and sits down on the couch in the living room.

"Hey, boys," Sara whispers. She smiles, takes her shoes off, and joins Noah on the couch.

"No," I say, following them into the living room. "Not having it, Noah. You brought Sara here? Really?"

"Hey," she says, a little too loudly. "I'm right here, Gaige. Don't talk about me like I'm not here."

"Sorry, Sara," I whisper angrily, as I turn from Sara to Noah and back again, "but, um, *this*"—I swirl my open palm in her face—"isn't happening."

"We need all the help we can get, Gaige," Noah says. "Come on. You know it's true. Sara's great at—"

"Did you *tell* her?" My angry stage whispers make me sound unhinged. I sit on the edge of the coffee table in front of them and lean toward them, demanding an answer. "What the fuck, Noah. A girl? She's not invited into this."

"Whoa, now," Sara says. She gets in my face, clearly ready for a fight. "What the hell is it with you gays, always attacking straight girls like this? Is there anyone more sexist than a gay white male?"

"*You gays*?" I stare at her, astonished, and turn to Noah. "Are you gonna let her talk to me like that? *You gays*?"

"You have to keep your voices down," Noah says, ignoring my question. "You're about five seconds away from your old man coming out here with his freak on and kicking everyone out. That what you want?"

He's right and I hate him for it.

"Why the hell did you bring Sara here?" I say between clenched teeth, trying to be quieter.

Noah shrugs. He's got this damn smile that always gets him out of trouble. Like, everywhere. He uses it against me now.

"I just thought we could use the help, broseph. Things were pretty hot in that cellar today."

He's got a point. And also, he knows his smile is working.

"I'm not completely useless, Gaige," Sara adds, looking hurt for the first time as she puts her anger aside. She shrugs and offers me a smile of her own, a much less persuasive one. "We've been doing some research, if you wanna hear about it."

"Take back the *you gays* comment first."

"Then stop taking your anger out on the straight girl who's only trying to help you in the first place. You take back the *girl* comment."

"Take it back, Sara. I call bullshit."

"Of course you do." Sara gets up off the couch, brushes past me, and walks to the door. "Can you play out your hissy fit on our way there, though?"

"On our way where?" Logan says, reminding me that he's still here.

"Like I said, we've been doing some research. I think it's time we all paid a little visit to this *bookstore* of Gaige's together." She air-quotes bookstore in the most annoying way as she sneers in my direction. Didn't mean to go from friends to enemies so quickly, but here we are.

"It's true, Gaige," Noah says. "We found out some things about your friend Chalek."

"Like what?" I ask, doubtful.

"Like, I was right about him being gay. Did you know that his partner—" He stops abruptly and screws up his face in thought. "—one Robert Anthony Martin, was presumed to be one of Chalek's victims? He just vanished one day, and his body was never found. How do you like that?"

I don't say anything, but I'm already thinking about something Mael said earlier, something about Chalek desperately wanting something on the Other Side and how he'd stop at nothing to get it. What if the something *is* a someone?

"*And*, did you know that he and this Robert guy were listed as the architects of that whole string of stores down there on Elm? They literally built that place. You know what that means? They probably found that shit down there and built the stores on top of it to keep it for themselves."

"I don't see how any of this is going to help," I lie, not willing to let things go, even if Noah did just blow my mind. Chalek and his boyfriend stumbled upon hell and built their curio shop on top of it to trap it inside? What the actual fuck?

"Come on, Gaige," Noah says, tearing me away from the

accidental death stare I have on Sara. "Let's just get out of here before we wake your parents. We can argue out all our shit on the way there. You know this new information changes everything. I mean, sounds like this Robert guy is one of the people who went inside and never came back out. Tell me you weren't considering going back there already, anyway."

I don't even want to tell him that it's exactly what Logan and I were going to do. I'm suddenly quite happy to be the argumentative asshole of the group. But he's right. We can argue outside.

I shrug and get up from the coffee table. "OK," I say, sounding just as petulant as I feel. "We can leave. But Sara still has to apologize for the dig."

As we step out into the hallway, Sara mumbles something under her breath about not apologizing for saying something that is one hundred percent accurate.

I bite my tongue until the door is locked and we're walking toward the bank of elevators down the hall.

"I'll apologize for what I said as soon as you apologize for saying *girl* like I'm a plague you wanted to avoid."

Noah looks at me and nods, as if to make sure I see that he's in total agreement with Sara. There's a slight smirk on his face. In case I didn't get the message, he adds an emphatic "For real, dude," as he hits the button for the elevator.

Before blasting forward with a response, I think back on the conversation. OK. So that *may* have happened.

"It's OK, babe," Logan says, patting my back. "I was right there with you. I think it's dangerous, and maybe Noah should have thought twice before bringing—"

"Says the other gay," Sara barks as the elevator arrives and we all get in. She presses the button for the ground floor and then hits the doors closed button repeatedly, possibly like she's severely pissed and taking it out on the button.

"I think this conversation has run its course, don't you, Noah?" Noah says. "Yes, Noah. Yes I do. Maybe we can segue back into the Chalek conversation and let this one die on its own while we're all still alive."

"Sounds like a plan," I say. I smile, turn to Sara, and say, "You may have a point. OK, I'm sorry. That was, I guess, some toxic masculinity holdover I didn't realize I was carrying. I'm sorry. Just… super stressed right now. Of course four heads are better than three. Sorry."

"Me too. I'm sorry too. You know I love the gays," Sara says. The elevator arrives on the ground floor, and the doors open. Sara extends her hand. "After you. Gays before beauty."

Chapter Thirty-Two

WE'RE SITTING ON THE TRAIN, making our way to the bookstore, before anyone brings up the elephant in the room again.

"So, remember what I said about Chalek when you first told me his name?"

"You said a group of vigilantes attacked and killed him," I say, nodding.

"Yeah, well." Pause for dramatic effect. "I may have been slightly misinformed about the details of that story."

"Only slightly, babe," Sara says, coming back to life. She's been staring out the window, maybe trying to calm down. She swivels to face me. "Turns out he wasn't buried at all."

Now she scooches closer, like she's dishing hot gossip. I lean toward her as she continues.

"Sara actually found out all the other stuff, too," Noah says. "Right after she corrected me on the angry mob bit. Her Google-fu is slapping. She has a theory about Chalek and his partner."

"We'll get to Robert later," Sara continues, smiling at Noah in thanks for giving her credit where credit is due. "First up, we tried to figure out where the dude was buried, but we kept hitting a wall. Then we realized it was because they never found a body *to* bury. The neighborhood vigilantes definitely attacked him. Apparently, they tore him apart. Like, limb from limb. It was an instant bloodbath when they finally got their hands on the guy.

"But when the authorities broke up the crowd and everyone dispersed, they went to retrieve the body and, you know, do their archaic crime scene shit. Only, there was no body."

Sara stops her narrative long enough to say, "This is our stop. Let's go."

Talk about dramatic pauses. Sara knows how to use a cliffhanger. Logan and I race to catch up with her and Noah as they bail out of the train and walk toward the stairs.

"Hey," Logan says. "Wait up. Don't leave us hanging. What happened?"

Sara stops halfway up and raises a finger to the impatient Logan. "Climb, Padawan. Don't speak." She climbs the long staircase. Logan turns to me, shrugs, and takes my hand as we walk.

This gives me time to think, and when we reach street level, I already know how the story plays out. I have experienced this exact same thing with Chalek myself.

"So, at first they thought maybe the angry peasants had buried the killer in an unmarked grave, owing to his dirtbagginess and all. I mean, he clearly deserved that ending, based on everything Noah told me and what I've read," Sara says.

We head toward Elm Street. I'm beginning to wonder what we will be met with this time. Bookstore or no bookstore—that is the question.

"But the unmarked grave story has never been verified," Noah says, pushing himself into Sara's narrative, wanting a piece of the glory. "It's just the perceived ending of Chalek. Never verified."

"I beat the ever-loving shit out of that dirtbag down in the cellar one night, not long ago." As I say this, they all stop and look at me. Mostly they look disbelieving, doubtful, but I ignore their doubt. I look at each of them, making sure to evenly spread my condescension. "Thanks for the three votes of confidence, guys. It's true. I tore my hands apart punching his skeletal face. He was gore and blood and everything."

I hold up my hands and show them my scabbed knuckles. But let's face it, most of us are a bit scraped up from our various dealings with Chalek.

"Until he wasn't," I continue. "His face was gore and blood until it wasn't. Next thing I know, he's standing in front of me without a scratch on him."

"So let me get this straight," Logan says as we arrive at the intersection of Elm and Yonge. Almost there. I glance down Elm, but we're still too far away to see if there's a light in the storefront. "There was no body because Chalek allowed everyone to take out their anger on him, torture him, and do god knows what to him, and then he simply got up, brushed it off, and walked away? Holy shit."

"Yep," I agree. "Holy shit is right, babe. That's what he did the other night, anyway. He can even use that gunk to rewrite himself."

"So, I guess the real question is, how do we stop someone like that? And, like, is he even stoppable?" Logan asks.

"That's why I'm here," Sara replies. She laughs. "Hi. I'm the voice of reason. I'll be here to mock any and all negativity. Nobody is unstoppable. There has to be a way. We just need to find it. All villains have a weakness."

"Yep." I can't disagree with her logic, but I also have an urge to point out some logic of my own. "And so do all the superheroes, so there's that."

Just as we arrive at the building, Noah turns to me with a scowl on his face. "Let it go, Gaige."

"What? I did. I'm just saying. Chalek isn't the only one with weaknesses. And he has probably figured out ours by now. I mean, you know, besides the obvious ones. Like we bleed and break and die and whatnot."

"Yeah. You let it go. Sure you did," Noah says, shaking his head in disgust. "Sorry, Sara. I didn't realize he was this much of a douche."

Just as I'm about to protest, I catch a glimpse of Logan, who stands beside me shaking his head. I have no friends in this battle. Apparently, we don't argue with Sara.

"It's time to work together," Noah says. "And looky here. It would appear that there's a new bookstore where nary a bookstore stood before. What do you know? So, we all in this together or what?"

I look at the bookstore and turn back to the group. With a shrug, I let go of our earlier spat as much as I can.

"Guess this is happening." Something tells me we won't have a problem getting in this time. I put my hand on the door and push.

Chapter Thirty-Three

THE CACOPHONY OF BELLS STARTLES both Logan and Sara. I'd laugh, but I'm not really in the mood.

"Nice touch," Noah says. His voice has the same effect on me that the bells had on the other two.

We enter the store, and I point out Lilith, who sits atop one of the long bookshelves. Eight rows of them, just like there should be. As before, all of the books range from black to gray to brown in tone, and most of them don't have any writing on their spines. Could it be true that each one represents a person Chalek chose to feed to his Dark Ichor? I want to point to everything and say, "See, I told you! See? Bookstore!"

I stabby-point at all the things but say nothing. I just point and sneer, hoping they get my meaning. My friends stand gawking at the store, mesmerized by its impossible existence and its stage-set phoniness.

"It's different," I whisper. Looking around, I can see slight variations from my previous visits. The lights flicker madly now that we've entered the store. There's also a shimmer of fog about our feet, even more fog than was here during my first visit, when

I thought of mornings fishing with my dad. Everything looks less real.

"It's awfully quiet," Noah says. He unfreezes and walks down one of the long aisles of books. "And what is that stink? It smells like—"

He stops in his tracks and turns back to look at us.

"Yep," I say, because I know exactly what he's thinking. Like the place inside the book. He's never been there, but he's been somewhere eerily similar that smells exactly the same. Everything we see here must be formed by the slimy goop.

"Like that fucking crypt in the cellar. The place that bastard locked me up in. That's what smells like this. That tar."

Yep. Nailed it. Before I'm able to agree with him, though, a peal of gravelly, cancerous laughter bursts out from somewhere within the depths of the building. It fills all the spaces so that there's no way to escape it.

"What the hell was that?" Sara says. She takes a few steps back toward the front door and bangs against the hanging bells. As they jangle into motion, she lets out a short, startled scream.

"It's OK," Noah says. "He's trying to scare us. It's what he does."

"It's working," Logan says. He retreats to Sara's side, and she nods at him in agreement. "I feel like we're done here. Like, maybe we should just go and not come back."

"We're in too deep for that, sweetie," I say. I hold out my hand and gesture for him to join me. We have to go deeper into the store. We have to confront Chalek, or he's never gonna stop harassing us. "We're in the bookstore that isn't here. There's no turning back now. We're *all* in."

"I was afraid you were going to say something like that."

To his credit, he steps forward and takes my hand. Before fully accepting his fate, though, he turns back to Sara with a pleading look and holds out his free hand to her.

"I suppose it's a little late for me to agree with Gaige on the whole girl thing, eh?" Sara asks.

Unexpectedly, Logan lets out a little yelp of laughter that clearly leaves him feeling uncomfortable. Everything sounds a little off in here, a little discombobulated. He says nothing, just shakes his hand in her direction, urging her to take it.

As Sara puts her hand in Logan's, I pull on his other hand and begin to walk down the aisle of books toward Noah. We're doing this.

Lilith jumps down off the bookshelf and begins to follow us; her curiosity is getting the better of her. She falls in at the end of our little conga line of terrified lunatics as we walk into a trap of monumental proportions. I hope she has nine lives, and that she spares a few of them for us hopeless adrenaline junkies.

"Remember what I said before," I say as we arrive at the washroom. "He's weaker when he lets us all in. This place isn't like it was the first time I was here. It's *weaker*."

Noah looks at me quizzically. I gesture toward the ceiling with a nod.

"The lights. They're flickering like mad. The fog. It all looks so *cloudy*, staticky. He's struggling to keep it here because it's not just me, now. This happened as soon as he let you guys in the other day. It all became less real, less here."

"Well, let's hope it's all a little less murder-y too, then," Noah says. He tries to follow up his words with a chuckle and a smirk, but they come out wrong and he grimaces with regret. He turns on the washroom light.

Wonder of wonders, the door in the floor is already propped open. If that isn't an invitation to madness, I don't know what is.

"Wait. So that's where we're going?" Sara says. "You didn't tell me about crawling down into a hole. Wow. OK. Well, you guys really know how to have a good time, don't you?"

"You ain't seen nothing yet," Logan says. He lets go of both of our hands and shivers exaggeratedly. "Ugh. I did not see me ever going back down there."

"Same," Noah says. He goes to retrieve the flashlight, but it's not there. "Looks like phones."

He pulls his from his back pocket and holds it up in victory before turning on his flashlight app and shining the light into the gaping hole in the floor.

"Wait," I say, pushing myself in front of Logan. "If we're gonna do this, I kinda need some sustenance first."

"Huh?" Logan says. At any other time, the look of confusion on his face would be comical.

"He wants you to kiss him, Padawan," Sara says. We all chuckle a bit before she breezes past me and says, "Not a bad idea."

So, before they go down into the murderous dungeon of doom, our four heroes stop everything to have a two-minute make-out session in the abandoned washroom of a bookstore that doesn't actually exist. Good times.

"Just what I needed," I whisper as I pull away from Logan. "Let's do this. It's time to slay the dragon."

"One sec," Noah mumbles, still lip-locked with Sara.

"Come on, loverboy," Logan says. "Chalek's probably getting a bit impatient. No doubt he has a lot of *surprises* waiting for us down there in the underworld."

"The Other Side world," I say without even thinking.

"Huh?" Sara asks as she and Noah finally disentangle. "The what?"

"That's what Mael calls the place inside the book." Saying it was nothing, but hearing it, I get how bizarre it sounds. "There's the Other Side, the Outside World, and, they call the goop Dark Ichor. I take it that Noah didn't tell you absolutely everything?"

"I'm not sure Noah *knows* absolutely everything," he says in self-defense. "Though I do enjoy Mael's nod to Greek mythology. Ichor was the blood of the gods. Dark Ichor? Perfection. Go, Mael."

"No time now," I say, ignoring his explanation. His explanation wasn't for me, anyway, since he already told me about the connection the other day. I take out my phone and turn on my flashlight app. Holding it over the opening in the floor and illuminating the old ladder, I make the first move. "Time to visit hell."

"How can I refuse when you put it that way?" Logan says. The look of terror on his face erases his attempt at casual banter. He's deathly pale, and his hand trembles as he holds out his phone. The bright light of his flashlight temporarily blinds me.

I smile, look away, and start the descent into Chalek's creepy, dank cellar.

Chapter Thirty-Four

NOBODY SPEAKS AS WE GO down the ladder. Once we're all on solid ground, I look around to see which cellar Chalek is giving us tonight. Looks like the old one, with the bare bulbs hanging from the rafters. Like the bookstore upstairs, though it seems to be just barely here. The lights are dim and flicker constantly. He's struggling to hold the facade in place. There's a light fog near the floor, making it difficult to see our own feet.

Fog is also coming down in tendrils from the escape hatch leading back up to the washroom. As I watch them snake down and wrap themselves around the ladder before joining the fog on the floor, the door slams shut. With the violent slam comes a sprinkle of dirt from the cellar ceiling.

"*That* wasn't scary," Sara whispers. She shivers for emphasis. "What the hell was I thinking?"

Noah moves in closer to Sara and puts an arm around her shoulder.

"I think we have to start at the place where we saw the stuff seeping out through the wall. Mael told me the substance is what Chalek uses to control things. He can transform it."

"Can't we just talk to this Mael person and ask them how to stop this madman? Sounds like they've been helpful so far."

"They're inside the book, Sara," I say. "Not like we're going to bump into them in the cellar. Besides, Chalek messed them up pretty badly last time we saw them. I don't even know if Mael made it. I mean, I think they were already dead, technically, but it looked like Chalek might have killed them again. If that makes any sense whatsoever."

"Not really," she says. "I guess I'll have to take your word for it. But why are we in the cellar when we could have gone inside the book? Noah told me about the book. Seems like a great starting point to me. Where is this *magical book* of yours, anyway?"

I can't help but pick up on Sara's passive-aggressive tone. I think she may still be a bit pissed at my earlier display of toxic masculinity, as well as a titch skeptical.

"At this point, I can't even remember the last time I had it. It's all a blur now. I didn't bring it with me."

"What the fuck, Gaige?" Noah says. He stops walking and turns back to give me a look of incredulity. He shines his flashlight into his own face to make sure I see the look. "You came to the fucking climax, and you didn't think to bring the book that literally gives us access to the battlefield? What the actual fuck is wrong with you? You are broken, dude. Why are you wearing that useless backpack of yours if you aren't carrying the book inside it?"

"What?" I say. I hate the defensive, apologetic tone in my voice. "I don't leave the house without my backpack. You know that."

"We need that book, Einstein. I mean, Jesus. I thought that was a given."

"Don't freak out on me, Noah. Now is not the time."

He turns and storms off toward the part of the cellar where the goop was. He doesn't look back. Clearly, he's pissed. Sara shakes her head in disgust and follows him. Great. Let's just infight and make it easier for Chalek to win. Perfect!

"On your bed," Logan says, dropping the words like a bomb as he breezes past me. He follows Noah and Sara into the near darkness, lighting his way with his phone flashlight as he goes. Subtle.

"What?" I say. I bring up the rear, stumbling on the uneven floor before grabbing the wall to regain my balance. "Damn. Shit. What did you say, Logan?"

"The book, Gaige," he says, not turning back to face me while he speaks. "The last time you had it, it was on your bed. When we went in there together. Not gonna lie, I also thought you would have brought it. Seems like an important part of *all this.*"

By the time I get to where they all stand in front of the leaking wall, Noah already has a clump of the tar between his thumb and forefinger and is rubbing it between them, like testing its stickiness will reveal the big secret surrounding its origins. *It's goop from hell, Noah. Mystery solved.*

"I guess I just thought we would confront Chalek together and try to end this. I don't know what I was thinking. Of course I should have brought the book. Obviously. OK. My mistake. I'm sorry."

"Hey," Noah says. He puts his free hand on my shoulder. "We'll figure it out. It's OK. You're right, anyway. It must be more about this shit than the book, right?"

Before I respond, a huge crash comes from somewhere up above us. Like, a demolition crew just took out the store huge. It shakes the entire cellar like a muffled explosion. In its wake, there's a shiver of falling dirt all around us.

"What the fu—"

"Shhh," I say, cutting Logan off as I reach out protectively to pull him in behind me. The flickering lightbulbs die all at once, and we are left with only the beams from our phone flashlights. Some of the walls begin to change, become darker, more luminescent. Like the other place. Things begin to take on the same sheen of black as the Other Side.

"What's happening?" Sara says, just barely holding back a scream that comes out as a splintered moan. "What is this stuff?"

"Just don't touch it," I say. "Damn. He's doing it. It's happening."

"I'm going back to check on that noise."

Noah, of course. He's halfway back to the ladder before I have a chance to stop him. I run to catch up. I would rather not split up. It doesn't seem like a great idea at this juncture in our ghost-hunting careers.

"Wait," I say. "We shouldn't separate. Chalek's probably trying to distract us."

"Guys," Logan calls out from behind me.

"Stay there, Logan. We'll be right back. Stay with Sara. And don't fucking touch anything."

I get to the ladder and Noah's already at the top. Black tar drips from all around the door in thick, ropy strings. The whole ceiling is black where the stuff is slowly gurgling down. It's already all over Noah as he pushes himself against the door, trying to get it open. I know from the last time we tried that the door isn't going to open.

"Noah, it's not happening. Just leave it. When the time comes, we can leave from one of the other stores."

"Gaige? That you? Hello, there? Gaige?" It's Chalek. He's up in the washroom. His sing-song tone drips with mischief. "What are you kids doing down in my cellar? That's not nice. I just don't know what I'm going to do with you boys. You all just make me so angry, invading my space like this. This is trespassing."

Noah climbs back down and comes to stand beside me. He looks at me and shrugs slightly, as if to ask, *What do we do now?* He's basically covered in the goopy shit. He looks like he did when we walked through it yesterday. Was it yesterday? I can no longer remember.

"I thought he was getting weaker," I whisper. This doesn't seem weaker. He seems just the opposite of weaker, actually. If his game is to close the gap between the Outside World and the hellscape inside his book, it certainly looks like he's figuring things out. "I need that book."

Noah just shakes his head and frowns. Clearly, I've failed him. OK, then.

He walks over to where the others stand, farther down the cellar. The substance is oozing in everywhere. The cellar is literally transforming into the place inside the book.

"Is this what you're looking for?" Chalek whispers into my ear, his voice filled with gravel and death. He reaches around from behind me, and the book comes into view. There's a disconnect as I feel actual relief to see it this time. What is wrong with me?

"You keep misplacing this thing, and that insults me, you petulant boy. One should treasure gifts more than this. One should not misplace or mistreat them. I don't know why I bothered trying to be nice to you in the first place, boy."

I yank the book from his grip with both hands and scramble away from him as fast as I can. When I turn to flee, though, my foot slips in a recently-deposited pile of sludge. I go down hard on one knee; the pain is instant and unbearable. I drop the book in the muck and rub my knee to try to ease the pain.

"Watch yourself there, young Gaige. It's a mite slippy-sloppy to walk on, I'd say. Best be careful or you'll end up breaking a thing or two. Snap, snap."

"Get away from me, you freak."

"Now, that's no way to talk to new friends."

"Let him go, Chalek," Noah says, backtracking to my side and helping me back to my feet. On my way up, I snatch the book and hold it close to me. I wipe it on the front of my shirt. Suddenly, I'm more concerned about it than I ever was. Something tells me it's still an important key to the puzzle. I pull my shirt up and tuck the book down inside the front of my pants, where it bulges comically. I can't let it leave my person again.

"I didn't lay a single digit on the boy, and I'm sure he'll attest to that fact."

"Just back off, old man." I admire Noah's bravado, even though I can see right through it. A friend knows when a friend is fighting through his own fear to stick up for you. "Step off."

We back away from Chalek, who stands still as a statue, smiling the slippery little smile of a comic book villain. Oh, man, I hate this guy so much.

Walking down here is more difficult now. As the Dark Ichor keeps pouring in from all directions, the cellar looks more and more like the other place. I'm afraid we're running out of time.

Whatever he was cultivating in those little prisons he trapped us in, he's now found a way to bring it to the rest of the cellar.

But I'm not yet ready to give up on Mael. They have something to do with ending this, too. I know they're still there on the Other Side, still whatever they are if not alive. Waiting for my return, maybe even hoping for it. I have to see them one more time.

"Sara, Logan," I say, sloshing toward them with Noah at my heels. "Come on. Let's go." I wave my hand for them to join us.

"Wait," Sara says. "We haven't done anything yet. We can't just leave. We have to do something to stop this."

"Listen to the girl, Gaige. Shouldn't you try to stop this mess from happening? Looking a bit icky-sticky down here in the Other Side, don't you think?" He laughs, and I know by the way he said Other Side that he's mocking Mael's word for the other place. "My, my. Me-o my-o. We should find that godforsaken leak in the world and fill it in somehow, patch it up, so to speak. Things are not looking good, boyo."

"It's not gonna work, Chalek," I spit. "You'll never bring that place here. It doesn't belong here. Whatever *this* is, it's not that place. This is just another one of your cheap tricks."

"Are you sure about that, though, young lad?" he replies. He pulls the trick where he appears at my side in an instant. He blocks my way before I get to the next connected cellar. "It's looking a lot like it, dontcha think? Why, I could just see Mael having the time of their life down here, couldn't you?"

"Leave Mael out of it," I yell, and immediately regret my defensive outburst. I glance over at Logan guiltily. He's definitely noticed my protective tone. Can't take it back now. "You've done enough to them already."

"Ooh," Chalek says. I know right away that he's picked up on what just happened. He did orchestrate it, after all. "Am I detecting a bit of a love triangle here? Your boy toy looks just about fit to be tied about this Mael character. Do I smell jealousy, mayhap?"

He laughs. Every time I hear that laugh, it grates my entire being.

Logan steps forward, putting himself right in Chalek's face like he doesn't even understand the concept of fear. Chalek stops laughing and actually takes a step backward, away from Logan. The look on his face says he's just discovered fear for the first time.

"You can't come between us, old man," Logan says. He puts his finger in Chalek's face as he lays into him. "I don't know what you're doing or how you're doing it. Or even how you're alive, if that's what you are. But you can fuck off if you think your little game is gonna come between us. It's not happening, old man."

Go, Logan. My heart swells at his defense of our relationship, like he's taking on a school bully in the hallway between classes or something. Defending my honor. It takes me a few seconds to realize that Chalek's play at fear was performative, though. His fake fear melts away from his features as he breaks into a big shit-eating grin.

Chalek reaches up and grabs Logan's stabby, pointing finger so quickly that neither of us has time to react. He pulls it backward with one quick yank. Something in Logan's finger makes a loud pop, and I know it's bad right away. Logan yelps and crumples to the floor in agony while Chalek continues to yank on his finger.

I practically stumble from the instant feeling of nausea that flows through me as I see Logan's finger pointed in a direction it shouldn't be able to point. The look of excruciating pain on Logan's face just makes the nausea worse.

Chalek looks at me and laughs, pulling back harder on Logan's finger. He knows this is hurting me almost as much as it's hurting Logan.

From out of nowhere, Noah comes flying through the air and lands right on Chalek's shoulders. As Chalek stumbles forward, he lets go of Logan's finger, and I'm able to step in and pull Logan out of the line of fire. Noah and Chalek go down in a pile of twisted limbs and land with a squelch in the goop that's gathering on the floor.

Even as Noah's fists pummel the sides of Chalek's head, I know it's a wasted effort. This is exactly how Chalek allowed me to take out my anger on him the other day, and it only served to exhaust me. Still, it feels good to see the old man getting some payback, even if it will have zero effect on him in the end.

I turn my attention back to Logan, who's screaming into the crook of his arm while shaking out his other hand with the bent-back finger. I don't know if it's broken, but it's definitely dislocated. A finger should not point in that direction, ever.

"Stop moving it. Logan. Stop. Hold it still." Sara comes to his rescue, attempting to be the voice of reason. "Logan. Stop shaking it. You're just making it worse. Let me see."

"Oh my god," he screams. "It hurts. Holy shit, it hurts. Ow, ow, ow. Fu—"

"Shut up!" Sara yells, taking hold of his forearm and stopping him from pointlessly flailing his arm about. She looks at the finger, grips it in her hand and holds it steady. "This is gonna hurt. Do you hear me, Logan? This is gonna hurt like hell. But don't take it out on me."

"What? What do you mean? Shit. Oh my god."

I glance over at Noah and Chalek. Noah's still pummeling him, sitting on top of him and flailing blindly with clenched fists. Chalek is still allowing it to happen.

As I return my attention to Sara, she gives me a steely gaze. I don't know what she's planning to do, but I know what she wants. Support. I get closer to Logan and try to hold him steady. I wrap my arms around him and squeeze.

"What was that?" Sara says, looking off down the hallway. It's almost comical, how easily her distraction technique works. Logan looks away, and as he does, she heaves on his finger. With another loud pop, it goes back into place. Logan lets out a bloodcurdling scream and tries to shake me off of him.

I hold him for a few more seconds as he bucks and shouts. Eventually, he calms down, looks at his finger, and sees that it's back to its correct position. He looks up at Sara with gratitude.

"How'd you do—"

"Gymnastics. Eight years." Sara says. She puts a hand on Logan's shoulder, soothing him. "I've seen a few dislocated fingers in my time. Even had one myself. Painful, right? If we make it out of here, you'll have to go to urgent care to make sure nothing's broken, but it should be good for now."

"Holy shit," Logan says, still looking at his finger in amazement. "Thank you so much. That was—"

"I know," she says, smiling.

Chapter Thirty-Five

"HEY YOU GUYS," LOGAN SAYS, redirecting his attention as I get up and wipe myself off as best as I can. "Where's Noah? Where's the old man?"

"Oh, shit."

It's happened again. Noah's nowhere to be seen. He was right beside us, having his way with Chalek. Shit.

"Guys, I think we have a few problems right now. Look at this place."

Sara's right. There's so little left of the cellar, it's terrifying. As I look around, I get this eerie feeling. It's almost as if I'm back in the place behind the words. If I didn't know I was in the cellar—if there weren't still a few traces of it left—I would think I was inside the book, where Mael is trapped at the threshold of Chalek's Other Side.

The cellar is now almost completely coated in the substance from the Other Side. I recall Mael's warning about Chalek's main goal, to bridge the gap between the two places so he could bring something back out of hell. If what I'm seeing is any indication, we're almost there.

"Noah! Noah!"

Sara's screams for Noah startle me back to reality.

"Noah! If you can hear us, say something!" Logan shouts. He's on his feet now, and making his way deeper into the cellar. He turns right, down a hallway and away from the connected cellars, and I scoot after him so I can keep my eye on him.

I get a really bad feeling as I watch him move farther and farther into the luminescent darkness. In the Other Side, we're not supposed to breach the threshold—if we do, we can't come back out. I want him to stop moving right now, before he goes too far.

"Logan! Wait!" I call.

"Noah! Shout if you can hear—" Logan's words are abruptly cut off as he leaves my line of sight completely and dissolves into the darkness.

"Oh my god," Sara whispers from somewhere beside me. I hadn't realized she'd even caught up with me. "Did you see that? Gaige, what's going on? What just happened? Logan just—disappeared."

She sounds like she's at the brink of a nervous breakdown. I reach out to put a hand on her shoulder, hopefully calm her down a bit, but as I reach out, she darts forward to where Logan just vanished.

"Sara! No!"

She stops just short of the place where Logan disappeared. I look down at her feet and, for the first time, I see a line carved into the ground there.

"Don't move! Don't fucking move, Sara," I shout. I cover my face with my hands and scream. I just give in to the need. This is my limit. That's it. I'm out. Seeing the line Mael dug into the ground in the other place? Here? In this place? It's just too much.

Something grabs me by the shoulders, and I find myself being violently shaken. I think at first that it must be Chalek, finally taking pity on me by deciding to end my torture and make his last fatal strike. When I tear my hands away from my face, though, it's Sara looking back at me. She's come back from the threshold.

"Pull yourself together, Gaige," she says. Her voice is flat and calm, exactly what I need right now. "Now is not the time for a breakdown. We can all do that together once we get out of here. Snap out of it!"

She actually slaps me across the face. Like, as hard as she can. I can feel a welt begin to form as she grabs my face in both of her hands and stares into my eyes.

"Ow."

"OK. I'm sorry. Maybe that was overkill," she says, letting go of my face. "Sorry. I've seen people do that in the movies. I just didn't know what else to do. Your screams were freaking me out. I'm sorry."

"No, no," I say. "We're good. I think I needed that, actually. *I'm* sorry."

"Tell me what happened, Gaige. Where the hell have they gone? How could they just disappear like that? I don't think Noah was very good at telling me what's going on here, because I don't remember vanishing acts in his recap."

"Did he tell you how I start to read the book and then fall inside and go to an alternate reality? Did he tell you about how

Mael keeps saving me from going in too far and getting trapped with the other kids?"

"He told me some of that. Not everything, I don't think. Maybe."

"Well, see that mark on the ground?" I don't even bother saying floor, because down this hallway? This must be ground zero. The place has now fully transformed. It's ground beneath our feet, here—black, luminescent, sticky ground. I walk toward the line, pointing at it obsessively all the way. "Do. You. See. That. Line?"

"Yes. Of course. It's deep. I can't miss it."

"That mark was dug into the ground by Mael, when they told me I couldn't walk past it or I would go too far in to get back out. That line is supposed to be inside the fucking book, not here in Chalek's cellar. Logan just crossed that line, Sara! Logan crossed the line that can't be crossed!"

By the end of my diatribe, I'm shouting every word, spitting them at her as though she's the one I'm furious at, terrified of. We both look down at the line, mesmerized.

"But that's imp—"

"Impossible? You would fucking think so, wouldn't you?"

"Gaige." The voice comes from beside us, where there is nothing but goop-covered wall. I step away from the wall as the luminescence begins to glow around a familiar frame, making them stand out from the blackness. By now, I would know that silhouette anywhere.

"Mael!" I yell, as they emerge. It's discombobulating to see this, because it's basically the same place they emerge from, in relation to the line on the ground, back in the Other Side.

As Mael reaches forward, fully free of the wall, Sara flinches away slightly. I've never seen Mael covered in the goop before. It sticks to them here, too.

"Why are you here? Why did you bring others? You know that's a bad idea, Gaige. The last time you brought someone with you, Chalek was almost able to follow you inside. He comes closer each time, especially when it's more than one person. You shouldn't have done this. You both have to leave."

When Mael stops talking, they look down at themself, clearly stupefied that they're covered in the ichor that didn't stick to them in the other place.

"We're not in the book, Mael," I say, but judging by the look on their face, I think they've already figured that out. I pull up my shirt front to show them the top of the book sticking out of my pants. "We haven't entered through the book at all. It's right here. With me."

"I don't understand. Come, come. Come away from there." They gesture for us to move away from the line, allowing us the space to retreat farther from danger. Swiping at the tar covering them, they say, "I don't know what you mean. You're here."

I look around me. There's absolutely no denying where we are, and I know that the place inside the book is the only place Mael can exist. They told me as much.

I turn back to Mael. "I mean, we're in the cellar of Chalek's bookstore. In the Outside World. We entered the cellar, and it's slowly transforming into... this."

"He's done it. He's bringing the Dark Ichor back down here," Mael says. "He's halfway there, Gaige. He just can't figure out how to move back and forth between here and the Other Side.

I don't know what's on the other side of that line, but I know it's bad. And if he's able to bring something back from there, I don't even want to think about what might happen. He's doing it!"

I don't even have to ask Mael what they mean. The stuff Noah and Sara told me about earlier comes back to me. Sara's research. Robert Anthony Martin. That's what this whole science experiment gone wrong is all about: getting inside. For over a century, Chalek has been trying to figure out how this world works in order to get his boyfriend back.

The goop is all around me. I can see exactly what Mael means. Not only did Chalek somehow survive all these decades of madness, he's now managing to do exactly what he's been *trying* to do the whole time. Or so it seems. Either that, or he's invited this Other Side world into our own for so long that it's finally decided to take him up on the offer. I can't begin to imagine what that would mean. It couldn't be good.

Chapter Thirty-Six

"Maybe," I say. "But maybe not yet. If we go back down this hallway to the end, it's still cellar, still a combination. It's not all gone yet."

"Show me," Mael says. They turn away and begin to walk toward the end of the hallway, where it joins the rest of the cellar. "He's trying, Gaige. But maybe it's not too late."

"It's never too late," Sara says. I wish I had her confidence. I'm all about believing it might be a little too late to put the genie back inside the bottle. This is not looking good at all. Broiled chicken can't return to the coop, and all that.

Mael turns to Sara and smiles. "No. I hope not. I'm Mael."

"Hi Mael," Sara says. "I'm Sara. Gaige's friend."

"Batcaver," Mael says, beaming. They turn and smile at me.

"Huh. Yeah," I say. Sara scrunches her face up, questioning. I laugh and say, "I guess so. Yeah, she is."

We continue and follow Mael out of the darkness, but when we come to the junction at the end of the hallway, they stop dead in their tracks.

We look out into the rest of the cellar, glancing in both directions. The route back toward the bookstore looks luminescent, practically fully transformed. Looking in the other direction, though, I can still see dirt walls, cement walls, even bare bulbs hanging from rafters. I shine my phone's light in that direction. It's mostly cellar.

"I don't think I can go any farther," Mael says. The eager look on their face is agony. I can see that they just want to turn that corner and escape from their nightmare; but I can also see that they're terrified of doing so, fearful that it would mean the end of them. To leave their nightmare would be the end of them. I think that's something we both realize.

"I don't think you should try," I reply, seeing the hope and anticipation in Mael's face. I give them the most sympathetic look I can muster. I'm so sure they're right, but I don't want to say it out loud. It's too painful. "Stay right here. Don't move."

I take Sara's hand and we turn right, toward the interconnected cellars.

"Gaige," Mael calls from behind us. "You should go upstairs. Go see if it's like this up there, too. Outside."

"If we even can. I'll check. We got out through another store the other day."

"But we can't leave the others behind," Sara says. "We have to find Noah and Logan."

"We'll come back for them, I promise," I tell her, hoping all the while that I'm not wrong. I don't even know if there will be a way back in if we manage to get out. But I'm with Mael. I have to see what's happening upstairs. That big bang we heard earlier sounded more like an explosion than a shelf falling over, or something simple like that. "I just need to see what's going on up there."

I lead her to the cellar door that worked for us the last time, the one that leads to the abandoned greeting card store.

"Aren't you worried about Logan and Noah?" Sara says as we arrive at the ladder. "I don't want to leave them down here, Gaige."

"And we're not going to. We'll come back." I hold my phone out ahead of me, climb to the top of the ladder, and push open the door. Remembering that it's the spring-loaded one, I hold it open with one hand while I climb up through to the storeroom above us.

Once I'm up, I hold the door open and gesture for Sara to follow me. I shine my beam down on her and can see by the look on her face that she's reluctant to do so. I hope she's wrong. I hope we can get back in.

"Why don't I just stay here on the ladder? I can hold the door open and wait for you to get back."

I'm not going to take the chance of separating from the very last person in our group. Two of us down is enough. I shake my head and gesture again for her to follow.

She grimaces but relents. I help her through the door in the floor and release it once she's clear. It snaps back into place with a sound like a gunshot, loud enough to make us both jump. Clearly, our nerves are shattered.

Chapter Thirty-Seven

"COME ON. WE'RE JUST A couple of stores down. It'll only take us a minute." We walk through the store to the front door. That's when I remember that an alarm went off the first time we opened it. Shit.

When I hesitate at the door, Sara pushes me from behind. "Come on. Let's go. What's wrong?"

"The alarm." I turn to face her. "When Noah and I left this way, the alarm went off when we opened this door. It was deafening. We didn't get very far before we heard sirens. We're fucked."

"At this point, I'm pretty sure we're fucked no matter what we do. I say we do it and worry about the sirens later. Who knows, maybe we could use some saving right about now."

She might be right. She doesn't give me time to think it through, though. As she finishes speaking, she unlocks the door, pushes on it, and shoves me out onto the sidewalk. Sure enough, the cacophony of the alarm fills the night.

I pocket my phone and run toward the bookstore with Sara at my heels.

We duck inside before we hear any sign of sirens. When the door slams closed behind us, I hear the familiar bells rattle against the glass of the door.

The bookstore is basically gone. I take it Chalek has bigger fish to fry than keeping the facade of an imaginary bookstore in place. We're back to the abandoned building, even though the bells remain on the door. There's no other trace of the store. At the back of the empty space, streaks of goop surround the washroom door, dripping sludge all over the place. Not much of it has made its way beyond the threshold of the washroom door, though.

I push the bathroom door open a crack. The goop hangs off everything in here. Like maybe it exploded in here somehow?

"Oh, shit," Sara says from somewhere behind me. "What does this mean? What is this stuff, anyway?"

"Mael's Dark Ichor. The stuff that gives Chalek all his power. Possibly the reason he's been able to stay alive all this time? This stuff allows him to transform everything. It's what he uses; I just don't know how. He can rewrite matter with it."

"Sounds godlike to me. I agree with Noah. Great name for it. We have to get back down there before the street is filled with cops and we no longer have the option. Have you seen enough up here yet?"

She's so right. I'm guessing we have somewhere between two and ten minutes to duck back into the card shop and out of sight before it's all over.

"Come on. Let's go." I grab her hand and yank her toward the front of the store. By the time we make it to the door, though, there's a disturbance behind us.

"You're not gonna leave us here all by our lonesome selves, are you, kids?" Chalek says. I turn in time to see him emerging from the washroom. The door screeches against the floor as he opens it. Miraculously, he has no tar on him at all. "Where are you kids off to? We've only just begun."

Sara reaches the door and slams into the bells, making them burst into life and join the already chaotic noise of the alarm down the street.

I know that time is running out. And as much as I hate to turn my back on Chalek, I also know we have to get out of here. We need to get back to the cellar. Any second now, this place will be swarming with emergency vehicles. I can already hear them in the far distance.

"Gaige," comes a hoarse whisper from behind us. Logan's voice sounds so piteous, it stops me in my tracks. My relief is instant. Logan's made it out of that place in one piece. I turn around and there he is, standing in the doorway Chalek has vacated. He's wobbling on his feet, smeared from head to toe with tar, but here. Alive. Logan.

"Logan!" I run to him as he begins to crumple to the floor, and he falls into my embrace. I'll hold him forever—I'm never letting go. We sit on the floor together as I smother him in hugs. "Are you OK, baby? What happened? Where'd you go?"

He raises his head and looks me in the eye. Then he smirks, and the corner of his mouth lifts into a sneer. No. Shit. Fuck.

"*Are you OK, baby?*" Chalek's voice comes out of Logan's mouth in full-on mockery. Logan's face melts away, and his entire body becomes the shimmering sludge before it transforms and reorganizes, and I'm left holding Chalek.

He bursts into maniacal laughter as I let go of him and shoot backward, as far away from him as I can get. I crab crawl across the floor before I'm able to get back to my feet.

"*What*?" Chalek whines, feigning disappointment. "Didn't you like my portrayal of your pretty boy, Gaige? Awwww."

"We have to go *now*, Gaige," Sara yells. She's holding the door open and gesturing for me to come. The sirens are two or three blocks away at the most. "Now. Ignore him."

Him is the old man sitting cross-legged on the floor, laughing his ass off and slapping his big bony hands on the floor as he loses it. He's so amused by his latest shitty trick.

I run out, and Sara follows me to the sidewalk. The door slams, and the bells jangle against the glass. As we duck into the card shop, I have a moment of clarity.

We need fire. Lots and lots of fire.

"Please tell me you have a lighter in your pocket, Sara," I scream as I hold the door open and gesture for her to slide in under my arm. I know she imbibes pot occasionally, much to Noah's chagrin. "You've been amazing so far. If you have a lighter on you, I'll never doubt you again."

She smiles as she removes her phone from her pocket and turns on her flashlight. "I do not," she says.

Just as I'm about to give up hope, melt into the floor, and die from despair, she slowly trains her flashlight along the counter at the front of the store. There's a ton of shit on the counter—an old-fashioned cash register, a mile of mouse droppings, a collapsed stack of paper bags, a cup full of those silly pens topped with little troll dolls that have brightly-colored, fuzzy hair. Right beside the troll pens, there's a little cardboard box. And inside that box, there are about a half dozen lighters. "But we can *buy* one!"

I laugh despite the fact that I've never been this stressed in my entire life. In fact, I laugh so hard I'm afraid I might lose my sanity. Sara laughs with me but also keeps her head, runs to the counter, and grabs a handful of lighters.

She puts her phone back in her pocket, tosses me a couple of lighters, and says, "What did you have in mind?" She rolls her thumb along the roller of a lighter and presses the little red button. A flame bursts forth. She turns it on high. "Oh, look! It works."

"Those cop cars are really close," I say. I look around at the garbage strewn in every direction and am grateful that it's mostly paper of one kind or another. Displays, greeting cards, boxes, posters. The store is strewn with combustibles. "Just light everything you can get to. Let's start at the front of the store, by the door, and work back to the storage closet. Let's light it up!"

She doesn't stop to question me. Before I'm even finished talking, she's started three or four little fires. A cardboard display at the entrance, half crushed and still holding a few old Christmas decorations that have also been smashed. A Charlie Brown poster on the floor with a pile of other posters and papers. She's quick, touching corners of paper or cardboard wherever she can. I join her. Both of us run around the store with our two-fisted lighters ablaze, starting a hundred little fires.

The sirens are so close now, they're obviously on Elm. I glance out the front window and see flashing cherry-red lights reflected on the street. The cops are here. Shit. I hope it's enough.

As if in answer, Sara begins to cough and gag. "Shit. Smoke's thick. We better get downstairs. They're here. We have to go."

We make our way to the storage closet at the back of the store, still lighting things on fire and pulling more things over along the way, hoping they will catch.

"You realize we literally just burned down our only known exit, don't you?" Sara asks as we get to the ladder. We both drop our lighters and reach for our phones. "I hope whatever you have in mind isn't us dying in that creepy cellar, Gaige. I'm trusting you right now."

"Wish I could say the same," I say, mostly to myself. "It's a stall tactic. That's all I got. Stall the cops. They won't enter a burning building. I don't *think*."

"Are you serious?"

"Sort of. But also, not really." I pat my front, feeling the book's bulge in my pants. "The book has something to do with this, and I have an idea. It might not be anything at all, but it's worth a shot."

I gesture for her to go first. Even as she puts her feet down into the hole and starts down the ladder, little tendrils of smoke reach the storage room. Before her head is even through the hole, the smoke begins to fill the little room.

"Quick, quick," I urge. I gag on smoke and cover my face with the front of my T-shirt. "Go faster."

As Sara lands on the cellar floor, I straddle the ladder and climb-fall down as quickly as I can. Then, after a second of reflection, I scramble back up the ladder and pull the door in the floor closed to keep the smoke from entering the cellar.

"What now, Sherlock?"

"Um…"

"I don't think that's an option, Gaige. *Um* isn't going to cut it at all right now."

"OK, let me think," I say as I return to the cellar. "Search the bookstore for signs of the impending apocalypse? Check. Run back to the card shop and attempt to burn it to the ground while trapping ourselves inside? Check. Step back into Chalek's hellscape without reinforcements or any actual, feasible plan? Check."

"Helpful," Sara says with a sneer as we continue back through the cellar. "Noah's always telling me about you, but I never actually believed him. I always stood up for you when Noah needed to sound off with his frustrations. I don't think I'll be doing that anymore."

I hear crashing sounds and more sirens upstairs. I'm guessing the fire department is up there with the police, and they're working on putting out a fire or two.

"Oh, wait," I say with exaggerated aha flair, holding my index finger up in victory. "Bring magical book to the party in the hopes it holds a key to our escape? Check!" I lift my shirt and pull the book out of my pants. "Ha!"

"Nice trick," she says. "But what are you going to do with it?"

"He's not going to do anything with it. He's going to give it to me. *I'm* going to take it off his hands for him."

We both turn in the direction of the voice. A kid stands farther down the cellar, at the junction with the hallway where Logan disappeared.

"Who are you?" Sara asks. We both shine our flashlights at the kid as we slowly—and cautiously—make our way toward them.

"It's me, Gaige," they say. But they don't have to tell me. I already know who they are. The voice doesn't match the face, but I know the voice. I've heard it enough by now; I placed it instantly. "It's me. Mael."

As we get closer, I examine their face more closely. Same black hair, but their face is different. They're paler, and their features aren't as sharply defined.

Mael shrugs and smiles. They still have a cute smile, definitely. *Stop it, Gaige. Stop it.*

"Chalek must have given up on the facade," Mael says. "Probably has more important things to do. Or he realized it wasn't working the way he wanted it to. Doesn't matter. I'm back to my own self. Come on. Bring the book with you."

Mael gestures for us to follow them down the hallway, and I don't even know why I don't hesitate. I look down at the book in my hand and prepare to follow them.

Before my feet move, though, I glance back at Sara for affirmation. Her shrug suggests that we don't have any better options and we might as well follow them—so we do.

Chapter Thirty-Eight

"GAIGE!" LOGAN SQUEALS. HE AND Noah are squatting at the end of the hallway with their arms around each other. "Sara!"

"What are you guys doing? What happened? Where did you go? Are you OK?"

Sara's questions are like the rat-a-tat-tat of a machine gun as she runs to embrace Noah. Both boys are covered in goop from head to toe. Only their faces are wiped relatively clean. They rise to their feet to greet us.

"Logan," I say, letting out a long sigh of relief. Mael steps aside as I run to Logan and squeeze the life out of him. He sobs silently into my shoulder. When I finally pull away, I grab his face and look in his eyes. "You're never allowed to scare me like that ever again. Agreed?"

He smiles and shrugs. I let go of his face and wipe away his tears. When we kiss, I feel like I can't even remember the last time our lips met. Days ago? Weeks? Months? Nothing will ever compare to Logan kisses.

Mael clears their throat, bringing me out of my Logan-induced dream state. I drag myself away from his lips and return my attention to Mael. The four of us wait for them to speak.

Before they do, though, I notice with concern how shaken this *new* Mael appears. Their stricken look sends an ache through me.

"Sorry," Mael says, collecting themself. "I just… I never had that. What you and Logan have. What your friends here have." They look at all of us like they're going to break down in tears, but quickly shake it off.

"Sorry, Mael," I say. "It's not fair."

It's not enough, but I don't know what else *to* say. It's not fair that they've been trapped in hell for decades while the world went on without them.

"It's nothing," Mael says, trying ineffectively to wave it away. "Back to the book. You need to give me the book, Gaige. There isn't much time. Chalek's winning—look at this place. The Other Side is opening; it's almost here. There's something he wants in there, and he'll bring it out no matter what it means to the rest of the world."

How do I go from sympathy to mistrust so quickly? Almost absentmindedly, I put the book behind my back—even though I'm pretty sure Mael's right, and the thing Chalek wants from the Other Side is actually a person. Robert Martin.

We make eye contact. Mael couldn't hide their look of desperation if they tried.

"Don't give it to them, Gaige," Sara says, eyeing Mael suspiciously.

"No," Noah says, stepping forward in Mael's defense. "It's OK. Gaige, Mael saved us. They got us back from that place. You have to trust them. They must know what to do. They only want to help."

"But I was going to go inside," I say, as if that's a valid excuse, or plan, or alternative. And what the hell am I going to do when I get there? Especially with Mael out here.

"No." Noah is adamant. Before I have time to argue, Logan jumps in to the conversation.

"Trust them, Gaige. I wouldn't be here if Mael hadn't gotten me out of that place. They had to drag me out kicking and screaming. I didn't want to leave."

"What do you mean? We're still *in* that place. Look around you, Logan. We're in it."

"No," he says, holding my gaze. "No, we're not, Gaige. It's coming, but it's not here yet. This is only remnants. Chalek's not strong enough. There's still time to stop it." He grabs my shoulder and forces me to listen. "Do you remember that time you came with me to my uncle's place?

"Remember? We went for a walk while my dad helped his brother with something on his farm? We spent the whole day just walking, losing ourselves in the beauty of the place. We came to that big open field that you called *our* place. That's where I went when I was inside, Gaige. I saw it. The big oak tree, too. We sat under that great big tree—the only tree for forever. A lone tree in a never-ending field. We made out under it all afternoon. Remember?"

How could I have forgotten? But I did, didn't I? Because it's exactly what I saw in the Other Side, but I couldn't place it. *That's* what the meadow was. I knew that place was familiar, from my memories. It was a place Logan and I found together. Our perfect, happy place. And it's the same vision Chalek showed both of us, something we share. That has to be a sign, right? That he used the same thing to entice both of us?

"Mael almost sacrificed themself to bring me back from that place. I fought them, but they hauled me back. Mael saved me without even giving a shit what it meant for them, Gaige. We can trust them. We have to. What else is there?"

"The book opens the portal, Gaige," Mael says. Their face is like a porcelain doll's, slightly less pretty than Chalek's version but still beautiful. I would have fallen for this kid without the enchantments. "I've never stepped inside the book like you have. I need to take it because I need to go inside Chalek's world. I need to enter this new opening. And when I'm in there, I need to open the Book of Dreams, let myself fall inside, and hope like hell it works the way I think it will."

Even as they're speaking these words, I'm formulating the chain reaction their plan might cause. I'm not crazy about where they're heading.

"Like a black hole," Noah says, suddenly amped by Mael's words. "You open the portal when you're already inside the place where the portal takes you. It'd be like matter falling into a black hole, collapsing in on itself. The book would be gone. The world would go with it."

"Chalek's world. Only the Other Side world will be gone," Mael clarifies. "Not this one."

Noah practically dances with glee. Then he mimes crumpling up a piece of paper and tossing it away.

"Oh. Oh, that sounds like something. Yes," Sara says, bubbling with relief. Clearly, she sees a way out. Which it might even be, but still. At what cost?

As I prepare to disagree with this plan—based solely upon the fact that Mael would also be discarded in this scenario—a forearm wraps around my neck, and before I can tear myself away, I'm in a viselike chokehold.

Chalek is back.

"Ut-tut-tut. I would not do that, young lady," Chalek cautions Sara, halting her approach. As Logan comes at him from the other side, he says, "And, mister man, you do not want to come an inch closer. Your lovely boy here will have a whole new blowhole for you to gnaw on if you do."

Logan stalls mid-step, his face seething with rage, hatred, and fear. The sharp edge of a long blade pushes against my throat as Chalek uses me as leverage to keep the others at bay. He backs slowly away from them, dragging me with him.

"You," Chalek says to Mael. He gestures toward the end of the hallway behind us, where the new threshold is. He continues to drag me backward in that direction, his left forearm around my neck, his right hand holding the blade a little too snugly against my throat. "You sick and nasty little cretin. Move it. Walk. You've pushed too hard this time, little one. I should have ended you long ago."

Chalek flips us around so we're facing the threshold, turning his back to the three behind us as Mael paves the way before us. They're walking to their doom, and I have no way to stop them. I should have just given Mael the damn book when they first asked for it.

But I still have the book. There's that. If it's an ace in the hole, I'm not letting go of it. Chalek will have to run the blade across my throat and kill me first.

"You're going in there, do you hear me? I feed it, and it allows me to understand it more. That's the deal. You're next, Mael."

Mael keeps backing up, getting closer and closer to the line they dug into the ground, while Chalek bounces us back and forth, tossing me about like a ragdoll as he tries to keep his eyes on everyone at once.

"You want to understand it so you can save Robert," I say, hoping the statement has the shock value I'm counting on.

"What did you say?" Chalek yells, putting more pressure on the blade at my throat. "Don't you say that name, boy."

"Robert's not coming back, Lurch," I say. He continues to drag me closer to the edge, pushing Mael out in front of us.

"Shut your farking mouth."

I no longer know where my phone is, or I would shine my flashlight at Mael to see how close they are. The luminescent walls feel as though they're closing in on us, pulsating, becoming. I'm not even sure Mael needs to cross the line. It feels like everything around us is already the other place, the Other Side.

"You did all this," I say, trying to gesture toward the madness about us. "All this, just to try to save your boyfriend. You killed so many innocent people. You poisoned yourself. You're going to hell for—"

"Enough. I've heard enough. You know nothing, silly empty boy. Stop talking. Robert's still there. I can feel him. He's there. They're all there. They just need a way out."

"And what about the ones you buried in your cellar?"

"Gaige, I've had my fill of you."

"Believe me, Lurch, I feel the same way. Those bodies, they

were your first attempts. Your first failures, before you even figured out a way in."

"There were growing pains in the beginning. This world was Robert's baby, not mine. I made mistakes. Those people, though, they didn't die for nothing. They helped the cause. And now I'm almost there. Almost ready to bring the inside out, so to speak."

I can still hear the racket upstairs, the sirens, the crashing. They must be putting out the fire now. I wonder if—I hope that—the fire got big, big enough to engulf the bookstore, the entire block. I hope it's a fucking inferno up there.

As Mael makes it to the line, they turn back and look at me. Their eyes penetrate mine, and I know they're trying to tell me something, but it's hopeless. I'm not a mind reader, and they're not Chalek. They're just a kid. A lost, terrified kid.

"You bring that nightmare place into the world, Chalek, and it's over for everyone. Are you too far gone to even realize that?"

"You're wrong, boy. I just want Robert back. It's been a long haul. You're not going to stop me now. We're almost there."

When I look over Mael's shoulder, the tall grass comes back into view. The walls of sludge, Mael's Dark Ichor, evaporate, and the dungeon beyond the line becomes an oasis. A breeze makes the grass dance. The wildflowers sway. It feels like I'm watching the words in the book fall and spiral, becoming sentences and memories and dreams.

Just when I think I'm still in control of the book—our only way out—Chalek eases it out of my grip like he's taking a toy from a sleeping baby. I feel it go, but I can't stop him. Now that he has the book, he releases the pressure on the blade and his chokehold. He begins to back away toward Noah, Logan, and Sara, leaving me at the threshold with Mael.

He's unconcerned with me because he knows I'm mesmerized. He's holding me in a trance. Mael begins to lean into the dark place, to edge closer and closer over the line. I don't know what they see on the other side, but I know they're tired. Too tired.

As Chalek backs away from us, I try to look away from the threshold, but I just can't. I can't force myself away.

Mael steps past the threshold into the Other Side. The luminescent glow about them makes them stand out against the backdrop of the field. It also makes the oasis shimmer and lose clarity. Mael waves their arms frantically, jumps up and down erratically. Because they've entered the vision, they're breaking its spell on me. They're intentionally shaking it out of existence with their flailing.

I turn away from it all, from the field, from the flowers, from Mael. I see Chalek slipping out, past Noah. Only Logan and Sara stand between him and his escape with the book in hand.

"CCCHHHHAAAAALLLLLLLLEEEEEEEEKKKKKKK!"

Chapter Thirty-Nine

I SCREAM HIS NAME SO loudly, it feels like my eardrums shatter. I fall to the slick black ground, spent from the effort.

Chalek turns back, stunned to see me looking at him, to see his power over me destroyed.

At the very moment he takes his eyes off of Sara to look at me, she jumps.

I should clarify: Sara vaults. Sara motherfucking flies. She has somehow propelled herself off of Logan and sprung through the air. When she lands on top of Chalek, he doesn't even see her coming. She sits high on his shoulders. It reminds me of the shoulder rides my dad used to give me when I was a little kid, so I could see the Santa Claus Parade over all the adults in the way. It's just like that. Bam. Go, Sara!

Then Sara folds her legs and squeezes. She's literally gonna choke out a grown-ass man with her thighs while I look on in admiration.

"Don't just stand there," she yells at everyone as Chalek struggles to grab her legs with his bony old hands. He chokes and curses and swears. "Get him!"

We all come to life at once, scrambling from both directions toward Chalek and Sara. She now has her hands over his face and claws ruthlessly at his pale white flesh, attempting to blind him to anything else going on around them.

Noah gets to them first. He runs at Chalek's legs and dives sideways like he's sliding into first. Both of his feet hit the side of Chalek's leg, and the crack of old man bones fills the long hallway. Bullseye. He takes him out at the knee.

As Chalek screams and goes down, Logan runs in and jogs right past them. It takes me a second to realize that he just snatched the book from Chalek, ripped it clean from his hands as though it were a baton in a relay race.

Chalek crumples to the ground, taking Sara with him. He's reaching for his leg before he even realizes that he no longer holds the book. Logan steams past me, book in his outstretched hand. He's ready to hand it off.

I quickly glance at Mael and see them turn and begin to walk deeper into the darkness, to where I once saw the oak tree standing. They don't turn back.

Even with Chalek's injuries, he manages a hard swing in Sara's direction as they land in a heap. He knocks her off of him, struggles to get up on his one good leg, and then plows past Noah, dragging his bad leg behind him. Noah's not his target. Not just yet.

In an instant, Chalek is healed and new again, like Noah didn't just shatter bones. I see that he plans to run after Logan, to get the book. I jump into Chalek's path.

"Boy," he says. He can't hide his desperation. "You can't stop me."

"That won't stop me from trying, Lurch."

"We're a duo, this *goop*, as you call it, and I." He tries to push past me, but I hold firm. "We're symbiotic. It won't let you win. I'm its master. It bends to *my* will. It's your turn to enter the book, boy."

"Eat shit, old man. You're lying. You know nothing about this *goop*. It owns you, just like it owned your boyfriend. And you're letting it." He pushes me again. Ignoring him, I look for Logan. He's reached the line on the ground and stands looking into the glistening darkness at Mael, book in hand. Mael is some twenty feet away, watching us.

Chalek takes a swipe at me from behind, pushes me, and attempts to throw off my balance. But I stand my ground. I won't let him get to Logan.

Mael shouts something at Logan. I can't hear them, but in response, Logan waves the book above his head. Then he swings his arm back and throws the book toward Mael with all his might.

"Noooooo!" Chalek bellows as he watches it arc into the depths of the darkness and land in the sludge next to Mael. "You farking boy. I'll kill you."

Chalek shoves me aside and rushes toward Logan. I run to join Logan at the line and grab hold of his hand as Chalek blips out beside us. Logan is no longer his target. Chalek has one last chance.

When Chalek reappears several feet from where Mael stands with the book, I'm afraid it might actually be over for us. If Chalek gets his hands on the book, he'll stop Mael's plan, and we'll all be fucked.

Mael stands shimmering in the darkness, the open book in their hand. They raise their free hand to offer us a little wave. Sara and Noah have joined us at the line. We're all covered in goop from head to toe. There is nothing for us to do but wave back at Mael. I glance over at Logan guiltily before ending my wave by blowing Mael a kiss.

As Mael takes the book in both hands and looks into it, Chalek moves closer, hand outstretched, to grab either Mael or the book. He shouts out in desperation as Mael stares into its open pages.

As Chalek closes the distance between them, he makes a last-ditch effort to stop the kid he wouldn't let walk away. But it's too late. He's missed his opportunity. The book falls to the ground as Mael fades away, beyond its words. Mael is inside its swirling, inky blackness. They've gone to the place beyond the words.

Chalek opens his mouth to scream once more, but nothing comes out. Slowly, the tendrils of ropey slime around us begin to flow toward the open pages of the abandoned book on the ground and pour inside. It's a trickle at first, but gradually it builds and builds to a torrent as it's sucked inside the open book. Of course Mael was right. They had to open the portal to the Other Side once they were already *in* the Other Side to create the disaster that would save the Outside World while locking the Other Side away from it. But now it's all pouring in on top of them. Surely, Mael is gone, lost. Dead.

The penny drops for Chalek. He turns his glare toward us before bending down and reaching for his precious book as Mael's Dark Ichor streams into it in gulps and waves. He's desperate, now, to stop what cannot be stopped. He can't save the book, and he can't save his Robert. He can't even save his precious inky substance from itself.

"Holy shittin' Jesus," Noah whispers. He's standing beside me now, holding Sara's hand.

Chalek lifts the book from the ground. It shudders and shakes in his grip as a reverse fountain of luminescent goop flows into the portal within its pages. The goop pours in from every direction and rushes toward the book in Chalek's hands. It slithers up his legs, covers his torso, and begins to engulf him on its way inside.

In the midst of this, something floats up out of the book. It's a bright blue swirl of light, almost too dazzling to look at. Then it blips into a shape that is unmistakably Mael. They glance about them, and their gaze finds us. A smile forms on Mael's face just before they float up through the ceiling and disappear.

"Mael is free," I whisper as we watch in awe. As the book continues to suck up the darkness, other kids begin to swirl up out of its pages. One after another, they come into view: dazzling blue lights that take on the shapes of more and more kids. They float noiselessly up and out of the book, through the ceiling, and beyond. "They're all free. They're out."

The last flickering swirl of light is a dark bruised purple, not bright blue like all those before it. It slowly forms into a young man, who struggles to reach up and grab onto the boy who comes out before him. He fights to be a part of the upward flow.

"Robert!" Chalek screams. He can't take his hands off the book. The being that came from the pulsing funnel of ominous dark purple light looks back at Chalek. There is a moment of recognition, and he gives up reaching for the boy who went before him. As that boy floats away and vanishes, Robert swoops toward Chalek and gloms onto him in desperation.

A tremor begins to move through Chalek's body. It's slight at first but quickly gains speed. His face blurs in and out of focus as the shaking becomes more and more violent. I can no longer see the dark swirl of Robert that surrounds him. It's as though they have blended into one.

An endless, helpless moan leaves Chalek's throat. Though reunited with Robert, he is finally helpless. He cannot blip out or save himself while he's in the grip of the book. He's gone too far this time. The old man wanted too much, and he's gone too far. He's trapped.

He can't let go, now. The inky goop he's spent his life feeding and protecting has no allegiance. It uses Chalek as the final stop on the highway to the inside of the book.

What was it he said to me all those days ago? *I tried to warn you not to dance with the devil. Now you're dancing, young fella. Now you're dancing.* That Lurch-faced motherfucker is dancing now! And his Dark Ichor? Definitely the devil.

The book in Chalek's hands begins to glow with the red-hot light of a supernova. He holds it out in front of him as it collects the last of the Ichor matter around it with a violent, relentless, vacuuming black-hole hunger.

The fierce glow from the book travels out into Chalek's hands, up his arms, and throughout his body until he himself is lit with the fiery light of a thousand suns. For a split-second, Robert bursts up out of Chalek's frame, no doubt in an attempt to escape Chalek's fate. But in the next instant, either gravity, fate, or Chalek himself pulls him back down inside, and he disappears again. Chalek's face tilts upward, and his mouth is still open in an endless scream when the light bursts out of his throat and shoots up in a display of impossible brightness.

Right in front of us, Chalek explodes into the nothingness, becoming one with the goopy black tar before he, too, slips into the endless stream retreating inside the book's open pages.

The ball of fire that is now the book grows and swirls and shudders until all the Ichor is gone, sucked inside. The light dims, and the book slams shut, falls to the ground, and folds into itself with a violent boom that shakes everything in me.

Amidst the falling dirt and debris from the blast, I close my eyes and fall backward onto the cellar floor.

Chapter
Forty

WHEN I OPEN MY EYES again, Sara and Noah are in a heap beside me, and Logan is huddled against the wall on my other side. I reach over to grab his hand in mine. I don't even remember letting go of it.

There is nothing left of Mael's Other Side or of Chalek's Dark Ichor—it's all faded away. We're left in a shitty old unfinished cellar that smells only of old cellar. Even the goop that recently covered our bodies is gone.

The noise upstairs is louder now. It's no longer muffled by the miles of distance between the Other Side world and our own.

"What's that noise?" Sara asks, finally breaking our extended silence. "Shit. Something is still dripping. It's not over yet. Something's happening behind us."

With a sick feeling in my gut, I recall Chalek's teasing water leak when he trapped us inside the walls.

With Noah quick at her heels, Sara runs to check it out. I help Logan up. He's the last to get to his feet and looks disoriented still, lost between the two places. I don't know how we made it to the other side of this nightmare, but I don't care. He's here. We're together.

"Shake it off, babe," I whisper, bringing him in for a hug. "We made it. We're OK. Chalek's gone."

He hugs me back and slowly returns from the edge. We dust ourselves off and follow in the others' footsteps. This needs to be over. Like, I'm at my limit, and Logan has clearly passed his.

When we reach the ladder that leads to the bookstore, I know immediately what the dripping is.

Water. It's just water. That's all. Not Chalek. Not the Other Side. Just plain old water. It gushes in around the closed door in the floor. There's a small pool of it at our feet.

The fire department. They've been spraying their hoses at the strip of stores upstairs. The fire *did* spread. How about that? Take that, Lurch.

Logan looks back at me with a huge smile before he turns and heads up the ladder. He reaches the door and gives it a push. When it opens, more water gushes down into the cellar. All of us turn away to avoid it pouring onto our upturned faces.

After a few seconds, it stops flowing, and Logan climbs up through the opening. Noah drags himself up next. He looks back and holds out his hand for Sara to join him.

A little while later, we're all sitting on the curb across the street from the blackened buildings, marveling at the destruction Sara and I caused with our little lighter escapade. Whoa. Powerful stuff.

"I'll never doubt you or Girl Power ever again, Sara," I promise, turning to her. "I'm sorry. That was shitty of me."

"It's OK, sweetie," she says. She's staring at the strip of stores, mesmerized by the scene. "Once you know, you know."

"You're a motherfucking superhero, girl," I say, patting her on the back. "Did you see yourself leaping through the air like that? Whoa. Total goddess!"

She bursts out laughing, and Noah pulls her in for a side-hug. "That's *my* superhero goddess. Fearless, beautiful, and all mine."

While they focus their attention on each other and move closer together for a kiss, I turn to Logan, who sits at my other side.

"Do me a favor, babe," I say to him. He's wrapped in a blanket, brought to him by one of the paramedics who insisted on examining us after we emerged from the cellar of the abandoned store. "If I ever want to check out a new bookstore anywhere in the world, ever again in my life, just say no. Drag my ass away from it."

"Come on, Gaige," Logan says, laughing. He swipes my dangling bangs out of my eyes and gives me a *get real* look. Cupping my cheeks, he says, "You'll never change. If there's trouble out there, you'll find it. It'll find you. Doesn't have to be a bookstore that isn't there. Whatever it is, it'll find you."

He kinda has a point, but I pull away and smack him on the shoulder all the same.

"Thanks for the vote of confidence, creep," I say before leaning back in for one of his famous Logan kisses. I think I'll make this one last for an eternity—or at least long enough to destroy my memory of the last week or so of my life.

Have I mentioned how good Logan kisses are? Like, phenomenal. They give me wavy-gravy legs. His tongue melts me like water over sugar.

THE END

Acknowledgments

MANY THANKS TO THE MUSKOKA Novel Marathon organizers for giving me the space and comfort in which to write a partial first draft of this book. Best seventy-two hours ever! Can't wait for the next in-person whirlwind marathon!

It's been such a great opportunity for me to work with CB Messer and Candysse Miller of Duet Books again! CB found the perfect wrapping for this story, and Candysse is always there for every little thing I pester them with. I feel so supported by this team.

And many thanks to Annie Harper, another pivotal member of the Duet Books team, for guiding me gently through the editorial process with *Book of Dreams*. I appreciate her kind words, encouragement, and guidance. I'd also like to thank my copy editor, Zoë Bird, for their phenomenal work on this manuscript. Their spot-on edits were a special kind of magic.

I'm so grateful for the feedback I received on the partial first draft of this story. Thank you to those early readers: Grace Ombry, Jeanne Pengelly, Dale Long, and, my silly, lovely Orange mutual, Mel Cober. This book has changed a lot since then; I hope my early readers will be able to find tendrils of the earlier version in the final story.

Thank you, Michael, for the ideas, the talk-throughs, and the time and space to write.

And thank you to my daughter, Ashley, for yelling at me for years to *Save those kids from the cellar!* I listened. I dove back in. As usual, it takes a community to grow a book.

About the Author

KEVIN CRAIG IS THE AUTHOR of several young adult novels. Their most recent title, *The Camino Club*, was the 2021 Silver Winner of the Independent Book Publishers Association's Benjamin Franklin Award. Kevin is a five-time recipient of the Muskoka Novel Marathon's Best Novel Award. They are also a playwright, and have had twelve plays produced for the stage. Kevin lives in Toronto, Canada. An avid explorer, they love traveling the world with their significant other, Michael.

CONNECT WITH 🌐 ktcraig.com
KEVIN 🐦 KevinTCraig
ONLINE 📷 kevinthomascraig